~THE~
LAST DOGS
THE VANISHING

THE
LAST DOGS
THE VANISHING

by

CHRISTOPHER HOLT

LITTLE, BROWN AND COMPANY
NEW YORK   BOSTON

Text copyright © 2012 by The Inkhouse

Illustrations copyright © 2012 by Greg Call

Little, Brown and Company

Hachette Book Group
237 Park Avenue, New York, NY 10017
Visit our website at www.lb-kids.com

Little, Brown and Company is a division of Hachette Book Group, Inc.
The Little, Brown name and logo are trademarks of Hachette Book Group, Inc.

The publisher is not responsible for websites (or their content)
that are not owned by the publisher.

First Edition: September 2012
Library of Congress Cataloging-in-Publication Data
Holt, Christopher, 1980–
The vanishing / by Christopher Holt ; illustrated by Greg Call.—1st ed.
p. cm.—(Last dogs ; 1)
Summary: When all humans in his world disappear, Max, a yellow Labrador
Retriever, searches for Madame Curie, who he knows will help find his people,
but as he and friends Rocky and Gizmo search, they face angry wolves, a gang of
subway rats, and the Corporation, a supposed "perfect" society for dogs.
ISBN 978-0-316-20005-9
[1. Adventure and adventurers—Fiction.   2. Labrador retriever—Fiction.
3. Dogs—Fiction.]   I. Call, Greg, ill.   II. Title.
PZ7.H7388Van 2012   [Fic]—dc23   2012001550

10   9   8   7   6   5   4   3   2   1
RRD-C
Printed in the United States of America

For anyone who has ever loved and been loved by a pet—be it dog or otherwise!

DARKNESS

———◆———

Max was running in a field.

It was a happy place, with tall yellow grass and freshly turned earth—the land surrounding his people's farm. He loved being there. So many smells! The scent of rodents and cows and summer ragweed and mud filled his nostrils. He liked to run through the long grass, stretching his legs as far as he could, running until he couldn't run any more.

He heard distant laughter. The crystal clear shrieks of Charlie and Emma, his pack leaders, the children who had been there to play with him ever since he was a young pup. He loved his pack leaders, and they loved him.

Max could see the children standing on the horizon, shadows in front of a setting sun. Distantly, Max remembered that they should be away with their parents on vacation—but he didn't want to think about that. It didn't matter. His boy and girl were waiting.

"Hey!" Max barked. "I'm here! Wait for me!"

The children's shadows laughed, the sound echoing across the field.

"Come get us, Max!" Charlie called.

"Come on, boy!" Emma shouted.

Max bounded forward, as fast as his legs would take him, so fast that his muscles began to ache. But no matter how hard he ran, he never seemed to get any closer. Max craned his head to look back behind him and saw that the fields, the farmhouse, and the barn were shrouded in a thick, inky blackness.

The blackness undulated, pulsing like a liquid, living thing. Wispy, smoky tendrils spiraled up and outward, becoming dark storm clouds that raced to overtake the robin's-egg blue of the summer sky.

The darkness was spreading.

Max turned back to Charlie and Emma. Soon the darkness would overtake them, too. He pushed himself to go even faster, but he couldn't possibly reach them in time.

Max's ears twitched as something clicked.

The sky exploded into a stark white, blinding him, burning his eyes.

No, not the sky at all—it was the lights on the ceiling turning on to signal a new day.

Max awoke.

CHAPTER 1

BRIGHT AND EMPTY

Max's head jerked up from the chilly concrete floor. He blinked his eyes, clearing them of the fog of sleep.

Max was alone.

He was snuggled against a ratty old blanket in the back of his cage—a kennel, the humans called it. It was quiet and cold, and Max's stomach growled endlessly, nipping at his insides until he ached.

It had been so long since he'd seen anyone. So long since he'd eaten the last of his kibble, two days since he lapped up the last of his water. Day by day he awoke to the click of a timer and the fluorescent lights on the ceiling flicking on, the buzz of them hitting his ears before the light shone into his tired eyes.

And day by day Max expected Vet, the man who was

supposed to watch after him, to come and refill his food bowl, to take his water dish to the big stainless-steel basin across the room and fill it with water.

But Vet never came.

It had been two weeks. At least, Max thought it was two weeks.

The first week had been normal, with Vet coming into the back room to feed and water Max as he did every morning, and to take him out to the field behind the farmhouse-turned-Vet's-office so that Max could run and stretch his legs.

The kennel was hardly Max's favorite place, but he'd grown used to it. Once every year, Charlie and Emma and their parents put him here while they went away. Why they didn't let him stay on the farm, he didn't know. But every visit, he was poked and prodded by Vet, who would lift Max's floppy ears and look inside and clean his teeth with a strange-looking brush. Vet's helpers would come brush his golden fur, combing out the burrs and matted hair. Eventually, after many days, Charlie and Emma always returned and everything went back to normal—that's what made the time with Vet bearable.

But this time was different.

By Max's count, the fluorescents had turned out six times and had turned on seven times since he'd last seen Vet—seven days. Seven days since Max had been out of his cage. Seven days since he'd had anything to eat.

4

His tongue and nose were dry. His stomach twisted with hunger pains. He was so tired.

And alone.

Vet's back room wasn't large, but it had enough room for four cages just like the one that boxed Max in. Each kennel was about the size of one of the closets in his family's home. Metal pipes made up the four corners, with chain-link fencing stretched between each pipe so that Max couldn't get out.

In Max's past visits, other dogs had been in the kennels: Cupcake, a fluffy Lhasa Apso who yapped complaints day and night about how her space simply wasn't *posh* enough; Shadow, a stocky black Chow who was mostly quiet and shy and kept to himself; Ariel, a wiry mutt who liked to gnaw and dig at the bottom of the kennel when she wasn't barking challenges at Shadow.

And Max's favorite kennel companion out of all his visits was an older female dog named Madame Curie, though Max just called her Madame. She was the same size as Max and the same breed—Labrador—only her fur was like the night sky, black and flecked with strands of white. She was all wise words and good humor, and talking with her always helped the days pass by faster.

Max especially liked looking at the sparkly golden symbol on her collar—three connected rings in a straight row. He'd never seen anything so fancy on another dog, and it glittered spectacularly even under the fluorescent lights.

Madame had been with Max right up until the day Vet had stopped coming. Max awoke one morning to find her kennel empty, its door squeaking on its hinges. She hadn't even said good-bye.

Since then, the other kennels remained empty.

Max barely had enough room to pace back and forth. His area was bare except for the torn blanket that he slept on to avoid the cold concrete floor, the empty food dish, the plastic water dispenser that used to fill his now-dried-up bowl, and the shed fur that formed little messy piles. Once he'd also had a rubber ball, but in a fit of hunger, he'd torn it into tiny pieces, which were now part of the mess on the floor.

And in the back corner was the place Max made his bathroom. He had been so ashamed the first time he'd been forced to go inside his cage. Ever since he was a pup, he'd been taught that his business was only to be done outdoors.

Beyond the kennels, Max could see Vet's examination room. The walls were lined with counters and cabinets, with sterile medical equipment hanging from pegs and lying in blue liquid. In the center of the room was a long table, its top shiny steel. On the other side of the room from Max's cage was the large metal basin with the faucet.

The faucet dripped.

Drip. Drip. Drip.

Each water drop pinged against the bottom of the

sink, and Max's ears twitched with each *ping*. His throat burned for water.

Max hadn't thought of it much at the time, but in the days before Madame disappeared, she'd started to act strangely. Muttering of something coming. Something dangerous.

"Be prepared, Maxie," she'd told Max in that serious, grave tone of hers the night before she was gone. "There is a darkness on the horizon. I can feel it."

Max had been chewing on his red ball covered with nubs. "I don't feel anything," he'd said with the ball between his teeth. "Are you sure it's not just an old dog ache?"

Madame had barked a friendly laugh. "Of course I feel it 'cause I'm old, Maxie. Old dogs have smarter bones that creak and rattle when bad things are going to happen." Laughter leaving her voice, she added, "I don't know what it is yet. But when I find out, I'll tell you. Be safe, little Maxie."

And now Madame was gone.

Everyone was gone.

His dreams showed the darkness she spoke about, or at least how Max imagined it looked. And even though his body ached, he couldn't stop worrying about where she'd gone, or what her cryptic words meant for his family.

Because if Max knew one thing above all else, it was that his family would never abandon him for two weeks unless something or someone was keeping them from him.

If only he had a way out, then he could find his family himself. A wave of exhaustion rolled over Max, and he padded back to his blanket. He turned in a circle and began to lie down, his eyes already halfway closed.

And then he heard something: a rustling of plastic and a creak of hinges.

Max's eyes snapped wide open. He darted to the side of the kennel, stuck his snout through the chain-link fence, and sniffed deeply.

A stench of fur and musk met his nose. He saw the small cat door that led from Vet's examination room into the main house. It was swinging back and forth, as though something had just darted through it.

And Max could hear a clattering of claws atop the concrete floor.

"Hey!" Max barked. "Who's there?"

From across the room, a muffled voice barked, "Whoa!"

There was a great noise—a clanging and crashing as things fell and hit the floor somewhere out of sight.

A creature darted from behind the table and raced across the room, back toward the door, a latex glove covering its head.

"Stop!" Max yelped. "Please, I need help!"

The little creature skidded to a stop mere inches from the cat door. It shook its head until the latex glove flew off, letting Max get a good look at the animal.

It was a dog.

A very small dog—no bigger than Max had been as a

8

puppy. For a moment he wondered if this was another Labrador puppy, but no, Max's limbs had been long when he was young, not like this little dog's short, stubby legs. The little dog's fur was also mostly a sleek black instead of the faded gold of Max's shaggier fur, and though both dogs had floppy ears, the ears on the smaller dog seemed much too big for his pointy little head.

Max lifted a paw and clung to the cage. "Please, can you help me?" he asked. "It's been days since Vet has been here. What happened?"

The other dog looked Max up and down with big, watery brown eyes that were surrounded by a pattern of brown fur. He tilted his head.

"Hey, you know if there's any kibble in here?"

Max's paw fell limp. That was the last thing he expected the dog to say.

"I don't know," Max said, unable to keep a pitiful whine out of his voice. "I'm hungry, too. And I need to find my people."

The little dog studied Max with one brow raised and his tail wagging slowly, seeming to take in Max's size. "You want food?" Looking away, the dog began to mutter to himself. "Of course he does. All anyone keeps asking about is food, food, food!" To Max, he said, "Well, tell you what—"

The dog stopped talking, and his ears flicked, hearing something that Max could not.

"Sorry, buddy!" the dog said as he began to back through the door. "Gotta run! Try to pinch the latch on the door. I've seen other dogs do it." And then the dog disappeared, the small cat door flapping behind him.

Max looked up at where the cage door met the pole that supported the fence. There was a gap there, enough space for Max to maybe stick his snout through.

Across the room, the faucet *drip-drip-drip*ped. The water was so close, yet so horribly out of reach.

Max's chest swelled with determination. If the little dog wasn't going to help him, then he was going to have to help himself. He was going to get out of this smelly, horrible cage.

And he was going to find his family.

CHAPTER 2
PRISON BREAK

◆

Opening the cage door was not as easy as Max had hoped.

Max leaped against the kennel's gate, his body hitting the chain link with a loud clang. He twisted his snout sideways and tried to force it up between the pole and the door, but the latch was too high and out of reach.

He dropped down onto the concrete, his eyes watering.

The little sausage-looking dog had made it sound so easy. And the latch itself did *look* simple enough. It reminded Max of chew toys he'd been given to gnaw on, just two little levers that he could bite and twist.

He could do it. He had to.

Max snorted in and out through his nostrils. The

next effort was going to have to count. Tensing his hind legs, Max leaped.

His paws slammed against the chain link. The gate rattled. He bent his front paws, straining to hold himself up while his hind feet scrabbled against the concrete.

Eyes wide, he forced his snout between the door and the pole. It was a tight fit, the cool metal pressing against his gums as he opened his mouth wide. The taste of acrid metal met his tongue as his mouth wrapped around the latch.

He bit down.

Resistance. There was something in the latch, some sort of spring. Of course. Human hands would need to press down hard to open the door.

Max's whole body trembled. His paws started to slip. The pain as the chain link cut into his feet was intense. His instincts yelped at him, telling him to let go, to give up.

In Max's mind, he saw the laughing faces of Charlie and Emma, saw the pulsating darkness muddy and erase their features. The faucet dripped, the sound plinking cruelly.

Growling deep in his chest, Max clamped his jaws down on the latch as hard as he could.

And the kennel door swung open.

Max tumbled forward, his paws pulling free from the chain link. He plopped heavily against the concrete floor, and, for a moment, the wind was knocked out of him. Max lay there, his chest heaving up and down, his eyes unfocused. Above, the bright light of the fluorescents flared.

And then Max realized it: He was free.

Free.

"I'm out," he barked. "I'm out!" A surge of energy flooded his limbs, and Max rolled over onto his feet, his tail wagging, a blur of golden fur.

Drip. Drip. Drip.

Water. Delicious, cool water. He could finally drink.

Max's head darted from side to side, catching his bearings. There, across the room. The giant basin where Vet filled the water dispensers and washed the smaller pets.

Max raced across the room and leaped up against the basin. He'd seen how Vet turned on the faucet. He pressed the lever down with his snout. So much easier than the latch on the cage.

Pipes groaned in the walls, and the end of the curved faucet let out a little gurgle. Then water. It gushed from the faucet, a strong, steady stream. It glittered in the light.

Max plunged his entire head under the faucet, letting the water slide off his pale fur and down his back. He pulled away, shook his head, and barked a laugh. Then he lapped out with his tongue, pulling the water down his throat, filling his stomach.

Soon he felt energy come back to him. His muscles

surged with strength. His middle grew fat, bloated with water, but he didn't care.

Finally, when he knew he'd had his fill, Max dropped down and sat on the floor. His tongue lolled from his mouth as he panted a smile. His nose was *wet*, for the first time in days, and the sensation made him want to roll around on the ground and get his belly rubbed.

Only that couldn't happen. Because there were no people here.

The strange situation he was in came back to Max in a rush. He was alone. Abandoned. And he needed to find out why.

There was that other dog. The little, funny-looking one with the short legs and the long body. Maybe he could tell Max what was going on.

Max stood on all fours and turned from the basin. The water still gushed from the faucet, but he left it on. He never wanted that faucet to be turned off again.

"Hello?" Max barked. "Little dog, are you there?"

His barks echoed through the sterile, concrete room. No response.

Across the room, past the large examination table, was the door with the little cat flap at the bottom. Sounds drifted from beyond the flap, thumps and maybe the yelps of another animal. Max padded across the room. His brows lowered as he examined the little cat door. Clearly, he would never fit through it. He wasn't the biggest dog ever, but he *was* big, after all.

But his head was certainly cat-sized.

Max shoved his snout through the cat door and twisted his head to force it out. He got through as far as his shoulders but couldn't really turn to look to his left or right. All he could see was the wooden floor and plain wall of the hallway.

Sniffing, Max's nostrils picked up the scent of the little dog. The smell was excitable, urgent, and tinged with the meaty scent of kibble. Max could hear clearly now—there was a commotion going on down the hallway to his right. A scrabbling of claws against wood, thumps, and little yelps.

"Little dog?" Max barked. "Is that you? I got out of the kennel. I opened the latch like you said!"

No response. The sounds of struggle continued. Unable to turn his head, Max snorted in frustration and pulled his head back through the cat door.

Sitting on his haunches, Max craned back his head to study the door. Its handle was a flat lever, like the one in the sink, only this one was sideways.

Max jumped up and pressed his paws down on the door handle. There was a click, and the door creaked open. *Easy!* Sticking his snout between the door and the jamb, Max shoved with his head, and the door opened wide.

He padded out into the hallway, the floor changing from cold concrete to smooth wood. To the left, a bunch of doors like the one he'd just come through. To the right, a pale turquoise door that swung on hinges. Max recalled coming through it. On the other side was the waiting room where his people sat on chairs until a woman behind a desk told them it was their turn to see Vet.

The noises came from beyond the swinging door.

Head hung low, Max slunk down the hallway. The closer he got to the waiting room, the louder the sounds became.

Max pushed past the swinging door slowly. For a moment, he dared to hope that there would be people in the room beyond, loud people with cages holding cats and ferrets and birds, like there always were when his people brought him here.

But the waiting room was empty and dark.

Dingy daylight streamed through the narrow slats of closed blinds. The room smelled strange, like nervousness and sadness and—was that what he thought it was?

Yes. He smelled fear.

It felt strange to be in the room all by himself. Aside from the lack of people, everything *looked* normal. The chairs were all lined up neatly against the walls. The magazines on the end tables were fanned out, waiting to be read. The desk where the lady usually sat was neat and organized. Next to the doorway was a small red machine on a stand with a glass globe on top. Charlie and Emma often begged their parents for change to put inside to release brightly colored gum balls.

But something was definitely not right. What had happened in here?

Max paused, listening. Uncertain, he took a step farther into the waiting room. The turquoise door swung back and forth behind him, squeaking on its hinges.

"Hello?" Max barked quietly. "Little dog? Are you in here?"

His barks lingered in the stale air, unanswered. For a moment Max wondered if he'd actually said anything at all.

And then, a heavy thud.

Startled, Max leaped back, the fur along his spine bristling. Ahead of him, something banged against the door that led outside. Something big.

A scrabbling of claws as something scratched at the door. Another thud.

Only then did Max see that a small wooden chest had been shoved up against the bottom of the door. That had never been there before—he was certain. People would trip over it. Someone had pushed the box there, but why?

Max remembered: Just like on the door to the back room, the front door had a little cat flap.

From beyond the door, Max could hear a deep, guttural growl. He stiffened. That wasn't the growl of a dog, at least not one from a nice home like his. It was the growl of something feral. Something wild.

And then, another heavy *bang*.

The chest in front of the door slid across the floor from the force of the blow, revealing the cat door. The creature on the other side fell silent, as though surprised.

Max backed away, his body low. Something bad was out there. Something *real* bad.

A furry white head burst through the cat door.

The snout was long and thick, matted with dirt and dried blood, crisscrossed with scars. The creature's gums were pulled back, revealing teeth stained yellow. Its pale blue eyes were manic, crazed.

A wolf. A very thin, very angry wolf.

And its rage-filled eyes were focused directly on Max.

CHAPTER 3

A WOLF AT THE DOOR

"You!" the wolf snarled, his voice guttural and his words clipped. "You are new. Where is the runt?"

Max backed away, keeping low to the ground, not taking his eyes off the beast.

The wolf snapped his jaws and shoved forward, struggling to get through the cat door. "Answer me! Now! The runt, the little *coward*, promised food!"

Max felt his tail and hind legs bump up against the swinging door behind him. For a moment, staring at the wild-eyed wolf struggling to wiggle through the tiny cat door, Max thought about turning and running. But this crazed wolf was after the little dog who'd given Max advice.

He couldn't let the wolf get in.

Max bared his teeth and took a step forward. "Who are *you*?" he asked. "You do not belong here!"

The wolf stopped struggling, panting because of his efforts. He was so thin that he had managed to get his shoulders partway through the small opening, something Max could never hope to do.

"You speak with authority, mongrel," the wolf barked, "even though you speak to Wretch. How brave of you."

"I'm M—" Max began to say.

"We do not need to know your name!" The wolf flicked his scarred white snout in the direction of the receptionist's desk. "Make yourself useful, dog, and drag over a bag of the little coward's kibble. Unless you, too, wish to suffer."

A threat. Max didn't like threats. A growl formed in his throat, but he kept it down.

"Who's 'we'?" Max said as he took another slow step forward.

Wretch jerked from side to side, pulling himself farther into the dimly lit room. "'We' are my pack. We are starving. You should know better than to question a wolf when he is starving."

Max sniffed. The wolf smelled sickly, damp—as if his matted white fur was hiding old wounds. He didn't seem so tough. Especially not stuck halfway through a door meant for a creature a quarter of his size.

Rising to his full height, Max lifted his tail and ears to show Wretch that he wasn't afraid. "Oh, yeah?" he barked. "If you're so hungry, why are you trying to get in here instead of going out hunting? Though from the way you look, you're probably too weak to even catch a mouse."

Wretch's head shot up. His black gums were bared again, his stained teeth dripping with saliva. A deep, angry growl rose in his throat. With one last lunge and shove against the front door, Wretch's starved, skinny body burst into Vet's lobby.

The wolf's momentum carried him directly toward Max, but Max jumped to the side just in time, letting Wretch slam snout-first into the wall next to the swinging door. Max was stunned—he didn't think the wolf could get in! But Wretch had ignored the pain, forcing himself through the door despite the bloody scratches now striping his flanks.

As Wretch recovered and rounded on him, Max wished he hadn't taken the opportunity to taunt the wolf.

"I—" he started to say.

"I warned you, dog!" the wolf roared.

And Wretch leaped.

Max reared back on his hind legs, and the two met each other chest-to-chest. Gripping Wretch around the neck with his front legs, Max flung his head from side to side to avoid the beast's vicious, snapping jaws.

Shoving forward with his hind legs, Max pushed Wretch away. The wolf tumbled backward, slamming against an end table next to a row of chairs and scattering a pile of glossy magazines.

Max fell onto all fours. He narrowed his brows and walked warily in a circle around Wretch, eyes not leaving his foe. "Leave now," he demanded. "This isn't a place for you. I will defend it and the little dog if I must."

Rolling onto his feet, Wretch matched Max stride for stride. They circled each other in the center of the lobby, between the chairs.

"You think you can take me, dog?" Wretch spat. "You? A pampered mongrel who cannot hunt for himself and must rely on *humans*?" He laughed.

"Says the wolf who threatens a little dog for kibble," Max replied. He was nearing the swinging door. The wolf was under the blinded windows.

Wretch grunted. "You know nothing, dog," he said, his voice low and serious.

"What's your favorite flavor?" Max said with a tilt of his head. "I like the meaty stuff. Wait, let me guess, I bet you're a big fan of the *kitty* ch—whoa!"

His hind leg met something slick and thin. The cover of a magazine. His paw slid, and, caught off balance, Max almost fell onto his side.

And Wretch, seeing his chance, leaped at Max, all claws and teeth.

Fangs met fur as Wretch clamped down on Max's neck.

Pain. Sharp, lancing pain as a tooth pierced his skin.

22

Max yelped, closed his eyes. He snapped at the air, and then his teeth met fur, and he bit down with all his might.

Wretch howled a scream and let go of Max's neck.

But before Max could let go himself, the wolf barreled forward again, driven by a savagery that Max couldn't have imagined. The room spun, and Max found himself with his back against the dusty wooden floor. Wretch towered over him. Max was helpless and could only watch as the wolf opened his jaws to bite down.

Max had to break free. Had to escape—to the swinging door, down the hallway, to the kennel. But he was stunned by his fall and couldn't move, and the teeth were coming closer—

"Hiiiiiii-*yah!*"

The high-pitched bark echoed through the lobby. Max turned to the side and saw the little black dog jump on top of one of the chairs and leap through the air, flinging his sausage-looking body against the gum-ball machine by the front door. He slammed into it with a resounding *clang*, then fell to the floor.

The gum-ball machine rocked on its stand, back and forth, before finally tipping over.

Right toward the wolf.

Wretch turned his attention away from Max just in time to see the gum-ball machine fall. Then the glass globe smacked against him, shattering into pieces. Brightly colored gum balls spilled out, clattering to the floor and rolling off in all directions.

Wretch yelped and jumped away. The half of the globe still attached to the heavy, red machine caught on the wolf's dirty white fur, and he dragged it away, shaking back and forth in an effort to pull himself free.

Max rolled onto his side and pulled himself up. Avoiding the broken glass and the gum balls, he bounded over to the stubby dog, who lay on his back, stunned.

The little dog's dark eyes were glassy, unfocused, and his tongue lolled out of his mouth.

Max looked back to make sure Wretch was still preoccupied, then sniffed the little dog and licked his brown patterned face. "Are you all right?" he asked between licks. "Did you hurt yourself?" *Lick, lick.* "Wake up!"

The little dog blinked, regaining his bearings, then sputtered. He swatted at Max's snout and snapped his teeth. "Yeah, yeah, I'm fine, buddy!" he yelped. "Stop slobbering on me!"

There was a series of loud crashes as Wretch flung the gum-ball machine from side to side. His yelps were high-pitched, in pain.

Max turned just as the wolf dislodged the broken gum-ball machine. Blood from cuts all over his snout and head ran over Wretch's fur and into his eyes, blinding him.

Wretch scrabbled and stumbled over the fallen gum balls. Tail between his legs, he lowered his head to dart back through the cat flap—and missed, bumping his wounded head against the door and leaving a bright red smear. Howling, Wretch tried again, found the flap, and forced himself through.

The sausage dog grimaced. "Yeesh, that looked painful." He sniffed at a chipped green gum ball. "And he made such a mess of the place, too. Wolves!"

"Sorry," Max said, sitting by the front door. "About the mess."

"Well, don't sit down just yet, buddy!" the dog said, turning to him with wide eyes. "We gotta find a way to stop any more of them from coming in here." He scampered up to Max, looked from side to side, and said in a low voice, "They're after my kibble."

Max nodded. "But why do the wolves want dog food? Why don't they just hunt?"

Waddling past Max, the little dog studied the chairs and tables. "No time to explain now," he said. "Let's see, maybe if we . . . hmm, no, if the chest didn't keep them out . . ."

Groaning, Max got to his feet and followed the sausage dog. He had to walk very, very slowly to match his pace. The poor dog's legs were just so short.

"Excuse me," Max said.

The little dog ignored him, instead sniffing at a potted plant beside the receptionist's desk.

"Excuse me!" Max barked louder.

With a sigh, the other dog turned to him. "Yeah, buddy?"

"Can I at least know your name? In my head, I keep calling you the little sausage dog, but it seems rude."

The little dog seemed taken aback. He gaped. "Well, it *is* rude. I don't go around calling you the giant... gold...furry...dog thing." He looked back at the cat door and then the empty lobby area and sighed. "Yeah, I got nothing."

Max sat again. "What kind of dog are you, anyway? I've never seen a breed so...unique."

Flicking his ears, the dog winked. "I'm one of a kind, what can I say? The humans say I'm a Dachshund. And the name's Rocky."

Max wagged his tail and relaxed his jaws into a smile. "I'm Max. I'm a Labrador. Nice to meet you."

Turning to resume his search, Rocky said, "Yeah, well, wish it was under better circumstances. Just imagine, a few weeks ago I'm thinkin', I got it made! I got me a new pack leader, and her dad, Vet, is some sort of animal doctor! I get to hang out and meet a bunch of other dogs, and, best of all, these guys got tons and tons of kibble in back. Tons of it, every flavor you could want!"

With a grunt, Rocky leaped up onto a plush chair next to the receptionist's desk, putting his paws on the desktop to look over the pens and pads of paper. "Then all of a sudden, the humans disappear and the wolves are getting bossy and—not what I signed up for, you know what I mean?"

Max stiffened. For a moment he couldn't say anything

and just watched as Rocky bounded down from the chair and began to head back toward the front door.

"The humans?" Max finally said. "All the people? They disappeared?"

"Well, I don't see any around. Do you?" Rocky asked. "I—"

Rocky's ears flicked. He spread his legs wide and held himself low. "You hear that?"

Max shook his head. He sat up and walked to stand next to Rocky. His claws clinked on the wooden floor.

"Shh, hold it down, big guy," Rocky whispered. "Listen."

And Max heard it. The sound of a dozen or more padded feet crawling over grass, of wolves huffing for air as they surrounded the building.

Wretch's pack. They were here.

"All right, they ain't gonna be happy!" Rocky barked. Looking up at Max, he said, "Hey, see that cabinet by the door?"

Max nodded. It stood floor to ceiling and was made of wood. The doors were shut; Max didn't know what was inside.

"I see it," Max said. "You think...?"

"I do, buddy!" Rocky said, rushing over to the side opposite the door. "I bet a big, strapping dog like you could knock it over easy! Just like in the movies!"

"Movies?"

"Your pack leaders don't watch movies with you?"

Rocky shook his head. "Tragic. Anyway, come on, give it a shot!"

"I don't know," Max said. "It looks awful heavy. I haven't eaten in a week and I'm not feeling so strong. . . ."

Rocky jumped up and put his paws against the cabinet, straining to push it over. When it didn't budge, he fell back onto all fours and gulped for air. "Come on, buddy," Rocky said. "I promise, you tip this over and I got tons of kibble for you. I'm telling you, Vet left behind enough to feed us for the rest of our lives!"

Max tilted his head, trying to figure out a way to get the cabinet over.

A head burst through the cat door.

Surprised, Max jumped. The head belonged to another wolf, this one bigger and even uglier than Wretch. It, too, had a scarred snout—three great gashes of pale white flesh that its gray fur could not cover.

The wolf caught sight of Max. "You!" he bellowed, scratching on the other side of the door. "You are the one who harmed my pack mate. Dolph will make you sorry!"

"Oh no, not Dolph!" Rocky yelped. He leaped up and down next to the cabinet. "Come on, Max!"

Dolph pulled back, and then something struck the door. Max could swear the wooden door buckled from the force of the blow.

"I will tear you limb from limb!" Dolph howled outside the door. A chorus of other wolf voices took up the cry. Max felt his tail tucking between his legs, but then he stopped himself. *No.*

"Okay!" Max barked to Rocky. "I'm going to do what you did before."

"You're gonna what?" Rocky asked.

But Max didn't answer. He'd already run to the side of the lobby opposite the chairs, gum balls, and broken glass. He spun on his paws and studied the cabinet. Near it, against the wall under the shuttered windows, was a chair.

"Let us in and your deaths will be swift!" Dolph howled, shoving his head through the cat flap. His pack mates were still thudding and scratching against the door.

Max ignored him, focusing on his goal.

"Here goes," Max barked, welling up all his remaining strength. With a deep breath, he bounded forward.

And leaped.

Onto the chair. Carrying forward his momentum, he leaped again. Slammed his body against the side of the cabinet.

With a groan and creaking of wood, the giant cabinet leaned sideways. Slowly at first, then gravity took hold, and it tilted over and fell onto its side in front of the door with a crash that made Max's ears ring. Dust from the floor billowed up in little clouds, and broken splinters flew off the cabinet from the force of its collapse. The wooden doors fell open, and a big television set tumbled face-first onto the floor with a soft crunch of glass.

Hacking, Max got to his feet. He blinked to get rid of the dust in his eyes.

"I didn't hit him on the head, did I?" Max asked.

Rocky emerged from beneath the couch against the wall, shaking his head. Max's ears twitched, and he could hear the giant wolf, Dolph, on the other side of the door, roaring in anger. The rest of his pack joined in, howling loud and long.

"Too bad," Rocky said, waddling up to Max's side. "I really hate that guy. But hey, buddy, you done good. No more wolves are coming in that way."

Max's stomach rumbled, and he grimaced. "I'm glad," he said to Rocky. "Now can I have some kibble?"

"Of course, big guy!" Rocky said as he led the way to his kibble store. "Anything for my new partner. With me as the brains and you as my muscle, we're gonna make a great team!"

CHAPTER 4

KIBBLE AND BITS

Rocky's stash of kibble was through a door behind the receptionist's desk. It was some sort of storage area with metal shelves lining the walls. There were people things on the higher shelves, stacks of paper and boxes of pens, but Max didn't care one bit about those.

Not when there were bags upon bags of delicious, meaty kibble stacked atop one another. A mountain of food.

Rocky waddled into the room, saying, "Here we are, Max, all the—"

The smell of the food overwhelmed Max. He ran forward, diving headfirst into the nearest bag. He bit into the paper and yanked his head back and forth.

The bag tore, and little brown pebbles of kibble poured free, clattering against the linoleum, skittering into the corners.

Max chomped down, taking huge mouthfuls of the food and chewing it only briefly before swallowing. His stomach groaned, begging for more, more, more.

"Hey!" Rocky jumped up and down next to Max's head. "Leave some for the little guy!"

Max swallowed a mouthful and panted for breath. His gut ached now, but it was a good kind of ache—he'd been so hungry for so long.

A nip at his front heel. Max let out a yelp and looked down. It was Rocky, of course. The dim daylight that streamed from the lobby and into the dark storeroom glinted off his shiny black fur.

"You done?" Rocky asked. He looked at the floor littered with torn paper and crumbs of kibble. "Ugh, so messy! You bigger guys don't care much for cleanliness, probably 'cause you're so high up, you don't have to crawl through it. Well, I do, buddy, and let me tell you, it ain't a good time!"

"Sorry, Rocky," Max said, tearing his eyes away from the piles of food. "It's just been so long since I've eaten, I couldn't stop myself."

"Are you all full now?" Rocky asked.

Max nodded.

"Good." The small black dog turned and walked out

of the storeroom. "As long as we keep those wolves away, you won't ever starve again. Come on, let me show you the digs."

Max padded behind Rocky, strength returning to his tired limbs. As they rounded the receptionist's desk, he took in the catastrophe that was the destroyed lobby with fresh eyes. The last time he'd trashed a room this badly he'd been a puppy, and his pack leaders' parents sure hadn't been pleased with him.

"So what's the story with the wolves?" Max asked as Rocky led him back to the swinging turquoise door.

"Oh, those guys." Rocky snorted as he shoved past the door and into the dark hallway. "They've been coming around ever since the people went away. Kept threatening to tear me limb from limb, blah blah blah—I mean, who woulda thought they could actually get in and do anything? I would have ignored them, but they wouldn't stop slamming against the doors. So I dragged a bag of kibble or two to the kitty door to make 'em shut up, until I realized that if I kept doing that, I'd have no more food for me!" Rocky stopped and peered back over his shoulder. "Er, I mean for *us*, big guy! If I'd known you were in the kennel, I'd have stopped by sooner."

"Thanks," Max said. "I'm not sure how much longer I could have lasted trapped in there."

"No thanks necessary, buddy," Rocky said as he continued down the hallway to a door at the end. "Anyway, I shoved that chest in front of the door today to keep

Dolph and other wolves like Wretch from sticking their ugly mugs in the kitty flap, but I didn't know they'd figure out a way to break through."

"You couldn't have known," Max said. "Thanks again for knocking down that gum-ball machine."

"Don't mention it. We're a team now. Ah, here we are."

Rocky stopped in front of a closed door. It was at the very end of the hallway opposite the turquoise door. Max had never been through this door before.

The little Dachshund angled his head to look up at Max. "Follow me and I'll show you where my pack leaders live. There are so many beds to sleep on and so many toys to chew—oh, buddy, you gotta see it, you just gotta!"

Max raised one of his fuzzy eyebrows. "How do you open the door?"

"I don't." Saying that, Rocky turned from Max—and jumped through yet another cat flap, which Max hadn't noticed.

"That's not going to help me!" Max barked. Then he noticed that the door handle was the same lever style as the kennel's. Wagging his tail at his good luck, he jumped up and pushed down the lever. The door swung ajar.

Darting through, he caught the tail end of Rocky laboring to pull his long, short-legged self up the carpeted stairs. Max raced past the smaller dog, easily bounding up the steps.

His nails clattered against stone tiles when he

reached the landing. The stairs opened up into a large, light-filled kitchen. Everything seemed in place and clean: dishes stacked neatly inside cabinets with glass doors, people food in boxes lined up on the counter. The only thing that seemed out of place was a coffee pot filled with brown liquid, an empty mug beside it.

"Hey, wait up!" Rocky called from behind Max. "I— oof!—can't get up these steps as fast as you."

Dread filled Max's gut as he stared at the undrunk coffee—whoever had made it had left in a rush. The dream of the seeping darkness came back to Max, and his heart began to race.

Max padded out of the kitchen and into a neat dining room walled with windows, and then into a hallway. All the doors here were wide open, so he peeked into the nearest one.

It was a child's bedroom. The narrow bed was unmade, its pink-and-white sheets all tangled. Toys— dolls missing their heads, a little plastic oven, a half-chewed toy horse—were strewn across the floor. A closet door was open, as were all the drawers of a dresser painted with pink horses. All the clothes were gone.

"There you are," Rocky panted as he squeezed past Max into the room. "This was my pack leader's room, Vet's daughter. I get to sleep on her bed now that she's gone, and she left all her toys for me to play with. Considerate of her." The dog waddled to a chest at the foot of the bed, jumped atop it, then jumped once more onto the bed. He turned in a circle, then plopped himself down in the center of the sheets.

Max sniffed at the empty drawers. There was that vague mix of scents he'd smelled in the lobby. Urgency. Fear.

"Where did she go?" Max asked. "Where did all the people go?"

Rocky peered down at Max over the edge of the bed. "No clue, buddy. I was sleeping out in the living room one morning, and then my pack leader, Tracy, came and woke me up. She hugged me hard, and I licked her face and ran to get breakfast. Next thing I know, I go downstairs and the humans are rushing around all nervous-like before running outside. And they haven't been back since." Rocky dropped his head onto his paws. "But I'm sure they'll be back. They always come back."

"So Vet and his family had time to make sure you were fed, then?" Max asked, unable to keep his fur from bristling. "Why did they leave me locked in a cage to go hungry? Why would they do that?"

"It can't have been on purpose, big guy," Rocky said. "In fact, I saw Vet go into the room with the kennels the morning they left, and next thing I know, a big black dog with a shiny collar rushed out after Vet as he hurried away. Maybe he thought he'd set you free like the other dog, but your cage shut itself? Vet loves animals. He wouldn't have hurt you on purpose."

The big black dog must have been Madame Curie,

37

Max realized. So that's how she'd disappeared. But surely she would have noticed he was sleeping and that his cage was shutting, or had never been opened. Why didn't she wake him up before running off? Did it have something to do with her warnings?

"The black dog, did she say anything to you?" Max asked. "Did she say where she was going or mention me at all?"

Rocky tilted his head. "Now that you mention it, she did yell at me something about not letting 'him' follow her. I just assumed she meant Vet, since I didn't know you were here, too. Hey, maybe it was *her* who shut your cage!"

Max shook his head. "Why would she do that, though? Why wouldn't she want me to get out, too?"

"I dunno, big guy. But it makes more sense than Vet leaving you locked up." Gesturing with his snout, Rocky motioned toward the toys on the floor. "Just relax and have some fun. I like chewing on the little people dolls the best, even though their heads always come off. Or I got a nice bit of rope in the front room. Or—"

"I don't want to play with toys!" Max barked. "Whether Vet tried to let me out or not, my people still would have come for me if they had a choice. Something is wrong. I've got to find them."

Max turned and left the room. He had to find a way out. Padding down the hallway, he found himself in the big bedroom where Vet and his wife must have slept.

The room was just like the little girl's: bed unmade, dressers and closet empty. Misty gray daylight flooded through a large sliding glass door.

Max was across the room and nudging open the door when Rocky burst in. "Hey, whoa, hold on there!" he yelped as he scrambled to Max's side. "Where are you going, huh?"

Ignoring him, Max shoved the edge of the door with his snout. It gave, and cool air rushed through the crack. Shoving again, the door slid all the way open.

"Buddy, hey, buddy," Rocky said from behind Max, his voice jittery with nerves. "I don't think you're supposed to go out there. I tried it when I first moved here and got yelled at by my pack leader's mom. She was scary, let me tell you."

Max stuck his head through the opening and sniffed at the wooden floor beyond. The floorboards smelled of rotting wood and acrid bugs. It was a covered balcony, the bottom coated with dry, brown leaves. A low, slatted railing surrounded the balcony on all sides—with just enough space between each rail that a tiny dog like Rocky could slip right through.

"Max..." Rocky said.

Max looked back over his shoulder. "It's okay," he reassured the little dog. "They were probably just afraid you'd fall if they let you out on the balcony. But you're too smart for that, right?"

Rocky blinked. "Right, I'm glad you recognize that.

But why are you even going outside, big guy? There are wolves out there! In here is so much nicer. I guarantee it."

"I just want to have a look." Max took one step out, then another, crunchy leaves and painted wood under his feet. Humid air whooshed over his fur as he padded to the edge, where he rose up on his haunches and rested his paws on the railing.

Down below the broad railing opposite the sliding door, on the north side of the house, was a pool. Its water was murky—pine needles and leaves floated on its surface, and there were green flecks of something that looked moldy and spongy.

Beyond the pool was a big, open field, similar to the one surrounding Max's own home. That was how everything was around these parts, as Max knew—big fields dotted with the occasional home. Just past the flowing grass was the highway, lined with poles holding thick black wires, and past that a dark line of trees—the forest. Above it all was a gray, stormy sky.

Max shivered, sensing a dampness in the air—it would rain soon.

"All right, you see all you need to see, buddy?" Rocky asked, sticking his head through the doorway and sniffing. "Do you see your people out there?"

Max looked over the fields to the highway. He'd been trained long, long ago never to go across the strips of gray asphalt that cut through the grass—the highways and roads. All throughout the day, cars and trucks and big semis would grumble and race along them at superfast speeds, and if Max got in their way...

But the highway was silent, still.

"No." Max could not hear a single vehicle. "I don't see anything," Max said as he dropped back down onto all fours.

"Then it's best to just wait inside, right? Where it's comfortable and we have food."

Max went to the shorter, eastern edge of the balcony, which faced the road at the front of the house, where Vet had his office. Once more, he rested his front paws on the railing to get a look. He could see the edge of Vet's gravel parking lot, just past a high fence. The lot was empty, though there were rubber tire marks on the little road that seemed to lead to the highway.

"There's no one anywhere," Max said softly. It was all so *quiet*, in a way that Max had never known. He'd been around people his entire life. And even when they weren't around, his farm was a din of mooing cows and bleating sheep and buzzing flies.

But here: silence.

"Hey, big guy," Rocky said quietly as he came out and over to Max's side. "There's nothing we can do about it except wait for them. Come back inside."

Max let one paw drop from the railing, then the other. He sat back. Even though Rocky was standing beside him, he'd never felt so alone.

"I'm not giving up," Max said to Rocky without looking at him. "But it's going to rain soon. We should rest up inside. Then I'm finding a way out of here."

"All right," Rocky said. "Sounds like a plan I can get behind." Max watched as Rocky waddled back to the open sliding door, his tail wagging. "I got a really great rope we can play tug-of-war with, and then we can—"

Max and Rocky stiffened as sounds rose up from the front of the house, both of their ears twitching. Dozens and dozens of paws padded against grass and gravel, and several wolves began to howl in anguish and anger, their rage piercing Max's sensitive ears.

It had been silent here, in this abandoned home and Vet's office. Max had thought quiet meant that the wolves were gone.

He'd been wrong.

Max stuck his head between the slats of the railing. Rocky raced back and did the same. Below and to the right, in the empty gravel parking lot, a dozen or more gray and white wolves paced in small anxious circles. One stopped, a wolf larger than the others with three evenly spaced scars on his snout.

Dolph.

The wolf pack leader sneered up at the two dogs as the other howling wolves stopped circling and made a course to the road.

"You think you can keep me out?" Dolph roared up at them, his gums and teeth bared, his gray eyes

42

narrowed with hatred. "You think we will starve? We shall feast on your insides tonight!"

"Yeesh," Rocky muttered to Max. "And you wonder why I don't want to go traipsing through the fields? If it's not wolves trying to make a meal of your guts, it's bears or large birds or something."

"I shall wear your fur as my coat!" Dolph continued from below.

"Yeah, yeah, we get it," Rocky said.

"I shall put it on and pretend I am a pitiful dog, and my pack and I will laugh at how pathetic you domesticated beasts are! *We will laugh!*"

Looking up at Max, Rocky said, "Wolves! Always so crude, ya know?"

But Max's eyes were on Dolph's pack. The thin, sickly wolves weren't running across the street and into the fields as he'd expected. Instead, they'd circled one of the wooden poles, the one right at the edge of the parking lot. They barked and yelped as they scrambled over one another, almost as if trying to climb it.

No, not climb, Max realized. They were shoving at the base of the pole with all their weight. Already, the pole was leaning forward, the gravel and dirt at its base rippling from the force.

"What are they doing?" Max asked. Eyes wide, he looked down at Rocky. "What if they knock it over and use it as a bridge to get inside?"

Lifting a paw, Rocky swatted at the air dismissively. "Don't be silly, big guy! They couldn't possibly—"

From the lot, there came a loud, deafening *crack*. As Max and Rocky watched, the pile of wolves gave one last shove—and with a groan, the utility pole began to tilt toward the house.

"Or maybe they could," Rocky finished with a gulp.

CHAPTER 5

INFERNO

The pole fell slowly at first, creaking in protest as it leaned toward the house. The thick black wires attached to the top stretched taut, just barely keeping the pole from collapsing all the way.

"Maybe the wires will hold it up," Rocky said quietly.

The shoving wolves fell back, the entire pack looking up at the pole expectantly. It hung there, bouncing up and down from the momentum of falling and being snapped back up by the wires over and over again. The pole was taller than the house, like a giant tree stripped clean of its limbs, and it cast a long shadow over the parking lot.

"See?" Rocky said. "We're fine, buddy! No need to—"

Two of the power lines snapped, and with a

thunderous creak, the pole separated from its base and slammed down—straight onto the house's roof with a boom and an explosion of sparks.

The snapped lines whipped through the air, sizzling with electricity.

"Watch out!" Max barked, ducking down behind the balcony railing. Yelping, Rocky stumbled over his feet and hid behind Max's haunches.

The broken wires lashed and fell into the parking lot, where they sparked and coiled like live snakes. Beyond them, the pack of wolves howled in triumph, circling the base of the broken utility pole.

"What's happening?" Rocky asked. "Are they gonna climb up? I don't want my insides to get eaten! I need them!"

The thin, dirty wolves backed away, all eyes on Dolph. The big pack leader growled at them as he strode to the pole. Dolph stepped one paw on the pole, then another, gripping into the wood with his claws. Certain that he had his footing, he slowly started to walk up the makeshift bridge.

Max looked down at Rocky. "We need to get back inside and find a way to block this door. It's glass, so they can probably break through."

"How are we supposed to do that?" Rocky yelped. "We don't have enough time!"

An acrid smell met Max's nostrils, interrupting him before he could respond to Rocky. It was a familiar stench, one that reminded him of winters in front of the hearth back at the farm. But this smell was different somehow, heavier and dirty and...smoky.

Something was on fire.

From the road, the wolves once more began to howl. Bright orange flames stretched along the fallen utility pole. Dolph bared his teeth at the fire and stopped climbing. He was two-thirds of the way up, and the flames lit his face with an orange light.

"Whoa! Fire!" Rocky cried. Darting his head back through the railing, he barked in laughter. "Dolph!" he called. "Doesn't look like you thought this plan through all the way, did ya?"

"Uh, Rocky..." Max said. He couldn't see the fire yet, but he could *hear* it: flames crackling along the eaves above them.

Dolph roared, briefly taking his eyes off the bright flames. The wolf's eyes narrowed in defiance and rage.

One of the broken wires whipped up again and lashed Dolph's side. Yipping in pain and surprise, he lost his grip on the pole and tumbled through the air before landing in a heap on the gravel. The sparking wires snapped above his fallen body.

At first, Max thought the wolf might not get up. But Dolph slowly climbed to his feet, licking his wounds. The fire had engulfed the entire pole by now, running back along its length and sending a cloud of greasy black smoke up into the gray sky. Howling, Dolph backed away from the wires and the pole and rejoined his pack. He turned and began loping toward the field, his pack falling in behind him. Together, they cut paths through the long grass as they raced toward the faraway hills.

"Yeah, you better run!" Rocky barked, jumping excitedly. "And don't come back!"

"Rocky!" Max barked again.

"What is it, big guy? Can't you see I'm busy celebrating over here?"

"Rocky, we have to get out of here, too!" he barked. "The house is on fire!"

"What?!"

Now Max could feel the warmth and see the flickering light of flames as they burst out along the edge of the roof over the balcony. The fire was spreading—fast.

"What do we do now?" Rocky cried. He darted back and forth. "What are we gonna—oh, no! The kibble!" Looking up at Max, terrified, Rocky shouted, "Buddy, we need to save the kibble!"

Before Max could stop him, Rocky bolted back through the open sliding glass door into the dark bedroom.

"Rocky, no!" Max barked.

A foot-long piece of the roof, consumed by flames, broke off and fell onto the balcony. Immediately, a few leaves caught fire, shrinking into little black husks.

Max whined deep in his throat, head darting to look between the open sliding glass door and the pool just beyond the balcony. He needed to flee.

But he couldn't abandon his new friend.

Whipping around, Max bounded through the bedroom and into the hallway. Thick, oily smoke undulated against the ceiling, growing heavier and bigger, swirling down to shroud everything in blackness.

Just like in Max's dream.

Max's eyes burned and watered, blurring his vision. "Rocky!" he barked as he raced down the hallway, the heat drying his throat. "We need to get out of here!"

He was almost to the stairs that led to Vet's office and kennel below when the roof at the far end of the hallway in front of him caved in.

Shards of flaming wood and heavy beams fell from the ceiling, slamming against the carpet in a thunderous, roiling heap. Fire whooshed up the walls, so white hot that Max felt as if his fur were on fire. He crouched down, his belly to the floor, and backed along the hallway, keeping his head low as the heavy smoke grew even murkier.

"Rocky!" Max barked, certain that his friend was cut off, trapped downstairs. He took in deep, heaving breaths that hurt his throat, not daring to think of the little sausage dog, huddled in a corner with all his kibble, nowhere to run....

"Buddy, I don't think we can go that way!"

Max sighed in relief as the little black figure that was Rocky emerged from the smoke, hacking. His brown markings were dark with soot.

"I don't think going back for the kibble was such a good idea," Rocky said sheepishly.

From deep in the house came another boom as something heavy collapsed. And then a sound of windows shattering. Around them, flames crawled down the walls, flaring brightly and burning up the air in the hallway.

"Come on!" Max barked, galloping back toward the master bedroom. "We need to get out of here while we still can!"

"Don't have to tell me twice!" Rocky barked back.

They burst into the bedroom, Max's eyes and throat aching from the smoke and heat. It wasn't as bad in here, with the smoke swirling out through the open door. There was just one problem.

The entire balcony was burning.

The two dogs skidded to a stop, staring at the flickering orange flames blocking their escape. Behind them, the heat was immense, the whole house going up like a raging bonfire.

"What do we do now?" Rocky howled in fear, hiding his face. "I'm too young to die, big guy! I have plans! There's so many different brands of kibble I never got to try, and so many toys I never got to chew, and—"

"We jump for it." Max crouched low and took in a deep breath of what clean air there still was near the floor. "There's the pool just over the balcony's edge—if we can land in there, we won't get hurt."

"Are you kidding?" Rocky asked. "The balcony is on fire! We'll get burned up!"

"If we don't try, we'll get burned up anyway," Max said. He stood and tensed his hind legs, preparing to run.

Tail tucked between his legs, Rocky backed away from the burning balcony outside the door. "I can't, big guy," he said. "I just can't."

"Yes, you can!" Max barked. The wallpaper in the bedroom was burning now, curling up the walls in strips that instantly turned to ash. The smoke in the room was so thick that it was becoming hard for the two dogs to see each other. "You're a brave dog—you've shown that to me. Follow me. I promise you'll be safe. Now come on!"

Not waiting for an answer, Max barreled forward, his heart pounding. Every instinct in his body screamed at him to stop, to turn away from the flames, to hide.

Clenching his eyes closed, he jumped onto the balcony, the pads of his paws burning. Too late to go back now.

One huge leap.

And he was in the sky.

Distantly, behind him, Max heard a familiar voice cry out, "Hiiiiiii-*yah!*"

CHAPTER 6

THE ROAD HOME

Max was flying.

He felt like he would never touch the ground again. A crisp, cool wind rushed past him as he flew forward, away from the flames that seemed to be searing his back, away from the place of his days-long captivity. Away from the darkness and toward his people.

And then he was falling, his ears blowing up past his snout, the world spinning.

He slammed into the water.

Max landed so heavily that the air was knocked out of him and his belly stung. He sank beneath the pool's surface and instinctively tried to breathe, but the chilly, murky water gushed into his burning throat.

Panicking, he opened his eyes and slapped at the

water with his paws, struggling to reach the surface. Something splashed into the pool right above him, and the surge of bubbles was like a guiding trail. Max swam up, his head finally bursting out into the air once more. He hacked and coughed up water.

A moment later, Rocky's head popped up beside him. A wet leaf was stuck to the little dog's forehead, and like Max, he gasped for air.

"We made it," Max said, relief washing over him as he dog-paddled toward his friend.

"We made it!" Rocky repeated with confidence. "I always knew we would."

Max just rolled his eyes.

Together, the two of them swam through the leaf-strewn water to the edge of the pool. Behind them, sparks showered down, floating in the air and fizzing out as they met the water. The groans of the dying house and the whoosh of the devouring flames were thunderously loud.

The two dogs plopped onto the concrete that surrounded the pool. Max was so exhausted, he couldn't even bother to stand and shake the water off his fur. Instead, he rolled onto his side and watched Vet's house burn, the heat from the flames drying his body even from this distance.

The walls collapsed and the fire flickered, but Max's eyes were on the billowing cloud of smoke that filled the sky. It was so much like the darkness in his dreams—the inky menace that was coming for him and his pack leaders. He shuddered.

Rocky stood and shook, flinging water all over, then sat and watched the burning house with wide, forlorn eyes.

"All that kibble..." he said with a sniff. "Gone, just like that."

"Don't worry, Rocky," Max said as he got to his feet and shook himself. "Just be glad we're safe."

There came a loud crack from the sky, and both dogs yelped. The gray clouds had grown darker, and not just from the smoke.

"It's gonna rain," Max said. "We should find shelter."

Rocky looked at the empty field. "You have any idea where to go, big guy?"

Max looked toward where the wolves had disappeared, across the road that ran in front of Vet's house. "Anywhere Dolph and those wolves are not." Shifting his gaze, he tried to remember the way his pack leaders' parents always drove him to Vet. They usually came down the highway. It was as good a place to start for home as any.

"Follow me," Max said. "I think I can find my way to my house. We'll be safe there."

The sky cracked again. A fat pellet of water splashed onto Max's nose, another on his back. Max began to gallop north toward the highway, Rocky at his heels. As heavy rain started to fall, they burst from the grass, ran across the eerily empty highway—and headed toward the shadowy safety of the trees.

Max and Rocky were soaking wet again by the time they reached the forest.

Rainwater dripped from Max's nose and tail, and all his golden fur was matted and soaked. It was so cold out that he could barely contain the shivering in his legs.

The smaller dog had grown silent the farther they got from the destroyed house. Max slowed his gait as they padded through the underbrush between the trees, just to make sure he didn't lose Rocky. But the little Dachshund kept pace, even as his head was slung low and his tail was tucked between his legs.

Max wasn't sure how long they'd been walking, but it was growing darker and darker beneath the trees. Water plopped down from the canopy of branches above, but it was nowhere near as bad as the heavy rainfall out in the open fields.

When he could walk no more and his eyes were drooping with exhaustion, Max turned in a circle and lay down at the base of a tall tree between two thick roots. The bark was solid and a comfort against his back—no one could sneak up on him here. And there were lots of branches with wide leaves above, the better to protect them from the rain.

Rocky nudged Max with his snout. "We can't stop

here, buddy. We're still outside! There could be wolves around or—" With a sharp intake of breath, Rocky went rigid and looked up. Almost whispering, he said, "Birds. Big ones with an appetite for Dachshund!"

Max raised his head. "It'll be okay, Rocky. I sleep outside all the time, and no bird is going to try to snatch you with me right here."

Rocky's eyes went wide. "You sleep *outside?* Like some sort of wild animal?" Pawing at the damp earth, Rocky lifted his snout in disgust. "I mean, running around outside is fun and all, but only when you have *people* around and it's *daytime.* I *always* sleep in my bed or on my pack leader's bed. This is just"—he snorted—"messy."

Resting his head on his paws, Max closed his eyes. "It'll just be for tonight. Aren't you cold and tired? We should curl up together to conserve our warmth."

Rocky sighed, then Max felt him curl up against his belly. "Yuck, yuck, yuck," he muttered as he moved around again and again, apparently trying to get comfortable atop the damp grass. "The things I go through. What a world."

But Max could barely hear him. He was already drifting off. A distant part of his brain barked at him to get back on his feet, to keep moving, to *find his people.* But it had been such a long day—escaping the cage, fighting the wolf, exploring Vet's house, fleeing from flames....

Exhaustion swept over Max, and he slept.

Max runs through the overgrown fields by his people's farm, the dirt dry and hard beneath his paws, the smell of summer in the air. He's chasing after his pack leaders, Charlie and Emma, the two of them laughing and playing without him. Why would they play without him?

Nothing is right.

A darkness is behind Max, curling up into the sky, swirling and inky black like smoke pouring forth from a burning building.

This darkness isn't smoke. It is something much worse.

Max has to save Charlie and Emma from the darkness. But the more he runs, the farther they appear, until they are nothing more than two tiny, shadowy dots on the horizon, far, far away. . . .

Max's eyes snapped open. His head shot up, and he blinked, trying to remember where he was. He needed to be home. Charlie and Emma were in trouble!

The day before came back to Max in a flash. He was still in the woods with a little furry black sausage dog curled up beside him.

For a long time, Max lay there, surrounded by the damp scents of wet leaves and fresh mud, just listening to the woods. The rain had petered out, but he could still hear the *drip-drip-drip* of water falling from leaves.

There was a distant buzzing of insects and the croaking of tree frogs, but he didn't hear any birds.

And he didn't hear any sounds of people. No cars on the highway just beyond the woods. No music or TV noise from any nearby houses, if there were any this far in the forest. No one calling his name, searching for their lost dog.

Max couldn't help but whimper as he lowered his head against his paws.

He tried to go back to sleep. But he kept imagining he heard footsteps, only to dart his head back up to see nothing and no one in the black woods.

Beside him, Rocky rolled over and snorted, then rolled over again.

"Rocky," Max whispered, "are you awake?"

For a moment, Max's words hung empty in the quiet woods. Then Rocky grunted.

"Can you tell me more about what happened before all the people left?" Max asked quietly.

Rocky snorted. "Already did."

"But maybe if you tell me everything, even if it doesn't seem important, it'll help us figure out what happened."

With a whine, Rocky rolled around again, shoving uncomfortably into Max's gut. His back legs kicked dirt and leaves into Max's face, and Max scrunched his nose to keep from sneezing.

"They just left," Rocky grumbled. "They did people

stuff in the morning like always. Then fed me, let that black dog go, and left in a hurry."

"Is that it? Did you—"

"Buddy, that's all I got!"

Rocky jumped up onto his four stubby legs and stomped away. Plopping down six feet away, he flung a front paw over his snout in exasperation.

Max sighed. "I wish Madame were here."

"Who?" Rocky grumbled from beneath his paw.

"She was the big black dog you just said you saw leave when Vet did," Max said. "She was smart, so much smarter than me. And she kept talking about how she felt something coming. Maybe she knew something. Maybe..."

"Maybe she did," Rocky snapped. "But she isn't here, is she? Look, no offense, big guy, I'm sorry your old lady friend ran off. You seem nice enough and you helped me with Dolph and the fire and everything, but I'm not much in the mood to talk, since I can't help thinkin' this is all your fault."

Max blinked in surprise. "*My* fault? Why?"

Rocky got up and paced back and forth, spitting the words out in harsh barks. "I was doing just fine on my own before you showed up. I had the wolves under control, I had all the food I could eat, an actual *bed* to sleep on. Then you saunter in, pick a fight with Wretch, and next thing I know, my house is burned down and I have no food!"

Max's ears and tail drooped. "I didn't mean any

trouble," he said softly. "I just needed to eat, and now I need to find my people. I'm sorry about your house."

"*Sorry*s aren't gonna fill my belly, big guy!" Rocky said. He fell to the grass on his back. "What are we gonna eat out here? All that meaty, delicious kibble, burned to a crisp! It's a travesty!"

Max studied the underbrush around them. "Maybe I can, you know...hunt."

Rocky stared at Max, aghast. "*Hunt?* You mean kill something and *eat* it? That's pretty barbaric, buddy. I'm a domestic dog, through and through."

Max ducked his head. "I've never actually hunted before, but I have chased little animals around the farm, and it's better than going hungry. It doesn't seem too hard to catch something. I mean, if a wolf can do it..."

Rocky once more placed his paw in front of his eyes. "That's it, we're doomed. I'm going to starve to death out here in the woods with a big gold puppy who likes to set things on fire!"

"I didn't cause the fire—"

Rocky yowled, drowning him out. "Oh, what a cruel, unjust world! Why me? Why now?"

Ignoring him, Max stood and stretched his legs. It didn't seem quite as dark out now—the sky was growing brighter between the branches overhead—and that meant the sun was coming back up. And the rain-scrubbed air was clean—letting familiar, distant scents waft through the woods to meet Max's nostrils.

Max did feel bad about Rocky losing his home. He couldn't imagine what it would be like to watch his farm turn into a blackened shell, gutted by fire. He had to make it up to the little dog somehow.

But he still needed to figure out what was going on and where his people had gone. Maybe if he could find someplace or someone familiar, that would help. Or, with any luck, maybe he could find Madame and have her explain what her cryptic warnings had meant.

Lifting his snout high, Max took in big breaths of woodsy air through his nostrils as he turned in a circle. He could smell the scent of some wild dog who'd marked his territory nearby and the fading musk of small woodland creatures like squirrels and rabbits.

And floating on the breeze were the scents of a farm: hay and manure and grass and cows and pigs. Only... those last two scents were *wrong*, somehow, not the way the animals usually smelled. The stench, even from so far away, made Max's stomach roil.

He couldn't be sure it was his farm, not yet. But it was *a* farm, and it was worth checking out.

Still on his back, Rocky flung himself back and forth. "I was always a good dog," he yelped. "I never made a mess on the carpet. I let my pack leader's friends pet me even when their hands were all sticky. I even stayed off the couch. Mostly. So why me? Why?!"

"Hey, Rocky," Max barked. "I think I know where to

go. I can smell a farm. We can go there and see if my people are there, and—"

Rocky jumped up onto all four feet, ears perked up. "Will there be kibble?"

Max nodded. "There should be. They always have a big bag in the pantry for me."

"Well!" Rocky sauntered over to Max's side. "I knew I rescued you from the kennel and followed you out here for a reason, buddy! Lead the way!"

Max raised an eyebrow. "Weren't you just howling about how I ruined your whole life?"

Rocky snapped at the air. "I just get a little cranky when I'm hungry."

Following his nose from the highway, Max soon started to recognize sights that he saw through his family's car whenever they drove him to and from Vet's office. Hopeful, Max confidently led the way, and it wasn't long before he and Rocky broke from the line of trees and Max saw a familiar sight.

There, just off a gravel road that branched from the highway, was his farm.

The wide-open field was surrounded by the jagged black bars of an old wooden fence, and there was a bright red barn at the farthest end. And down a gravel road, his house, a big yellow home with white shutters and a porch that wrapped around everything and that he liked to crawl under.

The sun was shining brightly, warming up his golden fur, and there was barely a cloud in the sky. The yellowed grass of the fields behind the house waved gently back and forth in the afternoon breeze.

It was perfect. Everything was perfect. He was home, at long last. Home!

"We're here!" Max barked, his tail wagging. He leaped up and down, barking again, "We're here, we're here!" Why weren't Charlie and Emma coming out to meet him? "I'm home!" he barked.

Max barreled forward as fast as his legs could carry him. He heard Rocky protesting behind him—"Hey, buddy, I can't run that fast!"—but all he cared about was running through the front door, careering into the den, and slobbering all over Charlie and Emma while they petted him and—

But then he slowed and stopped in the middle of the gravel driveway.

Something wasn't right.

In fact, something was very, very wrong.

CHAPTER 7

NO ONE HOME

Max could smell the cows, but they didn't smell like they should—there were still the familiar aromas of cow and of hay, but those smells barely masked the stench of something putrid. And Max always equated the cows with a smell he could only describe as warmth. That smell was gone, not even a linger of it in the clear air.

There was no mooing. No clucking chickens, no belching pigs. Like the woods and the highway, the farm was much too silent.

"Thanks for letting me catch up," Rocky panted as he came to Max's side. "I—ugh! What is that stink? It smells *rotten*."

Swallowing, Max padded from the gravel road over the grass and up the slope to the fence. Peering between the slats, he saw a cow lying by the door of the distant barn—and recoiled at the sight.

It was dead. From the smell, Max guessed that the ones in the barn were probably dead as well.

Max had seen them all just two weeks before, standing around, chewing their cud, and staring at one another, bored, with big black eyes. And now they were dead.

Flies swarmed above the cow's body.

Someone—or something—had killed it and left it there.

The rancid smell made Max's gut churn and his eyes water. He backed away from the fence, his tail between his legs. Once he was back on the drive, the rise of the hill blocked the image of the dead animal in the yard and the dark, open barn that was so quiet when it should have been loud with bleating and cawing.

"What happened?" Rocky asked.

"I don't know," Max whispered. "I don't—" Swallowing back the bile that had risen in his throat, Max took off toward the house. The sun was shining and the breeze was blowing and the house looked as inviting as ever, and yet Max knew something was deeply wrong.

His paws against the gravel were the only noise as he ran. Max galloped down the road and veered off across the grass of the front yard. There was no car in the driveway. The windows were all dark. But maybe his people were in there, hiding from whatever had happened. Maybe they were waiting for him just beyond the door—

The car is gone.

Max leaped up the steps of the wooden porch and jumped against the front door, howling and barking, claws scrabbling against the painted wood. He barked out his pack leaders' names, knowing that even though they wouldn't understand his words, they would know it was him.

Dropping onto all fours, Max paced along the porch, the floorboards creaking beneath his paws. He raised himself up to look through the windows, but the inside of the house was dark.

"I'm home!" he howled. "Charlie! Emma! I'm here! I came back for you!"

"Um, buddy..."

Startled, Max jumped, then looked behind him. Rocky was struggling to pull himself up the porch steps.

"They have to be here," Max whimpered. "They have to be home."

Waddling up to Max, Rocky nuzzled his neck. "Hey, big guy, it'll be all right. I told you, the people are all gone. We gotta make do for ourselves till they get back."

"But why would they leave me?" The stench of the dead cow from the barnyard met his nose, and Max swallowed back his nausea again.

"I dunno, buddy," Rocky said. "But we should get inside and fill up our bellies. At the very least, we got us a home again."

Sighing, Max stood back up, his tail dragging and

his ears drooping even more than usual. "Come on," he said flatly, leading Rocky across the porch. "This wraps around the whole house. I think we can find a way in."

"All right!" Rocky barked. "Kibble time!"

Max wanted to be mad at the Dachshund—his people were *gone* and that cow was *dead*—but he had to admit, his stomach was empty, too. As he led the little dog to the back of the house, he reasoned with himself: If the car was gone, that meant his people had driven somewhere. They were safe, at least.

"Here," Max said as they reached the back door. "This leads into the kitchen. It's got a bottom half and a top half, see?"

Rocky stared up at the white door. "Fascinating," he said. "Can you get it open?"

Max leaped up and slammed his front paws against the top half of the door. It swung open easily. As he dropped back down to all fours, he said, "Sure can. The latch never works."

Together, the two dogs nosed a nearby deck chair over to the door, and then Rocky—with some assistance from Max—jumped up through the open top half. Max followed, landing heavily on slick linoleum on the other side.

Rocky was already checking out the place. The small dog sauntered through the kitchen and into the dining room, looking every which way.

"Not bad, not bad," he said. "Not quite as nice as my old digs, but it has a certain homey feel to it."

Max growled. "Glad you approve. Ready for that kibble?"

Rocky barked a laugh. "Look who you're askin', big guy!"

The pantry was ajar, so Max nudged it open with his nose. Before he even had the door open all the way, Rocky darted through, salivating so much that drool dripped from his lips. The entire pantry smelled of the kibble—meaty and slightly chalky. There were two bags in the back of the pantry, one opened and one sealed shut. Even though the open bag was three times as big as Rocky himself, the little dog had no problem tipping it over and spilling a feast all over the dusty floor.

The two dogs dove in, snapping up the little brown pellets. As they did, Max looked up at the rest of the pantry. The shelves were strangely bare—his pack leaders' parents usually kept the small room packed with cans of people food, piled high all the way to the ceiling. But there wasn't much left, just a few things like bananas with blackened peels and a few dusty boxes.

After their meal, Max led Rocky to the downstairs bathroom, where they took turns gulping water from the toilet. Rocky informed him that he considered toilet water quite a delicacy. "It just has that special taste, ya know?"

Full with water and kibble, Max let Rocky wander around and check out his home. But Max had a new mission: He had to find clues to where his people went.

He started in the kitchen and dining room. He found

a newspaper on the dining room table, but the pictures on the pages didn't tell him anything.

Next was the living room with the old stone fireplace in front of which he liked to sleep in the winter, and the white-tiled front entryway, where the stairs led up to the bedrooms. Nothing there, either. But as Max neared the den, a buzzing met his ears—something electric and familiar.

The TV was on.

Max padded into the carpeted den. Rounding the worn gray couch he'd spent many a night dozing on, he saw that the TV was glowing at the empty room. It wasn't showing any cartoons this time, and the sound was somehow shut off.

But what the TV showed was interesting enough.

"So do you think your pack leaders would mind if I chewed on some of their toys?" Rocky said, coming in behind Max. "They got some real juicy-looking—"

"Shh," Max said. "I need to watch this."

Rocky waddled to Max and sat beside him. "I don't see why I gotta be quiet when there's no sound to listen to anyway," he grumbled.

Max ignored him, too engrossed with the pictures he was seeing on the screen. A red, scary symbol kept flashing—Max knew in his heart that the symbol meant something bad. Between the symbols, there were images:

A highway like the one near the farm and by Vet's office, only seen from up high. This one was crowded

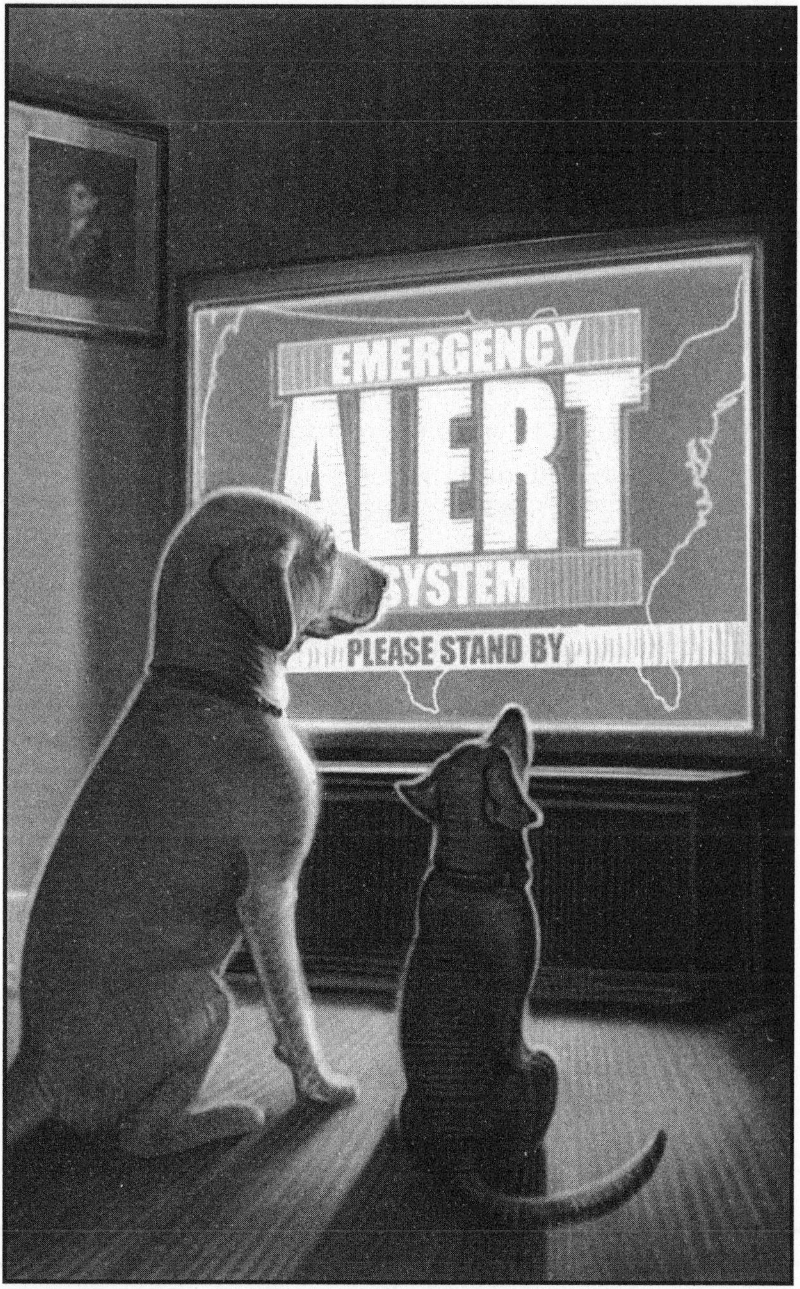
EMERGENCY
ALERT
SYSTEM
PLEASE STAND BY

with cars, so many that none could move. They looked like brightly colored ants trying to swarm over winding, asphalt logs.

A row of houses along a street filled with people—some wearing green clothes and scary helmets, waving their arms and guiding the people toward trucks like the ones his pack used when they moved the cows.

A map with a bunch of symbols Max didn't recognize. But there were animated arrows along squiggly lines that could symbolize roads, and the arrows all moved away from the center.

"What does it mean?" Rocky asked as he watched the silent images next to Max.

"I don't know," Max said, confused. "But I think the people in the helmets are making everyone get in their cars and drive away."

The image changed again. This time to a sandy beach. There were cars parked everywhere, and more people than Max had ever seen crowding the shores, staring out over the water. It reminded Max of his visits to the lake when his pack leaders' parents took them all fishing, but this lake was bigger than any he'd ever seen.

The image disappeared, replaced by the ominous red symbol. And then the same videos played all over again.

Max jumped up to his feet. "That's where we need to go," he announced.

"Where?" Rocky asked.

"The big lake. You saw the pictures. All the cars drove away and are at the giant lake now."

"That wasn't a lake, big guy. That's what they call the *ocean*. I used to be part of another pack, and we would go to the ocean once a year. I didn't like it. Too much sand."

"I don't care," Max said. "That's where our people have to be."

Rocky stood up, stretched his legs, and yawned. He then bounded up onto the coffee table, and from there onto Max's well-worn couch.

"But we just got here, buddy! Let's just hang out, play with some toys, eat some kibble, and rest up. I'm sure your people will be home soon."

"No," Max barked, harsher than he'd intended. Seeing Rocky's eyes go wide in shock, Max cleared his throat and said again, "Don't you see? They *can't* come back. There's too many cars, and the weird men in suits won't let them. We have to go to them."

Before Rocky could protest, Max padded out of the den.

"We'll spend the night here," he called behind him as he walked. "We'll rest and eat up. And then I'm going for my family, with or without you."

CHAPTER 8

WAGONS EAST

Max slept in fits and starts.

Being at home and surrounded by all the familiar smells of his pack was comforting, but the things he'd seen haunted his dreams. He found himself in the same nightmare, chasing Charlie and Emma as darkness blotted out the blue of the sky—but only for brief, flashy moments before his eyes snapped open and he discovered he was still in the empty den.

What he remembered in the flashes was different this time. Because it wasn't just Charlie and Emma on the horizon—it was Madame, too. She wasn't running away or playing. Instead, she sat patiently between Max and his pack leaders, her lips moving, silently saying, "I can take you there."

If only she hadn't darted out of Vet's office without him. If only she'd been more clear in her warnings. Maybe if he could find her while he traveled, she could help piece together the puzzle of the missing humans, instead of Max having to guess as best he could.

Max found that pacing in circles didn't calm him. Snacking on kibble and sipping more toilet water filled his stomach but not the emptiness that kept him awake and worried. His heart thudded much too loudly when he tried to lie back down on the den's couch, drowning out even Rocky's honking snores.

Finally, Max gave up. Even though it was still dark outside, he couldn't wait any longer.

He had to leave.

Max was in the middle of dragging a chair across the linoleum floor of the kitchen, its white wooden leg clamped in his jaws, when Rocky stumbled into the room, yawning.

Seeing Max, Rocky stopped midyawn, then blinked his big brown eyes once, twice.

"What are you doing, buddy?"

Max let go of the chair leg, leaving behind spittle-drenched teeth marks. "I couldn't sleep anymore. I'm putting this chair by the door so I can hop back outside and find my people."

Rocky blinked again, then shook his head. "You were just going to leave me here, big guy? After all we've been through?"

Max looked down, his tail drooping. "You said yesterday that you just wanted a place to stay safe until the people came back. I figured I'd leave while you were sleeping so you wouldn't feel like you had to come with me."

Rocky padded across the linoleum and shoved the chair with his head. "Awful generous of you, buddy," the little Dachshund said between shoves. "But I was just comin' in here to tell you that I've been thinking about what you said and what we saw on TV, and that I decided I'm coming with you."

"Yeah?" Max asked, and his tail began to wag. "But what about the kibble?"

"What about it?" Rocky asked. "We'll bring it with us."

"We will?"

Barking a laugh, Rocky shook his head. "See, you need me, buddy. I just don't think you're as concerned about eating as you should be! Anyway, I saw a little red wagon on the porch when we came in yesterday. That belong to your pack leaders?"

It did. There was a leather harness attached to its handle. Sometimes, Charlie and Emma would strap Max to it, and he'd run around the fields, dragging the wagon behind him and giving his pack leaders the best ride of their lives. He couldn't usually carry them for too long, because they were a little bit heavy, and the wheels always caught in the mud and against stone. But kibble weighed a lot less than two children, and roads were made for things with wheels....

Tail wagging faster and lips relaxed into a smile, Max said to Rocky, "I can't believe I didn't think of that!"

"Of course you didn't, big guy," Rocky said. "That's why I'm the brains of the outfit."

Max looked at the chair he'd dragged up against the inside of the double door, like the lawn chair on the other side they'd used to get through the day before. Through the open top half of the door, he saw that the sky had turned gray as the sun began to rise. "But how are we going to get a bag of kibble all the way up there?"

"Hmm," Rocky said, looking around the kitchen. "Good question."

It took several hours and a lot of dragging of chairs, furniture, and couch cushions before they'd managed to create a ramp. "It's like a soft mountain," Rocky said, testing it by waddling up to the edge of the door. "*Much* easier than trying to throw the bag over!"

After a quick breakfast of kibble and toilet water, the two dogs dragged the second, unopened bag of kibble to the mound of furniture and then, growling, tugged it all the way up to the edge of the door. Finally, panting a breathless "Hiiii-yah!" Rocky nudged the bag over the closed bottom half of the door. It landed with a crunchy thud on the porch outside.

That done, Rocky gingerly jumped onto the lawn chair and down. Max bunched his legs to join him, but then stopped to take in his home one last time.

It was strange seeing the kitchen so quiet. Max's food and water dishes were tucked in a corner, both empty. There were no dirty footprints from the children on the linoleum. No adult humans talking on the phone while pulling people kibble out of the cupboards and refrigerator. None of the enticing smells of human cooking. No bright lights for Max to lounge beneath, lying on his side and waiting for his belly to be rubbed.

He'd found his house again. But, Max realized, he had a ways to go before he found his home.

Turning away from the dark, silent kitchen, Max leaped onto the lawn chair and onto the porch.

"What took you so long?" Rocky asked, looking up from the bag of kibble.

"It's nothing," Max said softly. "Let's get this bag in the wagon and head out."

Noon was fully upon them when Max and Rocky walked down the gravel driveway toward the main road that ran in front of Max's farm. The bag of kibble filled the entire bed of the red toy wagon, which squeaked behind Max. He'd slipped into the harness okay, though he didn't like the way it was loose around his limbs. His pack leaders always pulled the straps tight around his front legs and chest. But he'd have to make do.

Rocky kept up beside Max, his legs little black blurs as he matched the bigger dog's stride. So far, the extra strain of pulling the wagon aside, their journey was going just swell.

Finally, the two dogs reached the main road.

Rocky darted out to the center and spun in a circle on the yellow lines that were painted down the middle of the road. "Ooh, yellow bricks!" he barked. "I've seen these in one of my pack leader's movies. We're supposed to follow them." Spinning to see the lines stretching both east and west, he barked to Max, "But, uh, which way do we go?"

Max looked to their right, in the direction of Vet's burned-out home—and the wolves. To the left was the direction his pack leaders' parents drove their car down most often. He didn't typically pay much attention, since if he was in the car, he was usually playing with his pack leaders in the backseat or putting his head out the window and having the wind—and all the wonderful scents it carried—blow past his face. But if he had to guess where the people would go first, he'd guess that direction.

Max gestured left with his snout, then headed to the center of the road to stand next to Rocky. "I think it's this way to where all the buildings are. The town."

Rocky looked up at him. "It's not very far, is it? I'm already exhausted just from hauling that wagon all the way out here."

"Hey, I'm the one hauling—"

"I'm not sure how long I can last without another

break, buddy," Rocky interrupted. "Just so you know." Spinning around to look both directions down the long, empty road once more, Rocky let out a small whine. "Oh, I'm already regretting this."

Max sighed. "It's not too late if you want to go back to the house and stay there."

Rocky looked uneasily behind them at the quiet barn that once held the cows. "Uh, no, I think I'd rather stay with you. Lead the way, big guy. Besides, where the kibble goes, I follow."

The sun blazed overhead, warming the asphalt beneath their paws and making heat rise up off its smooth black surface. The air shimmered around them as the two dogs marched along the empty, silent street.

It was strange to walk down the center of the road. Max had been trained long ago to never, ever go into the street unless he was led across it by one of his people. At first, Max felt guilty—like he should be walking on the gravel or grass on either side of the street. But the wagon rolled so smoothly on the asphalt, and no one else was using the road, and soon Max forgot to feel as if he was doing something bad.

Max and Rocky didn't talk much as they walked. Max was rapidly learning that Rocky's good moods lasted only as long as he was in the lap of luxury. Hiking down a long stretch of road with the sun beating down on their fur, for hours and hours, wasn't exactly glamorous. But to the little dog's credit, Rocky didn't whine. Much.

It was still so strangely quiet outside that it made Max's insides twist and turn in worry. If there were any birds, they had gone mute, and the result was that all Max could hear were his and Rocky's breaths and footsteps, the squeaking of the wagon wheels, and the buzzing of insects. The wide fields and clusters of trees on either side of the road provided nothing but the rustling of leaves and grass.

If it weren't for the images of people on the television, Max would almost wonder if all the people had just disappeared.

Of course, there was no way to know when those images he'd seen on the TV had taken place. One time when he'd sat and watched the television, the screen showed images of Charlie and Emma playing with Max— but they were both in the room, watching with Max!

It had confused Max until he saw himself chasing a chicken with Emma, and then he remembered that earlier in the week, one of his pack leaders' parents had pointed something at them—a tiny silver thing. Max figured it must have been a camera, like the ones that took the pictures of them framed on the walls, only this one took *motion* pictures. The TV just played back events that had already happened.

If the disappearance of all the people started with cars clogging roads and strange people in helmets, what happened after? What had they been running from?

Max was snapped out of his thoughts when his shoulders met more resistance than usual from pulling the red wagon behind him. He stopped, letting the wagon bump into his hind legs. Looking back over his shoulder, he saw Rocky lying atop the bag of kibble, head resting on his paws.

One of Rocky's watery eyes was open. As soon as the Dachshund saw Max looking back, his eye shut tight.

Max sighed. "Rocky, what are you doing?"

The little dog honked a snore and then flopped onto his other side, eyes still closed. "Can't talk," he mumbled. "Sleeping."

Max yelped. "No, you're not. You just talked! Come on, get down from there. You're making the wagon hard to pull."

Rocky lifted his head and opened his eyes wide and sad. "Aw, come on, buddy, please? Just for a little while! We can take turns. I can pull you next!"

Max looked from Rocky to the wagon to the harness. There was no way the little dog would be able to pull it for more than a few feet before collapsing in exhaustion.

Max sighed again. "All right, fine," he said. "But you owe me one."

His short spike of a tail wagging, Rocky rested his head back on his paws. "You got it, big guy."

Growling, Max turned his attention back to the road. Behind him, Rocky cleared his throat.

"Max, I'm serious," Rocky said softly. "Thanks for letting me rest. When you need me sometime down the road, I got your back. Okay?"

Max nodded slightly. "Okay. Now rest up. And try not to be too heavy."

As the sun began dropping from the middle of the sky, Max saw a car parked on the side of the road.

It was smaller than the vans and trucks his people drove, and it was the color of rust. The windows were rolled down, the doors flung open, the interior empty. There were no houses or buildings around that Max could see, just more empty fields and distant woods—no reason for anyone to park and leave their car for too long.

Slipping out of the harness, Max left the wagon, kibble, and a snoring Rocky in the center of the road. Padding softly, Max lowered his head and sniffed the asphalt as he neared the car. There were dark marks on the road, tracks that led to the car's four black wheels. The marks smelled of burned rubber.

Max crept closer to the silent vehicle, his heart thudding. He wished there would be people there, nice people who would let him and Rocky sit in the backseat and then drive them to their pack leaders. Maybe they were hiding on the other side. Maybe they'd left for just a minute to go into the woods and would come right back.

But it was clear to Max that there hadn't been people there in days. The car had been abandoned, and the smells of the strange people who'd once driven it were cold and unfamiliar. They'd just disappeared from their car, just like all the other people, just like *his* people. He was still just as alone, just as lost.

Whining deep in his throat, Max spun from the car and raced back to the center of the road. He slipped into the loose harness, and despite his aching muscles and dry tongue, Max bounded down the road, away from the horrible empty car, the wagon squeaking and bouncing behind him.

"Whoa," Rocky moaned behind him. Then again, "Whoa! Slow down, buddy! Whoa whoa *whoa*!"

There were signs on either side of the road ahead, white *X*s with blinking red lights attached. Max didn't see the metal tracks running across the road until it was too late. He bounded over them just fine, but the wheels of the wagon got caught, and the wagon flipped onto its side, sending the bag of kibble and Rocky tumbling to the ground. The harness pulled tight on Max's neck and chest, and he was snapped back to a stop.

Spitting out dirt, Rocky jumped to his feet. "The kibble!" he yelped, then went to examine the bag. With a sigh of relief, he sat back on his haunches. "Oh, it's safe. Whew."

Panting, Max climbed out of the harness and walked back over the tracks to Rocky's side. "I'm sorry. I didn't see the tracks there. Are you all right?"

Rocky sniffed his legs and backside, then wagged his tail. "I think I'm all right, buddy. Though you really ought to look out where you're going. What was the hurry?"

Max thought back to the abandoned car. The seeping darkness in his dreams.

"It's nothing," Max lied. "It's just that I think we're almost to town, and I can't wait to get there. Come on. Help me get this wagon over the tracks."

Max had been right: The town wasn't far at all. As twilight fell, he noticed that the roadside trees were growing closer together and to the road. The air became crisp and slightly colder. They passed a few street signs—big red ones that said something in white letters—and more lights that flashed yellow, blinking steadily and silently. Through the trees, Max could make out some houses hidden in the woods. If he remembered correctly from riding in his people's car with his head lolling out the window, there was a real town with stores not too far ahead.

Rocky jumped excitedly next to and around Max. "You took us the right way, buddy!" he barked. "I bet you all the people are close. And wow, we sure covered a lot of ground since this morning, big guy. I'm not even tired!"

Max was tempted to remind Rocky that the little dog had spent most of the day fast asleep. But his throat was too parched to bother barking back. They had plenty of food—what Max needed soon was a nice puddle of water.

"You know, I bet you one of the houses or stores around here is going to have a soft bed for us to sleep in," Rocky said as he raced ahead of Max and the squeaking wagon. "If we can find a new home each night, this trip won't be tough at all! Every home I've ever been in has had at least one bag of kibble hidden somewhere, too. In fact—"

Rocky stopped midsentence, his whole body going stiff, from his pointed snout to his short, spiky tail. The little dog's brown ears twitched.

Max slowed as he came up behind his friend. "What is it?" he whispered.

Rocky didn't have time to answer. The underbrush on either side of the road rustled, and then two large dogs appeared.

Both towered over Max by at least a foot and were even longer from snout to tail. They were sleek, slender beasts, but not thin or sickly like the wolves—no, these dogs had taut muscles beneath their shiny fur, and their long legs looked like they could propel them superfast.

The dog on the left was pale brown, except for black

fur that covered his broad snout and his two floppy ears. The other was dingy white with large black spots on his back and a narrow, pointed snout. Both dogs were big, but they were definitely different breeds, and the white-and-black dog looked much older than the brown dog.

But for all their differences, the two big dogs had a few things in common: Both were growling and baring their teeth ferociously.

And both were slowly and purposefully coming straight for Max and Rocky.

CHAPTER 9

GUARD DOGS

Lowering himself and narrowing his brows, Max took one step back, then another. His backside met the metal of the little red wagon. Ahead of him, Rocky stood still, his eyes darting between the two approaching dogs.

The younger, brown dog opened his wide jaws, revealing sharp teeth.

"Hark!" the dog shouted.

The older dog stopped growling and shot a look at his companion. "'Hark'?" he repeated, his voice deep and weary. "I guess that's one way to get their attention. Who do you think you are?"

The brown dog's fur bristled. Pointing his snout in the air, he sat down and placed a paw against his narrow chest. "I'm a guard dog, sir," he declared. "And I know from watching my pack leader that guards are meant to greet intruders by shouting, 'Hark!'"

"What does that even mean?" the older dog grumbled, sitting down as well. "Is that some sort of human version of barking?"

The younger dog opened his mouth as if to answer, then tilted his head in thought. "You know, I'm not entirely sure. But who knows why humans say anything?"

Rocky glanced back at Max with an expression that asked, *What's with these guys?* Max shook his head. He'd relaxed a bit, but he wasn't entirely sure what to make of these two new canines.

The older dog grumbled. "Now these two aren't afraid of us anymore. Your hark had no bite." He let out a small bark of laughter. "Oh, I should remember that for later."

"You and your jokes, old one," the young dog said with a shake of his head. The two of them had clearly spent a lot of time together.

Max stood to his full height. Taking a few steps forward, he said, "I don't mean to interrupt, but who are you two?"

The young brown dog leaped up onto all fours, shouting, "Hark! I am the Great Dane. This is the Greyhound. You two are entering the Enclave's territory!"

Rocky sauntered back to stand beside Max, then looked at the Greyhound. "Those are your names? Sound more like breeds to me. That'd be like me going around saying I'm the Dachshund or calling Max the Lab. Seems a bit on the impersonal side, if you ask me."

Groaning, the Greyhound got onto all fours, too. "The names of any dog in the Enclave are on a need-to-know basis, little one."

"Well, you don't have to tell us your names," Max said. "But I'm Max, and this is my friend, Rocky. We're just passing through. We don't mean any harm."

The Dane looked from Max to Rocky. "So you ain't wolves?"

"Do they look like wolves?" the Greyhound asked.

"Well, I don't know, old-timer!" the Dane barked. "Maybe they're baby wolves. You can never be too careful. I mean, I thought all humans looked alike until I saw those people in the baggy white suits with hoods." The large dog shivered as if trying to shake water off his fur, even though he wasn't wet.

The Greyhound shushed his fellow guard. "Don't talk about that. Need-to-know basis, remember?"

"Right."

Rocky paced slowly in front of Max and the wagon, looking from one of the big dogs to the other. "So, uh, we established we ain't wolves, big guys. And I bet you two could take us down no problem if we did try to cause trouble. So would you mind letting us pass?"

The Dane and the Greyhound exchanged looks.

"You just going through town?" the Greyhound asked in his deep, grumbly voice.

"Maybe a stop for the night to sleep," Max said. "But that's all."

The Greyhound sat back down and waved a paw. "Fine, then. Go right ahead."

The Dane whined briefly. "Old-timer, they seem domesticated like us, don't they?" he asked in a hushed voice. "Maybe we should take them to the Enclave and—"

"That's need-to-know!" the Greyhound barked.

"What's the Enclave?" Rocky asked curiously.

"Don't worry about it, little dog," the Greyhound snapped. "You want to pass and we're letting you pass. Now get, before the sun sets!"

"Come on, Rocky," Max urged, already padding forward with the wagon squeaking behind him.

The Greyhound stiffened at the sound of the squeaking wheels, noticing the wagon for the first time. He bellowed, "Wait!"

For a moment, Max considered bolting and racing down the road. He could see in the distance streets lined with tan brick buildings, the forested land on either side of the road giving way to people businesses. But Rocky with his stubby legs wouldn't be able to keep up with Max, and the weight of the wagon would slow Max down. Worse, the Dane and Greyhound seemed built for speed. They'd catch him for sure, and Max didn't want any trouble if he could help it.

So Max did as he was asked and stopped.

"What are you doing?" Rocky whispered. "These guys are weird. Let's just get out of here!"

Max didn't have time to respond. The brown Dane and the spotted Greyhound were upon them again, only this time they ignored Max and Rocky—they were sniffing hungrily at the kibble bag in the red wagon.

"What's this you got?" the Dane asked, snuffing the bag. "Ooh, is that beef flavor?"

Growling, Rocky leaped atop the bag of kibble. "Back off! This is our food."

The Dane looked as if he was ready to bare his teeth and snap back, but a warning bark from the Greyhound made him back down. Unlike the Dane, the Greyhound seemed much more interested in the wagon.

Rounding on Max, the Greyhound asked, "Where did you get this thing?"

"The wagon?" Max said. "It belongs to my pack leaders. I used to carry them in it using this harness." With his snout, he gestured at the leather straps around his shoulders.

"Interesting," the Greyhound grumbled, examining the wagon once more. "You know, we've been having dogs drag bags of kibble from the human stores to the Enclave. It's a lot of work and takes a long time. But with a—what did you call it? A wagon? Well, with a wagon we could carry back sacks upon sacks with no problem."

"You probably could," Max agreed. "If you knew where to get a wagon."

His eyes boring into Max's own, the Greyhound came to stand snout to snout with Max. "If we knew— that's right, pup. We got a lot of dogs back at our camp, domesticated dogs who were abandoned by our people like you and Rocky here, who could certainly use some help stocking up on food. Maybe we could borrow your wagon for a little bit? Since we so nicely let you pass. And since none of us want any trouble."

The old dog's deep tone was calm and considered. But the look in his dark eyes made it perfectly clear to Max that this wasn't a request.

Rocky leaped off the wagon to stand beside Max. "You can't let them take our wagon," he said underneath his breath. "How will we carry our kibble around?"

Max looked away from the glowering Greyhound and back at the younger and no doubt faster Dane, whose lips were pulled back ever so slightly to reveal his top row of sharp teeth.

Max's limbs were so tired from walking all day. His tongue was so dry. In his thoughts, he kept seeing the dead cow in the barnyard and the silent, abandoned car. He could certainly use a break. And maybe a side trip to whatever this Enclave was would help out some other dogs like him, who were lost without their human pack leaders.

"It'll be all right," Max whispered down to Rocky. Then, to the Greyhound, he said, "All right, I'm sure we can spare our wagon for a little bit."

The Greyhound backed away from Max, his long, skinny tail wagging and his ears hanging evenly, lowered. "Good choice, pup," he said as he turned and started toward the tree line. "Now, follow me. The Enclave isn't too far."

Dragging a wagon, Max soon discovered, was much easier on a flat, open road than it was in the middle of the woods. The wheels kept getting stuck on underbrush and roots and stones, and the uneven ground made the whole wagon rumble and tug at the harness straps.

But every time Max eased up to take the path more slowly, the big guard dogs would snap at his and Rocky's heels, making them walk faster.

"Watch it, buddy!" Rocky yelped at the Dane after one particularly close nip. "I may be small, but I ain't a puppy. I don't need you herding me."

"You're not a puppy?" the Dane asked, bewildered. "So you're one of those miniature dogs?" The big dog shook his head. "I'm sorry to hear that. We got some more of you small types at the Enclave. I always wonder how you get around with such tiny legs."

Rocky sniffed. "I get around just fine without needing to take up as much space as you oversize mutts. And I'll have you know, I have teeth and claws as sharp as any overgrown dog. So don't you test me, champ!"

The Dane growled. But he stopped nipping at Rocky's heels.

"Have you been guarding the road long?" Max asked the Greyhound, trying to calm the mood with polite conversation.

The Greyhound snorted. "Just since the people left. Everything that's gone down that road has had to go past us."

Max swallowed, an idea hitting him. It would be too easy—but if she was going to run in any direction after leaving Vet...

"Did you happen to see a Lab like me come through?" he asked. "She would have been older, and with black fur with white specks. She also has a collar that has three golden rings on it."

Grunting, the Greyhound nodded. "That sounds familiar. Can't say for sure. There's a good thirty of us here. But maybe."

"Are you talking about that old dog again?" Rocky whispered to Max.

Max nodded, unable to control his wagging tail even as the strain of walking through the woods was exhausting the rest of him. "I'm telling you, Rocky," he said, "Madame knows everything. If we find her, we'll be able to figure all this out in no time."

Mercifully, the trek through the woods didn't last much longer. The trees thinned out to reveal a small clearing. And as Max and Rocky entered, followed by the Dane and the Greyhound, a dozen other dogs of all different breeds halted whatever they were doing to look up at the newcomers.

Max stopped, taking in the scene. To his left were several bags of kibble tossed together in a haphazard pile, most torn open with little brown pellets spilling onto the forest floor. Next to the kibble, the earth had been dug up to make a trench, which was half full with rainwater. The mingling scents of damp fur and marked territory met Max's nostrils, mixing with the woodsy smells of leaves and dried mud.

On the opposite side of the clearing from Max, there were wooden planks leaning against tree trunks, as well as piles of torn sheets, rags, and human clothing, some arranged beneath the wooden slabs in nests and some just lying around. There were even a few pillows splattered with mud, and a single doggy bed that had a gash down its center, revealing fluffy gray innards.

In the center of the clearing was a wide, flat tree stump. The dogs in the clearing came forward to surround the stump now, all their eyes still on Max and Rocky.

They were all different breeds and shapes and sizes. There was a large, stocky dog with a droopy face and long brown-and-white fur who stood near the stacks of kibble, drool falling from his fleshy lips. Another dog was about Max's size, but mostly covered in a long tan coat except for fluffy white fur that ran from her chest to her pointed head and ears, reminding Max of some fancy human collar. A small dog around Rocky's size stood near the front of the pack, though her body was more proportionate and not shaped like a sausage; instead, she had shaggy black fur that covered her back and tan fur on her legs and face. Her snout was short with tufts of fur under her black nose and over her small eyes, and her pointed ears stood at full, perked attention atop her round head.

Max scanned the crowd, desperately looking for Madame's familiar face. But as far as he could see, there were no other Labs. He didn't get to look for long, though, because there was a disturbance in the group. All the dogs quieted and stepped aside, clearing a path for someone Max couldn't see.

"Quiet!" growled that someone.

A medium-sized dog covered with puffy, dirty-white fur pranced down the path and leaped atop the tree stump. His ears hung low on either side of his long, narrow face—a face with fur that was clipped short, making the puffy hair atop his head and covering his ears look like a hat that Max's pack leaders would wear during the colder months.

"Wisep—Ahem, I mean, *Greyhound*," the puffy white dog called from atop his stump. "Who are these two that you bring before us?"

The Greyhound strode past Max and bowed his head. "These are Max and Rocky, sir," he said in his low rumble. "They were left behind, like the rest of us. If

you'll look at the larger of the two, you'll see he has a contraption to carry kibble that I thought would be of interest to you."

The puffy dog looked over Max, then nodded down at the Greyhound. "Very good. Return to your post. You shall have your replacements soon."

Head still low, the Greyhound headed toward the woods, not looking at Max. The Dane followed, and the two disappeared back into the trees.

"Those big dogs are taking orders from *that* guy?" Rocky muttered to Max. "He looks like some stuffed toy my pack leader would keep on her pillows!"

The puffy dog cleared his throat with a growl. "So," he barked, "you have come to join us."

Max took a step forward, dragging the wagon deeper into the clearing. Several of the dogs, upon seeing the wagon, muttered among themselves.

"Not exactly," Max said. "We're traveling to look for our pack leaders—our people. We just agreed with the Greyhound to let you use our wagon for a short time to help bring kibble back to...wherever we are."

"Your people?" the puffy dog asked. "You're looking for the humans who abandoned you?"

Max worked hard to suppress a growl. "They didn't abandon me on purpose. I know them. They wouldn't."

The puffy dog closed his dark eyes and shook his head. "You poor creatures. I've been where you are, in denial of our new reality. But as you can see by looking around you, we're on our own now."

"And how do you know that, puffball?" Rocky barked. "How do you know any more than we do, huh?"

The puffy dog stepped daintily down from the tree stump and primly walked to stand before Max and Rocky.

"I know," he said, "because the same pack leaders who claimed they loved me my whole life spent their last days shouting at me before they chased me from my home and into the woods, leaving me to die. They told me to run away and never come back. And when I refused, they took it upon themselves to leave their homes to get as far away from me as possible."

The puffy dog paced back and forth in front of Max and Rocky, not taking his eyes from theirs. "All of us in the Enclave have similar stories, some worse and some not so bad. But we all know it to be true: The humans want nothing to do with us. So I created this new community where we can help one another survive in our new lives. Some still hope the humans will come back for us one day, and if they do, we will be here. If they do not, well..." The puffy dog stopped and looked directly at Max. "Then we'd better get used to being on our own."

"Who are you?" Max asked.

"My breed name, and how I am to be known to outsiders, is Poodle," the dog said as he leaped once more onto his stump. "The name the humans gave me is"—he snorted—"*Pinky*. But my true name, as I have discovered it in the Enclave, is Dandyclaw."

Max looked at the other dogs, who were staring back at him from the clearing, silent and listening. No one protested what Dandyclaw had said or disagreed about being abandoned. The looks of sadness on their faces said it all.

"Welcome to the Enclave, Max and Rocky," Dandyclaw barked. "Welcome to your new home."

And then he smiled—or showed them his fangs. Max and Rocky couldn't be sure.

CHAPTER 10

THE ENCLAVE

After his big speech, Dandyclaw dismissed the dogs who had milled around to gape at Max and Rocky, commanding them to get back to work. He then informed Max and Rocky that all dogs of the Enclave were "to pull their weight" each day, helping to keep their new home in order—including, starting right then, Max and Rocky.

"And what if we don't want to work to stay in your Enclave, huh, Dandypuff?" Rocky asked. "Like we told the overgrown mutts you had guarding the road, we're just passing through."

"It's Dandy*claw*," the Poodle growled. Then, taking in a deep, calming breath, the puffy dog sat down in front of his stump. "I don't mean to imply you *have* to stay here. I am no human, collecting dogs only to toss them aside once they are no longer to my satisfaction. But I invite you to stay for as long as you like and see how the Enclave suits you. I bet you will be surprised how satisfying working alongside fellow dogs can be."

"Always with the work!" Rocky whined. He plopped down onto his belly on the grass and covered his eyes with his paws.

Dandyclaw turned to Max, who had listened to all the speechifying in silence. Max wasn't sure if he believed what Dandyclaw had said about humans treating him and the other dogs so cruelly. But looking around the clearing at dogs digging in the dirt to make trenches or struggling with blankets to make more beds, he realized that maybe not all of them had pack leaders as kind as Charlie and Emma.

"Your contraption is genius," Dandyclaw remarked as he jaunted past Max and sniffed at the wagon. It was only then that Max saw the Poodle's tail—like his snout, most of the dog's tail had been clipped so that the fur was short. Only the very tip was grown out, shaped into a little decorative puff. Max stifled a laugh.

Instead, he said, "Thank you. But it's not really mine. My pack leaders hooked the wagon to the harness. And it was Rocky's idea to take it with us."

"That's me," Rocky called out, his voice muffled by his paws and the grass. "I'm the one with all the ideas. Don't see why the one who thinks up the ideas has to do the work, too."

Dandyclaw ignored Rocky, coming down to sit right in front of Max. "Still, a much cleverer way to keep yourself fed than how we've had to do it. I wonder if before night fully comes, you might show Sturdystep how to use it, and maybe make a run to the human stores to bring back more food."

"Tonight?" Max asked. "I've been walking all day...."

"Oh, I'm sure," Dandyclaw said. "But I bet you want your wagon back as soon as possible. And it would be a show of good faith to the Enclave before we share our food and beds." The Poodle narrowed his eyes as he looked past Max into the darkening trees, his lips parting to just barely show his front teeth. "I trusted some other dogs before who didn't prove themselves first. And I'm afraid the experience has made me less trustful."

Max's legs pulsed with distant aches, and his tongue was still so dry. But maybe if he had his fill of water first...and the town hadn't seemed so far....

"All right," Max said. "I suppose Rocky and I can take one more hike before the end of the day."

"Wonderful!" Dandyclaw said, leaping up to his dainty feet, his puff-tipped tail wagging. Then his tail slowed and drooped. "Oh, but I think someone of Rocky's size might just slow you down."

"Hey!" Rocky yipped, dropping the paws that were covering his snout. "My legs may be short, but you better believe I can make 'em move fast, Dandelion!"

The Poodle's puffy brows scrunched for just a moment.

"Dandy*claw*," he said between clenched teeth. "And all I meant is that maybe you could stay here and help set up beds for the night. In fact..."

Dandyclaw spun around, then leaped gracefully atop his stump. "Softspike!" he howled.

"Yeah?" a high female voice called from somewhere in the clearing.

Max leaned to peer past the trunk, but he couldn't tell where the voice had come from. All the other dogs had ignored Dandyclaw and were still busy digging and dragging wooden planks from out of the trees and wrestling with sheets.

"Softspike, come meet our new friends!"

"Oh! Yay! Okay!"

Across the clearing, a dozen rags flew into the air and a tiny black-and-tan blur burst from beneath one of the wooden lean-tos. The tiny dog Max had seen earlier, with the round face and the puffs of fur above her bright eyes and near her short snout, came to an abrupt stop right in front of Rocky, her nub of a tail wagging furiously behind her.

Rocky blinked open his eyes at the commotion, and seeing the girl dog towering over him, her little pink tongue hanging out, he jumped to his feet and backed away.

"Sorry!" she said. "I didn't mean to scare you. I just like meeting new dogs! New dogs just *love* me. I'm Gizmo. What are your names?"

Dandyclaw cleared his throat. "Your name is Soft-spike now, remember?"

Gizmo looked up at Dandyclaw. "Oh. Yeah." Looking at Max and Rocky, she said, "Anyway, like I was saying, I'm Gizmo—though outside the Enclave I'm supposed to be secretive and call myself the Yorkshire Terrier, though isn't *that* a mouthful to have to say all the time—but you can call me Gizmo, or Giz if you're really short on breath."

"Softspike," Dandyclaw said with a weary sigh. "We agreed on Softspike."

"Whoops," Gizmo said with a playful gleam in her eyes. "I guess I forgot again already."

Looking at the tiny, energetic dog, Max couldn't help but wag his tail. "I'm Max," he said. "And my skittish friend here is Rocky."

"Hey!" Rocky barked. "I am not skittish. I'm *cautious*. You gotta be when you're my size." Eyeing Gizmo up and down, Rocky added, "I also try not to run into new situations when I can scope things out first. You never know what's going to be waiting."

"Oh, he's right!" Gizmo said, her head a blur as she nodded. "I'm always having to watch out for big folks stomping all over the place not looking where they're going, though they don't scare me too bad, 'cause mostly they just want to get close to pet you. I love petting time. It's the *best*. I go crazy for ear scratches, just crazy."

"Yes," Dandyclaw said. "Quite. Anyway, Softspike, I

need you to show Rocky here how to make up some beds for him and Max to sleep on."

"Sure thing!" Gizmo said, her short tail still a blur of happiness. "Come on, Rocky. I'll show you all the best sheets and how to lay them just right. You'll think you finally got to sit on the best couch your humans never wanted you to sit on."

The little terrier was off in a flash, back toward the makeshift lean-tos and the piles of rags and sheets. Calling back over her shoulder, she shouted, "Hey, we can race! I bet I can get five beds done before you get two!"

"Great." Rocky sighed. With one wary look at Max, the Dachshund reluctantly followed Gizmo into the piles of blankets.

"She sure is something," Max said, wagging his tail as he looked over at Dandyclaw.

Dandyclaw sighed. "Yes, she always has such a . . . positive outlook. But you'll have time to meet her and the others later. Come, let me introduce you to Sturdystep."

"Actually," Max said, "I have a question before we continue. I'm not just looking for my people, but a friend of mine named Madame. Madame Curie. She's a Lab like me, only older and with black fur, and she wears a fancy collar. One of the guard dogs said she sounded familiar, but I haven't seen—"

"Madame?" Dandyclaw said, his voice cold.

Max nodded. "Yes, that's right."

The Poodle tilted his head as if in thought, then said,

"No, I can't say she's familiar to me. I'm afraid your friend hasn't been here. Now, shall I take you to Sturdystep?"

Something in Dandyclaw's icy tone made Max uneasy, but he couldn't tell if the dog was lying or if what he was feeling was just disappointment. Madame being here would have made the whole side trip worth it, even beyond helping the dogs with their kibble.

"All right," Max said after a moment. "Sure. Lead the way."

Dragging the wagon over the bumpy earth and grass, Max walked side by side with the Enclave's leader toward the edge of the clearing where the broken bags of kibble had been thrown into a heap. The stocky, long-haired dog with a wide, drooping face and ears whom Max had seen earlier watched with wary eyes as Max and Dandyclaw approached.

Nearing the trench filled with rainwater, Max couldn't help but stick his snout in and start lapping up the water, cooling his tongue and nose, filling his belly after the day's long trek. The water smelled strange and there were leaves and dirt floating in it, but Max couldn't find it in himself to care.

"Hey," the stocky dog bellowed, rushing toward Max so fast that Max was certain he meant to tackle him. But a sharp bark from Dandyclaw caused the burly dog to stop in his tracks.

"Let him," Dandyclaw demanded. "He can listen while he drinks."

With a nod of appreciation at Dandyclaw, Max went back to lapping up water. As he did, Dandyclaw explained to the stocky dog—Sturdystep—the plan for the evening. Max would show Sturdystep how to use the wagon, and together they would bring home more bags of kibble from the market before any other animals got to it.

"Fine," Sturdystep said after Dandyclaw was done with his instructions. Max wasn't surprised to find that the dog's bark was as deep and droopy as the flesh on his face. "We will go."

His puffy tail wagging in approval, Dandyclaw looked at the two dogs. "This day has turned out quite fortuitously. Now hurry up. Night will fall soon."

It didn't take long for Max to show Sturdystep how to slip into the harness, though while doing so, he discovered that the dog preferred to go by the name his pack leaders had given him: Brahms.

"Why does Dandyclaw call you all by other names?" Max asked as he checked the harness to make sure the straps were pulled tightly around Brahms's chest.

"He says that since the humans abandoned us, we should abandon their names for us," Brahms answered. "He says that in the wild, we find our true names."

Stepping back, Max asked, "And why does he have everyone call themselves by their breed names outside the Enclave?"

"Oh, that. Out there, I'm the Saint Bernard. Dandy-claw claims that if someone we don't trust knows either of our names, they can control us."

"Do you believe that?" Max asked.

"I don't know," Brahms grumbled. "Dandyclaw says it's happened to him before, so he's extra cautious. But if you think about it, don't you always come when someone calls your name?"

Max thought about it, and it was true—anytime a person called out "Max!" he came running.

"I suppose I do," Max said.

"Me, too," Brahms said. "Could all be superstition. But better to be safe, right?"

Leaving the Enclave clearing behind, Max led Brahms through the forest back to the main road. To the burly dog's credit, he took to hauling the wagon with ease—managing to navigate it between the dark trees and over underbrush without much trouble.

Of course, traveling on the road went much smoother. Max and Brahms passed the Dane and the Greyhound with nods of understanding, and from there it was only a few blocks to the nearest human store.

Brahms led the way, making a right turn down a side road and heading straight toward the market. The market sat by itself in a large empty parking lot, but the street leading to it had several smaller buildings huddled near the sidewalks. Max studied everything as they neared the store—there were no cars here. All the buildings that once glared brightly with fluorescent lights and all the shop signs that once glowed on the storefronts were dark and dim. Windows were smashed and glass was scattered over the parking lot. Trash tumbled through the street and into gutters, carried by an early evening breeze.

The scene was no different at the grocery store. Brahms showed Max the path he and other dogs had made through the broken shards of glass—"We dragged blankets to sweep the glass aside; that was Dandyclaw's idea"—so that they could get inside without slicing the pads of their feet.

The two dogs pushed through one of the swinging glass doors into the market.

The clacking of their claws against the hard floor of the market and the occasional squeak of the wagon's wheels echoed in the metal rafters high above. The last remnants of the fading sunlight seeped through the broad, broken windows at the front of the store, but they didn't penetrate all the way to the back. The shelves farthest from the doors were shrouded in shadow, save for some glass cases that buzzed and blinked with a dying lightbulb that wanted desperately to stay on.

Brahms expertly led Max down the aisles, winding past tipped-over shopping carts and avoiding shattered glass jars. Like the pantry back at Max's home, most of the metal shelves were bare. From farther back in the store, the stench of rotting meat and plants wafted. A constant buzzing of bugs came from the same direction, the tiny pests no doubt enjoying a spoiled feast.

Luckily, Brahms didn't take Max all the way to that section of the market. Instead, he veered down a side aisle—and Max stopped for a moment, surprised to discover that the shelves in this aisle were fully stocked. There were chew toys for dogs and cats and mice hanging from pegs. Boxes showing pictures of ferrets climbing through clear tubes. Cans with pink and orange labels with cat faces on them. And stacks upon stacks of dog kibble, ready for the taking.

Whoever had cleared out the rest of the store hadn't seen a need to stock up on pet supplies.

Max helped Brahms out of the harness, and, together, they clawed and nosed three of the largest bags of kibble so that they rolled off the shelf and landed in the bed of the wagon. It was hard, aching work, and Max was panting with exhaustion by the time they were done.

"That should be enough," Brahms decided in his low growl. "Don't want to overload ourselves."

Max shook his head as Brahms slipped back into the harness. "How did you manage to drag any of these bags all the way back to the Enclave?"

"It took a whole group of us," Brahms said, turning and pulling the wagon to face the door. "And the most we could get was one bag per day. We used a blanket, some of us dragging it with our jaws, others nudging the bag with our snouts." As he walked, the wagon squeaking behind him, Brahms barked out a laugh. "I have to tell you, this thing is a back saver!"

Night was fully upon them by the time Max and Brahms reached the main road and started back toward the Enclave. Max glanced over his shoulder at the small town, remembering how it had looked all the other times he'd visited—cars lining the streets and filling the parking lots, lights blazing from windows, people everywhere laughing and shouting and talking as they went about their business.

Now, the buildings were nothing but desolate, empty black shells. Max shuddered and raced to keep up with Brahms.

The path through the woods to the clearing was so dark that Max could barely see a few feet in front of him, but Brahms seemed to know the way by smell alone. When they finally made it back to the Enclave, the clearing was mostly still, silent. Dogs rustled in the blankets beneath the lean-tos, some snoring softly, others whimpering. Strangely, there was a camping lantern sitting on the edge of the stump, casting an orange glow that moths buzzed around. Max wasn't sure how it had turned on, but he welcomed the warm, familiar glow.

Max helped Brahms unload the three sacks of kibble near the stacks of the other bags, and then the two dogs ate their fill and lapped up rainwater in the trench. Brahms bid Max a friendly good-night, and Max, aching from snout to tail, crawled across the clearing to the mound of sheets he saw next to a snoring Rocky.

As Max curled up in his temporary new bed, he caught sight of Dandyclaw sitting alert atop his stump in the center of the clearing, the lamplight making his puffy white fur glow bright and milky. As silly as the Enclave leader's grooming was, there was no hiding the shrewdness in his eyes as he took in the new wagon and the pile of fresh kibble. The silliness, Max decided, went no deeper than the dog's fur.

Max awoke briefly in the night to discover the lantern turned off, the clearing now shuttered in darkness and the other dogs' shadows. Max was almost certain he saw Dandyclaw still sitting on his stump, in the same position he'd been in hours earlier, only now he was watching Max as he slept.

CHAPTER 11

BITTER WORK

It became clear the next day that Dandyclaw had no intention of letting Max and Rocky leave the Enclave.

At least, not anytime soon.

It started that first morning, after Max woke up entangled in people sheets with misty light glinting down through the treetops. Several other dogs were up, though many were still snoring beneath the scraps of wood and metal laid against the trees. Some disappeared south into the denser woods, which, Max concluded from the smells, was the designated bathroom area. He saw others marching dutifully into the trees at the west end of the clearing, through which he could see a moldering old shack that had been mostly torn apart—the source of the building material, no doubt.

A few lean-tos down from where Max had slept, a stocky white dog lay atop a mangled pile of pillows, softly howling a sad song up at the morning sky. Next to him, a squat brown dog with a squished face alternated sniffing the singing dog's backside and turning away to lick the grass and the bark of the closest tree with his fat, slobbery tongue.

Max's own tongue was dry once again, and the inside of his mouth tasted stale. Standing, he stretched his front legs and then his back legs, and opened his jaws wide in a yawn. Then, padding across the clearing to its eastern end, past Dandyclaw's empty stump, Max made his way to the trench next to the pile of kibble.

And found that almost all the water had drained into the dirt in the night.

"It never lasts long," someone grumbled beside Max. He turned to find wide, droopy Brahms nosing at the kibble.

"It doesn't?" Max asked.

Brahms shook his big head. "Either we lap it up too quickly or the ground sucks it all up while we sleep."

"What do you drink, then?"

Brahms gestured with his snout at the nearest edge of the clearing. "Get up early enough, and there's usually dew on the long grass and the bushes. It's never enough. But it helps until the next rain comes."

Max padded away from the empty, muddy trench to a patch of grass. Misty water droplets had settled on the blades, and Max licked it up. But all it did was make his throat cry out for more.

"Whaddya mean, I have to lick grass?"

Max looked back over his shoulder to see Rocky glaring up at Brahms.

"I thought you guys said this was a place for domesticated dogs, huh?" Rocky yowled. "Well, where I come from, we drink water out of bowls or toilets! Or bathtubs, if they ain't got bubbles in them. I was willing to give this trench a try, but I draw the line at eating leaves!"

Catching sight of Max, Rocky whipped his spiky tail back and forth in a blur. The little dog jumped up and down as Max came back to the kibble area. Other dogs were now circling the scene warily—the Great Dane, Gizmo, several dogs whom Max didn't know the names of but whose glassy, tired eyes told him they'd just been awoken by the commotion.

"Max!" Rocky cried out. "Hey, Max, buddy, big guy. Tell these guys we appreciate the bed for the night, but we need to be on our way. I mean, we certainly could have found us another house last night with a toilet to drink out of."

"You're going to leave?"

Gizmo darted forward from the forming crowd. Her tiny pink tongue lolled out as she looked from Max to Rocky.

Rocky's tail drooped as he looked over at the little

118

girl dog. "Sorry, Giz. Not that piling up sheets all night wasn't *superfun*, but this place ain't really my scene."

There came a commotion from the milling dogs, and they parted as the slender, white-puffed Dandyclaw marched up to the feeding area. "What's going on here?" the dog asked, glaring at Max and Brahms.

Brahms bent his head forward. "Sorry if we woke you up, Dandyclaw," he grunted. "But the Dachshund was complaining about the lack of water."

Dandyclaw sniffed, then went to the edge of the trench and looked down. With a sigh, he said, "It drained much quicker than the last time, didn't it?"

"It was warm yesterday," called a dog in the crowd whom Max couldn't see. "The sun always drinks the puddles fast."

"Hmm," Dandyclaw said. "Yes."

Max studied the dogs around him. There were over a dozen awake now, at least that he could see. The stocky singing dog lay next to Gizmo now, his squat friend panting madly beside him. Near them, a dog who looked like a white miniature version of Gizmo shivered endlessly. A few of the older dogs—two who looked like they could be related, their shaggy tan coats were so similar—took in heaving, disgruntled breaths, their eyes, ears, and tails all drooping. Everyone seemed exhausted, and surely they were all as thirsty as Max.

Max remembered his time trapped in the kennel in

Vet's office. Remembered being caged, knowing water was close by but unable to get to it.

"Well, you got an empty trench, and I got an empty belly," Rocky said, plopping down directly in front of Dandyclaw. "Me and Max let you borrow our wagon, like you asked. Time for us to leave, all right, Daintyclaw?"

"It's *Dandy*—" Dandyclaw started to say between clenched teeth. Shaking his head, he looked over at Max. "You think that this is all the kibble the Enclave will need, hmm? I thought we could spend the day sending teams to gather more."

"Hey," Rocky barked. "Not our problem."

"No, he's right," Max said diplomatically, not taking his eyes off the other quiet, sad dogs of the Enclave. "We can help at least for one more day. You didn't see the store, Rocky, but there's so much kibble just lying there. And it will take them forever to bring it all up here without the wagon."

Rocky dropped his snout to rest atop his front paws. "So we have to stay here longer? It *stinks* here."

"You get used to it after a while," the stocky white dog mumbled from his place in the crowd. His panting friend nodded vigorously, his bulging eyes looking in two different directions.

"See?" Max said, nodding at the other dogs. "They don't seem to mind. We'll only stay for a little while. And maybe we can find some water, too."

"Hey! Look!"

All the dogs turned as one to see little Gizmo standing on her hind legs with her tan front paws on the edge of the wagon, her nub of a tail wagging.

"What if we filled this wagon with water first?" she barked, her fuzzy eyebrows raised high. "Then we could carry it back here, and we could all fill our bellies. Does that seem like a good idea?"

Snorting, Rocky rolled his eyes. "No offense, Giz, but leave the heavy thinking to me, okay?" he said. "You're a master blanket wrangler, but problem solving is my area."

"Wait, hold on, Rocky," Max said, brushing past him to stand at Gizmo's side. He studied the wagon and sniffed the bottom of the bed, tiny kibble crumbs filling his nostrils with the smoky scent of bacon and beef. "There aren't any holes in the wagon bed, so it could work," he announced after a moment. "But how will we get the water in it?"

"What if..." Rocky started to say behind Max.

Max turned to find both Brahms and Dandyclaw towering over Rocky, staring expectantly. Rocky waved a paw in the air and said, "Naw."

"No, Dachshund," Dandyclaw growled. "What is it?"

"Go ahead, Rocky," Max said.

With a sigh, Rocky got onto all fours and waddled to the wagon. Gizmo dropped down from its edge and sat beside him.

"Well, most people buildings have hoses, right?" he

said. "Maybe we could put the wagon under one and fill it up? It could be a portable trench that doesn't lose the water."

Around the clearing, the other dogs mumbled to themselves, excited by the idea of this new toy the Lab and the Dachshund had brought into their clearing. Max could see their ears perking up, their eyes coming back to life.

"Seems worth a try," Dandyclaw said. "It would certainly keep our energy up for the day's work."

"Like I told you, Dandycane," Rocky said, nodding for emphasis, "I'm an idea dog."

"Oh," Gizmo said. "But I was the one who said we should fill the wagon in the first place. You know, when you said I shouldn't try to have ideas. Remember that?"

Rocky nodded at her. "True, true. But I *improved* that idea. And that's what counts, really."

With a roll of her little black eyes, Gizmo said, "If it helps you feel better about yourself to think that, I am happy to let you."

"Thank you," Rocky said.

"So, Dandyclaw," Gizmo said, turning her attention to the Poodle. "Can I have a new job today? Can I run with the wagon? I haven't been running in *forever*, and I bet I could help."

Dandyclaw shook his head. "No, I need you here, Softspike. The others need your morale."

The little terrier sighed, her ears drooping. "Yeah, I suppose so. I do like keeping the dogs happy." Perking back up, she barked to Rocky, "Well, come on, then, Mr. Idea Dog! I got some folding tricks to show you. And today we're going to try to beat my old record for sheets folded per hour!"

"Yippee," Rocky drawled. With a pitying look at Max, he waddled after Gizmo toward the back of the clearing, where a few of the bigger dogs were already working together to set up new lean-tos.

Most of the dogs dispersed then. As they wandered away, the stocky white dog took up a louder lamenting song, which was soon joined in by the two old-timers with the shaggy tan coats. Their howling arias filled the clearing as they marched to the broken-down shack through the trees. Meanwhile, the slobbery, squat dog and some of the others dove headfirst into a bag of kibble, sending pebbles of the food flying into the underbrush.

As Dandyclaw nipped at a few of the younger dogs, Max looked through the woods to the north to see the old Greyhound and his partner, the Great Dane, slinking through the trees to go stand post at the road—whether to keep guard or to find more dogs to bring to the Enclave, Max was no longer entirely sure.

For the task of bringing back water, Dandyclaw chose Brahms, Max, and another dog—the one Max had seen the day before with the puffed-out white fur on her chest and pointy ears. She was a Collie and preferred to go by her Enclave name at all times—Clearsight.

As Clearsight led the way, with Max dragging the wagon through the forest underbrush and Brahms taking up the rear, she spoke endlessly of how regal, far-sighted, and brilliant Dandyclaw was. Much like the Poodle leader's family, Clearsight's had tried to force her to run away. She had, but soon ran into the people in the baggy white suits, their heads hidden inside giant hoods with windows on the front. The memory sent a shiver running from her shoulders to her haunches.

"What are those people?" Max asked. "I heard other dogs mention them."

"We do not know," Brahms answered. "But they came after all the other people left. Some dogs say they saw others of us approach these ones for help, only never to return."

"It's true," Clearsight barked without looking back as she led them onto the main road into town. "One of the people in the baggy suits tried to capture me, but that was when Dandyclaw appeared with—well, he appeared. He distracted the thing so that the two of us could escape and hide in the Enclave." She sighed dreamily. "He is a true hero."

"Who did he appear with?" Max asked.

Clearsight continued to look straight ahead, barely

reacting to the question. "Oh, no one special," she said. "We don't talk about him."

The Collie turned the conversation back to the Enclave. It hadn't been more than a week since all the humans disappeared, she revealed, but under Dandyclaw's rule, it felt as though they'd been together for much longer. Currently, there were only a few dozen dogs in the camp, but Dandyclaw hoped for many more to come as the weeks went by. Most of the dogs had joined in those first few days after the people left, but occasionally there were stragglers like Max and Rocky, which was why Dandyclaw had dogs on lookout.

"And everyone is just happy to stay here?" Max asked.

"Well, not everyone," Brahms grumbled.

Clearsight shushed him. "Why wouldn't you want to stay?" she asked, turning her attention back to Max. "It's a home for dogs, by dogs. Sure, there were some mistakes made in the first few days. But...well, Dandyclaw won't let those mistakes happen again. I'm sure of it."

"I'm not so sure the old Lab thought she was making much of a mistake," Brahms grumbled under his breath.

"Wait," Max said, stopping momentarily. "Old Lab? Black fur? Was her name Madame?"

Clearsight nipped at Brahms's side before he could say anything. To Max, she said, "Maybe. I don't remember non-Enclave names."

"But I need to know," Max said. "She's a friend of mine, and finding her is important."

"Well...then ask Dandyclaw. Come on, now. We don't want to waste the day."

Max tried to press further as they continued their course, but neither Clearsight nor Brahms was willing to give much more information. Instead, they walked on in silence until buildings came into view.

Not that Max needed to know much more for certain. He was almost positive, between the Greyhound and Brahms, that Madame had been here at some point, even if Dandyclaw hadn't seen her. That meant he might find her sooner rather than later.

The trio didn't walk all the way into town. Instead, they passed a clearing between the woods and the back of the closest human building, rounded its side, and looked at the wall until they found a metal spigot. There was no hose attached, and the metal was dotted with rust. It took a few bites of strong dog jaws to latch onto the round, rubber-coated handle above the spigot and actually get it to turn. It was Brahms who finally managed to do so—and clear, crisp water burst from the spigot, pinging into the metal bottom of the wagon and sending water splashing.

Barking in delight, the three dogs jumped up and down, letting the water coat their fur and taking turns lapping directly from the gushing stream. Then they stood back, shook the water from their fur, and watched the water level rise in the wagon.

"Those tiny dogs are smarter than they look," Brahms said.

"And this wagon is the best thing that has ever happened to the Enclave," Clearsight said, her long tongue lolling from her pointed snout. "I can't imagine it ever leaving."

"Oh," Max said. "But Rocky and I can only stay for a short time. We'll find some way to make sure everyone always has water, though."

"Yes," Clearsight said, pointedly looking away from Max. "Of course."

The three dogs returned to the Enclave triumphantly and were soon surrounded by every dog in the clearing. So many crushed against the wagon's side that they risked tipping it over, and two of the bigger dogs almost got into a fight—but Dandyclaw intervened, barking at the group to take turns.

And when the wagon's bed was drained dry, it was back to work for the day.

Max, Brahms, and Clearsight took several trips to the store, taking turns hitched to the wagon. It was a long day and heavy work, but Max felt good about having a goal and helping his fellow canines.

Besides, the faster they stocked up the Enclave with kibble, the faster Max could get back to finding his people—and, if what he'd guessed was true, finding Madame's trail after she left this place.

It was on the last trip of the day when Max noticed the plastic and metal doggy bowls on a high shelf, almost hidden in the long shadows cast by the fading afternoon light. Brahms, Max, and Clearsight leaped up, over and over again, knocking the bowls with their snouts and paws until all the dishes clattered onto the store's tiled floor.

They took back one fewer bag of kibble on that trip to make room for the dishes—and when Max explained to Dandyclaw why, the Poodle leader was thrilled.

"So we'll let these fill up with all the rainwater," Dandyclaw repeated with a smile. "And then there will be no worries about our water draining into the dirt!"

"Exactly," Max said. "I just wanted to make sure that once me and Rocky leave, you won't have a hard time getting by."

Dandyclaw's tail wagged slowly and deliberately. "I appreciate it, I really do," he said. "But of course, who knows when it will rain again? And there's still so much kibble to be hauled up here. I do hope you can stay as our guests for a bit longer."

Max's eyes darted from the Poodle to Rocky, who was near the lean-tos tossing a knotted-up rag back and forth with Gizmo. He tried not to worry about Charlie and Emma, and Madame, and his dreams of darkness. Instead, he focused on the dogs of all shapes and sizes lying in their makeshift beds, shivering and alone, trying to make themselves feel at home in a place that was nothing like a home at all.

Neither his pack leaders nor Madame would look kindly upon Max if he left such unhappy dogs in need. As much as he wanted to leave and find them all, he would feel so terribly guilty.

"Sure," Max said, meeting Dandyclaw's dark eyes. "Of course we can."

Rain refused to come and fill the dog dishes littered throughout the clearing. And soon, "a little while longer" became a full week.

A week of waking with aching shoulders after hauling water and food to the Enclave. A week of listening to other dogs' stories of abandonment, and loneliness, and fear. A week of Rocky moaning about the state of his living space and the fact that he was asked to make *beds*, of all things, when he wasn't busy playing with Gizmo.

And a week of Dandyclaw keeping constant watch on Max. Waiting. But for what?

The supply of kibble at the store seemed endless, and it was always Max and some of the other bigger dogs making the trips to fetch the food, as commanded by their Poodle leader. Even though Dandyclaw was about the same size as Max, the Poodle never offered to go on these expeditions himself. No, he spent his days observing the Enclave clearing from his stump, handing out orders, and reaping the rewards of everyone else's hard work.

Max was as helpful as anyone. But he was beginning to resent how he was being used, especially since he'd made it clear several times that he needed to leave to continue his trek to find his people as soon as possible.

Brahms, sensing Max's weariness, let him have an afternoon off. Relieved, Max wandered into the woods east of the clearing, past the trench and the stacks of kibble. He wanted to rest, and he couldn't very well do that with Rocky constantly whining or chipper Gizmo challenging him to a race or Dandyclaw barking out endless orders.

After a short walk, Max found himself deeper into the woods, where the trees grew closer together and the bushes spiked up, untamed and wild. Perfect cover—no one would see or find him here.

Finding a nice, soft patch of moss at the base of a tall tree, Max scratched his back against the rough bark, circled twice, then plopped down and closed his eyes. His thoughts drifted to memories of lying in the laps of Charlie and Emma back home, breathing slowly and softly as they ran their hands through his fur, cooing about what a great dog he was. He imagined them there, the vision in his head so clear he could almost smell them—their excitable sweat, their hands sugary sweet from eating people treats, their hair the aroma of soap and wildflowers.

The aches in his muscles became distant and numb, and it was the most comfortable he'd felt in a long time.

As he started to drift off, Max took in a long, deep breath, inhaling the earthy scents around him.

But he smelled more than just moss and bark.

There was a wild musk. The dominating stench of marked territory. Tangy, acrid scents of blood and anger that burned his nose.

Wolf.

CHAPTER 12

RAINFALL

Max's eyes shot open, and he leaped onto all fours, his hair standing on end, his ears alert, blood rushing through his limbs from his fast-beating heart. The smell brought with it the horrible memories of fighting Wretch and fleeing the burning house.

And then Max realized that the smell was faded and old. If there had been a wolf here, it wasn't within the past few days. Still—there *had* been a wolf here. Recently enough that it might have seen the Enclave clearing? Max couldn't tell.

A sensation of being watched sent another shiver down Max's spine to the tip of his tail. The quiet, empty woods no longer felt serene and calm. Not worrying about the strain on his limbs, Max ran back toward the crowded Enclave as fast as he could.

Rain finally came that night.

Fat, heavy droplets splashed down from the canopy above, thudding steadily and rhythmically atop the metal and wooden lean-tos that all the dogs of the Enclave huddled beneath, burrowed into their blankets and rags. The stocky white dog—whom Max had learned the others called Lowchant—howled a lilting tune to the beat.

In the clearing, the droplets fell into the dozens and dozens of doggy dishes, filling them to overflowing.

Beside Max, Rocky shivered and dug into the bigger dog's side, trying to stay warm. Max didn't care about warmth—he was glad to at last have the sky give up all the water it had been hoarding. Now these dogs would have more than enough to drink. Around him, the dogs who hadn't yet awoken whined in their sleep, dreaming of their old homes.

Max was tired of this place, this depressing, exhausting Enclave. There was so much kibble that it would take months before the dogs could eat it all, and now all the dishes were filled with fresh water. As far as Max was concerned, if the rainwater wasn't enough, Dandyclaw and the other dogs could take a short trip to the spigot they found and lap directly from the source.

In the morning, Max decided, he was finally going to reclaim his wagon, and he and Rocky would at last move on. The longer he stayed here, the farther away his people might go, the colder Madame's trail would become. And finding them was his goal. These dogs could take care of themselves.

Only, when Max's eyes opened to take in the damp clearing the next morning, he realized something wasn't right. It took him a moment, but then he knew.

Brahms and Clearsight were gone. So was the wagon.

From the nest of blankets, Rocky yawned, then smacked his lips. "Is it morning already?" he asked drowsily. He was on his back, his tiny legs stretching up in the air.

"It sure is," Max said in a low voice. "And we've got a whole clearing full of bowls of water. Go drink up."

"Already on it!" Rocky said. Suddenly alert, the small dog turned into a blur of black as he raced to the nearest bowl.

Max scanned the clearing until he caught sight of the fluffy white fur and stupid haircut that could only belong to Dandyclaw. The Poodle, with a look of satisfaction, was marching daintily among the bowls of rainwater, taking in the Enclave's dogs drinking their fill. As if it had been *he* who had come up with the idea.

Stretching, Max got up from his bed, then marched across the clearing. Catching sight of him, Dandyclaw barked, "Ah, you're up at last. Good morning."

Max sat in front of Dandyclaw, blocking his path. "Where are Brahms and Clearsight?"

"*Sturdystep* and Clearsight are off to gather more kibble," Dandyclaw said. "I figured that you deserved a break for the morning, since your plan to catch water for everyone worked out so splendidly."

"Thank you," Max said. "But it's been days and days now, much longer than we ever meant to stay. Rocky and I really must be on our way. So when they get back, we're going to take the wagon and leave."

Dandyclaw lifted his top lip to bare his front teeth, half smile, half warning. "You want to *leave*? After all I gave you while you were here? After how the Enclave took you in?"

"All you *gave*...?" Max asked, incredulous. He couldn't believe what he was hearing. "I've been doing backbreaking work for a week to help you out!"

A little Corgi perked up at Max's loud bark, looking up midlap from a nearby water dish. Dandyclaw nudged Max and gestured toward the trees at the edge of the clearing. Sighing, Max nodded and followed the dog out of earshot of anyone else.

"I was hoping," Dandyclaw said in a low voice, "that your time among my Enclave would show you the reality of life now. We have all been abandoned. Alone, we wander the streets until we meet death. Together, we share our strengths of mind and body, and live peacefully. Why would you want to leave all this?"

135

Max growled. "I told you already. I *must* find my people."

"Your people either left you to die or are dead themselves!" Dandyclaw barked.

Max's fur bristled as he took a step back from the Poodle. "I know they aren't dead. You can't convince me they are."

Dandyclaw fully bared his teeth, for just a moment—then inhaled, long and deep. "Stay," he whispered. "Stay with those who need you. If I have overworked you, I apologize. We are both highly emotional, so I think we should take some time to think before we speak again. My brash actions in the past have lost me other useful dogs, and so I should know better."

"Lost you other dogs, huh? Like an old black Lab named Madame who you pretended not to know?"

For just a moment, Dandyclaw growled. He tried to cover it up as clearing his throat. "I told you, I don't know anything about a dog like that. You need to rest and calm yourself. I will assign other dogs to carrying the Enclave's wagon."

"The *Enclave's* wagon?" Max barked.

"Yes. My concern is only for those in my care. If you choose not to be . . . well, I wish you luck journeying without a supply of food."

Before Max could respond, Dandyclaw spun on his heels and darted back into the clearing. Max watched him go, a growl forming uncontrollably in his throat.

He had helped these dogs. This was how he was going to be repaid?

Max did not think himself an angry dog. He prided himself, in fact, on being a good boy, one who was friendly with every other animal and person he met.

But he had had enough of Dandyclaw and his lies about the humans and his miserable dog society.

Max marched into the clearing, past the dogs drinking from their bowls, past the stump, back to the little lean-to where he and Rocky slept. Rocky was there resting, though his head perked up as Max approached. "You look mad," he said.

"I am," Max growled. "Listen and don't argue. You and I aren't staying here another day. We are not going to hide in the woods when our people could be in danger."

"We're finally leaving?" Rocky laughed, giving a tiny jump. "Well, that's a relief, big guy! When?"

"Keep it down, Rocky," Max whispered. "And we'll leave as soon as Dandyclaw's back is turned."

"What about the wagon?"

"Forget it. We'll have to fight a whole camp full of dogs to take it back. It's easier to just leave it behind."

Rocky began to whine deep in his throat. "But our kibble!"

Max shook his head. "We'll find a way to get more. Plus, we'll travel faster without it. Now get ready."

It took half a day of pretending to rearrange blankets before Max saw an opportunity to sneak off.

He was at the kibble pile, eating his fill to prepare for his journey, when he saw Dandyclaw head past the lean-tos and into the southern woods to do his business.

Brahms was next to Max, the wagon beside him—and for a moment Max thought about reclaiming what was rightfully his. But he couldn't risk it. Not with the big Saint Bernard who would surely ask questions. Plus, there wouldn't be nearly enough time to get into the harness.

Instead, Max nodded at Brahms cordially, then casually walked into the trees at the north end of the clearing. He barked softly as he walked, signaling to Rocky, then crouched behind a bush to wait.

There came the padding of several small paws and leaves rustling—but the head that popped through wasn't Rocky's pointed black-and-brown snout with the floppy ears. It was the small, round face that belonged to Gizmo.

"Hello!" she yipped, chipper as ever.

Before Max could react, Rocky appeared beside her, spitting out leaves. "How did you get through that bush so fast, Giz? Blecch!"

"I went *under* the branches, not *through*," she said. "Seemed the smartest way to me. What, didn't think of that?" She giggled.

"Rocky!" Max said sharply. "What are you doing?"

"Don't worry, big guy!" Rocky said as he waddled out of the bush. "Gizmo is bored with this place, too. She wants to come with us."

Max looked at the two small dogs, both staring up at him expectantly. "I didn't realize you two had become such good friends."

"Well, I thought she was just a big fuzzball of chipper at first," Rocky said. "But I gotta admit, she's grown on me." The Dachshund looked over at his terrier friend with moony eyes—but she didn't seem to notice.

"I'm not too fond of Pinky the Poodle always calling me by a made-up name and making me do the boring work while the bigger dogs get to go run around town," Gizmo added. "I like you guys much better. Plus, I can never turn down a good adventure!"

"I can," Rocky said. "But not if it means staying here."

Nosing closer to Max, Gizmo lowered her voice and said, "And Rocky also told me all about how you are going to find your people. I've been lost from mine for . . . for a very long time. Do you think we can find mine, too?"

Max peeked up and over the bush. In the clearing, the other Enclave dogs milled about, none the wiser. There was no sign of Dandyclaw.

"All right," he said. "Of course you can come with us. Welcome to the team, Gizmo."

The little Yorkie's ears perked up, and her tail wagged

furiously behind her. "Yay! Thank you. You boys are going to just *love* having me around."

"I'm sure we will," Max said. "Let's go!"

Not waiting for any more chatter, Max turned and ran through the woods. He led the two smaller dogs parallel to the main road, so they wouldn't run into the Great Dane or the Greyhound standing sentry, but would still make it into town quickly. From there, they could hit the smooth streets once more.

Branches crunched and a flash of white fur darted in front of Max.

"Whoa!" Max dug his heels into the dirt to stop himself, sending leaves and dirt flying.

Before him stood Dandyclaw.

A furious, growling Dandyclaw. His lips were pulled back, exposing his pink gums and sharp white teeth.

"Where are you going?" the Poodle barked. "Where are you taking my dogs?"

"Uh, your dogs?" Rocky said, panting at Max's side. "I don't belong to you, Dandyclaw!"

"It's *Dandy*—" Dandyclaw started to bellow, then, realizing, said, "Oh. No matter. Any dog who comes into the Enclave becomes a member of my new society. For *life*."

"Whoa, there!" Gizmo yipped, shaking her head. "That's a little weird, don't you think? I don't remember agreeing to that. And I know for a fact I've seen a couple other dogs leave."

"Weird?" Dandyclaw spat, ignoring Gizmo and taking a step toward Max. "We were thrown out by the humans, and *I* am the one who rose up to keep us safe! Me! The least that can be expected of all of you is to stay by my side and keep the Enclave running!"

"I thought you only wanted us for the wagon," Max said. "We're just going to cause your Enclave trouble if you try to force us to stay."

"I don't want to force *anything*!" Dandyclaw bellowed, standing up for a moment on his hind legs. "You should be bowing at my feet, grateful that I gave you a warm place to sleep, a belly full of kibble, and water to wet your nose!"

"No offense," Rocky said, "but we were doing just fine without you. Seems to me it was *us* who helped *you* out."

Dandyclaw ignored him and dropped down to all fours. The Poodle almost seemed to be frothing at the mouth. "If I let you leave," he ranted, "then they may all want to leave, just like last time. But I can't have that. I can't!"

"Leave you, like Madame?" Max asked with a challenging growl.

"Oh, who cares about that old dog!" Dandyclaw barked. "She may have followed him, but who wouldn't?" He shook his head. "I still can't believe he left me, as though he could do better. All he accomplished was making the Enclave smaller. If more dogs leave, we'll become unable to support ourselves. We will fall prey to other beasts and to those humans in the baggy white suits."

"Who's 'he'?" Max asked. "What are you even talking about?"

Dandyclaw took a menacing step forward. "It doesn't matter, not anymore. Not when you're the one trying to go now. Worst of all, if I let you leave, you may lead those beasts and humans directly to us. You may spill our true names in moments of weakness, and we will be unable to resist the commands of our enemies!"

"You're crazy!" Max barked.

"I am the *savior of dogs!*" Dandyclaw howled, his barks echoing through the trees.

"Like the dog said," Rocky muttered, "crazy."

All four dogs stood silently, panting, glaring at each other in the green-tinged light beneath the trees. Max took in several heaving breaths, his eyes darting, trying to decide if he should leap at Dandyclaw's side and overtake the dog so that his friends could run ahead. But would Dandyclaw send other dogs from the Enclave after them? Bigger, faster dogs, like the Great Dane and the Greyhound?

But as Max breathed in, he caught scent of something in the air beyond the stench of doggy fear and anger.

Wolf.

No. *Wolves.*

Dandyclaw opened his jaws to begin ranting once more, but Max raised a paw. "Hush," he whispered. "Smell the air. Do you all smell that?"

Rocky huffed at the dirt beside Max, then jumped back. "Oh!" he yelped. "Wolves!"

Dandyclaw snorted. "I smelled that same trail when I followed you into the woods yesterday. At first I thought you had caught scent of me, but with the way you bristled, I knew it was the wolf smell. But it is an old trail. There are no wolves."

"Uh, Dandyclaw?" Gizmo said, raising an eyebrow. "You remember that it rained last night, right? A trail that old would have been washed away overnight."

"It can't be," Dandyclaw growled. "There can't be wolves here!"

Four pairs of ears perked up at the same time. From a distance, there came the sound of a wolf's howl. Then another, and another, rising up into a feral chorus.

"Take it from me," Max growled. "There can."

CHAPTER 13

A DARING PLAN

"My Enclave!" Dandyclaw cried, darting back and forth, unsure where to run. "They will destroy all I have built!" He halted in his tracks and bared his teeth at Max. "*You* did this somehow, didn't you? You led them here!"

"Hey!" Rocky snarled, leaping between Max and Dandyclaw. "Max would never do that. Never!"

The howls were coming from the southeast, near the forest line at the southern edge of town—but there was no mistaking that the sound was growing closer and closer.

"Go!" Max barked at Dandyclaw. "Go back to your Enclave, and prepare the other dogs for an attack. Run and hide or prepare to fight. The wolves will be weak but vicious."

"We will stand no chance!" Dandyclaw cried. "Few of our number have been in a true fight in their lives. We're *domesticated*. We used to live in houses! With people!"

"Well, if you really hope to stand a chance out in the woods," Max said, "you'd better learn how to fight, fast."

"Yeah!" Rocky barked. "Max took out a whole army of those wolves no sweat. The big guy knows what he's talking about."

"But..." Dandyclaw whimpered, ears and head drooping. The proud dog who had been standing before them only moments ago now looked weak and frightened. "But I don't know what to do...I need you...I need Precious...."

Gizmo went up to Dandyclaw and nuzzled his side. "Go back," she said softly. "Warn everyone at the Enclave, and make sure they are ready. We three will find a way to lead the wolves off the scent."

"You'll do that?" Dandyclaw asked.

"Heck no," Rocky yelped.

Max thought of all the dogs sleeping under their lean-tos, sad and abandoned, dreaming of all they had lost. He thought of Brahms and Clearsight, who were good dogs, friendly and strong and hard workers, who made for good friends while they hauled kibble. Of Lowchant and his simple squat friend, the old-timer twins, the Great Dane and the Greyhound, and all the rest. No matter what he thought of the Poodle who called himself Dandyclaw, he couldn't let those other dogs get hurt.

146

Head high, Max stepped up to Dandyclaw. "Yes," he said confidently. "We'll lead them away. The wolves are hungry and sickly, so they won't run as fast as we can. Thanks to the food at the Enclave, we are stronger and healthier than they are."

Dandyclaw's expression veered from mistrust to anger to amazement. Not saying another word, the Poodle darted between the three dogs and galloped back toward the Enclave.

"Okay, so what's the *real* plan?" Rocky said after Dandyclaw had disappeared. He looked at Max and Gizmo. "'Cause I'm not in the mood to have my insides eaten today. Doesn't sound pleasant."

"The plan is to lead the wolves away," Max said, already jogging ahead in the direction of the town.

"What?" Rocky yipped.

"Yup!" Gizmo agreed, darting to Max's side. "Oh, this is going to be *so* exciting!" Growling, she added under her breath, "It's about time I got to mess with those wolves."

"What?!" Rocky yelped once more.

"Come on!" Max called behind him. "We don't have time to waste. Let's run!"

"Gizmo, I thought you had some sense!" Rocky barked as he raced after his companions. "Unlike the big dogs."

"I'm full of surprises," Gizmo barked back, her eyes happy squints.

The wolves began to howl once more, the eerie

sound seeming to fill the empty spaces between the trees and the town, to roll over the landscape and quiet everything.

The three dogs soon found themselves bursting out of the tree line. They were in a square stone meadow just behind the first buildings of the town. There were patches of rectangular concrete, broken in places, with weeds growing up through the cracks. People garbage—plastic bags, broken glass bottles—was strewn about in the high, untamed grass, and at the far side of the meadow opposite Max, there was spray-painted writing on the backs of the town's buildings.

Max stopped, then searched the tree line to the south of the meadow and the town. Shushing Rocky and Gizmo, who were about to start talking again, he perked up his ears and listened.

Dozens of paws crunching over branches and leaves. Huffing, panting breaths. Feral growls.

And not a moment later, the first gray figures of the wolves flowed out from the trees, ragged shapes that swarmed together and apart and finally came to a stop at the opposite edge of the meadow. They seemed to be waiting.

They were as thin and sickly as Max remembered, but certainly they'd found something to eat in the week since he'd seen them last or they'd be dead by now. He couldn't help but count the beasts and wonder if there were now fewer members of the pack.

At last, the largest of the wolves shoved past those in front. The breeze shifted direction then, carrying the musky, wild stench of the wolves back to Max's snout. One wolf in particular.

"Dolph," Max whispered, recognizing his smell even before he could see the wolf clearly.

"Oh, no," Rocky whimpered, lowering himself to hide beneath the tall grass and weeds. "I was really hoping it would be some other pack. Any other pack. Not Dolph. I hate that guy."

"Dolph?" Gizmo asked with a tilted head. "You know these wolves?"

"You could say that," Rocky said.

Max shushed the two of them. "Keep low," he whispered. "Let's head toward the north side of the meadow, to the road. That way we'll have a straight shot into town, and they'll have to struggle through the tall grass."

The two smaller dogs nodded wordlessly. Lowering so that he was almost on his belly, Max led them slowly and quietly through the long grass facing the tree line where the wolves stood sniffing the air.

The road was in sight through the yellowed overgrowth—the same road that ran past the building where Max had filled the wagon with water so many mornings. He breathed in slowly, carefully. He needed to put as much distance between him and the wolves as possible. Gizmo and Rocky were already struggling to hike through grass taller than they were.

Air rustled Max's fur. The breeze had shifted, flowing south now.

Carrying Max's scent.

A wolf howled, the sound loud, aching in Max's ears.

"It's them!" Dolph bellowed from across the meadow. "The cowards who destroyed the food! The mutts that burned us! After them!"

Gizmo and Rocky froze in their tracks. Their eyes were panicked, and Rocky began to shake, nerves overtaking him.

"What should we do?" Rocky asked frantically, sniffing the air.

"*Run!*" Max barked.

CHAPTER 14

THE CHASE

Leaping to his full height, Max beelined toward the road, Rocky and Gizmo close at his heels. He bounded onto the asphalt, hot beneath his paws, and veered right to head east into the town and away from the Enclave.

"It's working!" Gizmo yipped in glee. "They're chasing us!"

"Ohhhh, it's working!" Rocky wailed. "They're going to catch us, big guy! They're going to torture us—or worse!"

"What's worse than torture?" Gizmo asked between pants.

"I don't know, but I'm sure they'll figure it out!"

Max dared a glance back over his shoulder. The wolves were thin, clearly exhausted, but their rage fueled them on. Already, they were almost all the way across the meadow, and Max and his companions had barely made it past the first two buildings.

"They're gaining on us!" Rocky howled, wind rushing through his fur.

"Just think of it as a race, Rocky!" Gizmo managed to squeak as she ran. "We just gotta beat them to the finish line—and you gotta try to beat *me*." Blinking, she added, "Oh, but what *is* the finish line?"

"Just follow me!" Max commanded. "And don't look back. I have an idea."

They reached the first street, the one lined with the empty, hollow storefronts, just as the wolf pack hit the main road. Max galloped to the right, heading toward the one building he knew the best: the grocery store.

Racing across the parking lot, Max leaped over fallen grocery carts while Rocky and Gizmo darted to the side to pass them. Max led them to the cleared path through the broken glass, then into the dark store.

"What are we doing in here?" Rocky asked. "They'll corner us!"

"Trust me," Max said.

Focused, Max darted down the front of the store, his nails clacking against the hard floor. Then he veered into the pet aisle.

"Oh, wow," Rocky said. "Buddy, oh, wow! Look at all this kibble! All these toys!"

"Ooh!" Gizmo barked. "Toys! No one ever said there were—"

Outside the broken windows came growls and howls as the wolf pack followed the dogs' scents toward the store. There came a high, sharp-pitched yipping, and Max dared a look behind him to see that some unlucky wolf had run directly over the broken glass and cut his paws.

"No time!" Max barked. "Come on! Help me!"

Leaping forward, he grabbed the nearest bag of kibble in his jaws, yanked it to the floor, and then wrenched back and forth until the paper packaging ripped and delicious brown pebbles mounded on the floor.

Spurred on by the sounds of their pursuers, Rocky and Gizmo did the same, grabbing another bag between the two of them, dragging it to the edge of the metal shelf, and tearing it open so that brown bits rained down. Max managed to get two more bags open and spilled all over the floor before he heard Dolph's deep growls echo in the metal rafters.

"They are in here! Avoid the glass, mongrels! *In here!*"

"Come on," Max said in a low voice. "Quiet."

"But look at all this *food*," Rocky said.

"You and kibble," Gizmo said, shaking her head as she turned to follow Max.

"Don't act like you don't like it," Rocky muttered back. "I saw you try to hoard that small bag of lamb flavor back at the Enclave."

"Guys," Max hissed. "Shush."

Dropping low to the chilly tiles, Max padded as softly

as he could to the rear of the store. The light that streamed through the broken front windows barely reached there, and the shelves were in shadow. Only one glass-doored refrigerator shed any light, but its fluorescent bulbs were flickering.

Just as they rounded the back edge of the pet aisle, the sound of dozens of claws clattering against cold, hard floor filled the store. The wolves walked softly, slowly now. Max could hear them huffing, following his scent.

Heart beating deep in his chest, Max waited. Rocky trembled beside him, and Gizmo's tail wagged in excitement.

"There are such bad smells here," a wolf growled at the front of the store. "Bad food."

"They are in here," Dolph growled back. "I can sense them."

The wolves walked on, coming closer and closer. *Clack clack clack* against the floor. Their noses snorting, smelling.

And then one of the wolves howled in glee.

"Food!" the wolf bellowed. "There is food here! Everywhere, food!"

The slow, calculated footsteps turned into gallops as the entire pack raced forward to see what the first wolf had found. There came starved cries of joy at the sight of the piles of kibble, crunches as the wolves dove in to eat their fill.

"Let's go," Max whispered.

The three dogs kept low to the floor and darted down the shadowy back aisle, careful not to let their own claws click against the floor. As they ran, they heard Dolph rage at his pack.

"This is a distraction! The dogs will get away! I command you to stop!"

"But, sir! There is so much *food*!"

Max slid against the slippery floor as he reached the first aisle, the one farthest from the pet aisle full of wolves devouring doggy chow. Veering right, he raced toward the front of the building, toward daylight, toward freedom. His tongue lolled from his mouth as he panted for air.

Max reached the front of the store, just in front of the checkout counters—and that was when Dolph, who had not entered the pet aisle, saw him.

"There!" Dolph bellowed. "They are here! Forget dry dog food! We shall feast on fresh meat!"

Dolph looked scarier than Max remembered, his gray eyes narrowed with rage and his chest heaving, showing a line of scorched fur.

"Go!" Max barked at Rocky and Gizmo. The two didn't hesitate, darting past a register and leaping out the front door in a flash.

Another glass-doored refrigerator, half the size of the one in his people's home, caught Max's eyes. It was set up right in front of the nearest checkout counter and was stocked with bottles filled with fizzy brown and green liquids.

As Dolph screamed at his pack to stop eating while he ran toward Max, Max leaped against the side of the refrigerator, just like he'd jumped against the cabinet back in Vet's office and Rocky had flung himself into the gum-ball machine. The refrigerator collapsed to the floor with a loud, echoing *boom*, and the glass door burst open. Bottle after bottle dropped to the floor, many bursting upon impact, filling the aisle with sticky liquid.

Not waiting a moment longer, Max ran to a broken window and hopped through to find Rocky and Gizmo already halfway across the parking lot. Behind him, Max heard Dolph howl in anger as he slipped and skidded among the fallen soda bottles.

With his last bit of energy, Max ran as fast as he could past the shattered glass and through the parking lot to his two friends.

"Did we stop them?" Rocky asked between frantic pants.

"Not yet," Max panted back. "But I think we slowed them down."

"This is great!" Gizmo yipped as they reached the main street and turned toward the unexplored side of town. "I haven't had this much fun in ages!"

Conserving their breaths, all three dogs ceased talking and focused on running as fast as they could down the main street. They passed street after street lined with abandoned buildings, nothing but broken windows and dark open doorways. After a while, the square buildings fell away and single-story human homes began appearing along the streets, set back on yellowed lawns. All quiet and dark. Some with doors hanging open and belongings strewn upon the grass. Others pristine and calm, as though someone still lived there. On one lawn, a child's tricycle lay upside down, its large front wheel squeaking as it slowly spun in the breeze.

Max considered veering into one of those houses— they were so much like the home of his people—and hiding with Rocky and Gizmo and resting for the night.

But then the howls came again.

The wolves had eaten their fill. Now they were on the scent of Max, Rocky, and Gizmo.

And Max knew that after all he had done to Dolph, the wolf was not going to stop his pursuit.

"Wow, those guys never give up, huh?" Gizmo said.

"I told you," Rocky cried. "I knew this would happen! What are we going to do now?"

"Let's wait for them," Gizmo said, growling and baring her teeth. She jumped around, shaking her head as though she had one of the wolves by his throat. "I'll fight them off! They won't stand a chance against me."

Rocky just looked at her and shook his head. "Girls."

Max stopped running, resting for just a moment to catch his breath. "There is a way out of this. Just...let me think."

Max strained to think back to the times he'd been driven into town with his people. The windows had been rolled down, carrying in the sounds of people laughing and talking in the streets, the outside air wafting with the aroma of barbecues and burning leaves. Sometimes Max had hung his head out the window, letting the wind run through his fur and over his tongue, but mostly he lay in Charlie's and Emma's laps, dozing.

And he also remembered riding past the town's bustling streets to a faraway lake, where he played with his pack leaders next to a cabin. The lake smelled of fish and mud and moldering wood, and he loved to bound up the banks, barking in glee as his people reeled in a fresh catch. Then there'd been a smoky fire in a rock pit, and meal scraps tossed his way, and chases after his favorite orange rubber ball into the cool lake water while the sun set on the horizon....

Max shook his head. He couldn't get lost in his memories, not now, not with the wolves growing ever closer. He commanded himself to think. When they went to the lake, the car always headed this direction, east through town. Then over a bridge, which crossed...

"The river," Max said. "We can lose them at the river!"

"What?" Rocky asked. "What river? How will a river lose them?"

"Same way most scents get lost," Gizmo mused. "Water. We can swim! I *love* swimming!"

The howls had grown louder, a stampede of wolves heading their way. Rest time was over.

"We can do it, guys!" Max barked. Then he resumed running down the center of the street. "We haven't come this far just to let a few wolves stop us!"

The three dogs ran as fast as they could, the world around them a blur—blue sky and white clouds bleeding into black street and green grass. Soon enough came a sound louder than either dog or wolf: the rushing of river rapids.

Max slowed, just enough to catch his bearings. Up ahead, around a bend, the road crossed over a bridge. And beneath the bridge was the river. The very wide, rushing, white-capped, deadly looking river.

"Oh," Max said. "That's a lot bigger than I remember."

"Doesn't matter!" Rocky yelped. "They're getting close!"

Indeed the wolves were. Dolph was so close that Max, daring a glance back, could make out the three scars on the beast's sneering snout. The wolves were a few blocks away but making up ground quickly. They'd regained their strength.

Suddenly, feeding them back at the grocery store no longer seemed the best idea.

"Over here!" Gizmo yipped, leaping up and down at an earthen trail next to the northern side of the bridge, just wide enough for a car to go down. There were two yellow poles on either side of the dirt road with heavy metal chains between them. "I think this leads down!"

Max darted forward, leaping over the chains. The dirt road sloped down, curving to meet the river's edge. As quickly but as carefully as he could, Max followed the old muddy tire tracks. Moments later, he, Rocky, and Gizmo found themselves in the shadows beneath the bridge and on the banks of the raging river.

"Wow," Rocky said.

"Wow," Max repeated.

"So exciting!" Gizmo said. "Are we going to swim now?"

Down here, the river seemed an impossible obstacle. The dirt road gave way to mud, which gave way to hard, wet rocks embedded in the riverbed. The river itself roared louder than any animal Max had ever known, the sound echoing through braces on the underside of the bridge and becoming all that he could hear. The water was a churning mass of brown and gray that peaked into white-tipped waves as the whole mass rushed to the south.

And the shore on the other side seemed miles away.

"They're coming," Rocky yelped, pacing back and forth in fear. "You have a plan, big guy? We're not really trapped down here, right?"

"Weren't we going to swim for it?" Gizmo asked. "I'm game if you guys are!"

"It's too fast, Gizmo," Max barked, struggling to be heard over the roar of the waves. "We'll never make it."

"Then what?" she yipped. "We're not giving up,

right? We can't! I'm not going to let some stupid wolves get the best of us!"

Faintly, over the sounds of the rushing rapids, Max could hear wolves howling above. They'd reached the bridge. And they'd find their way down to the river's edge in no time.

Max spun around, looking frantically for a way of escape. Maybe a drainage pipe, or a hidden path, *someplace* they could hide until he could find a better way of leaving behind the wolves.

The shore was empty.

Despairing, Max turned his eyes back to the river. That was when he caught sight of the garbage.

Farther down the river, just past the bridge, was a jam of logs and human junk, like plastic bottles and wooden crates. The water slowed and swirled around the garbage before rushing past again. From what Max could see, it ran at least most of the way across the river with gaps in places that the water could spill through. A narrow, accidental dam.

"I see a way out," Max barked. "Come on!"

"I'm coming, I'm coming," Rocky barked back.

The three dogs raced along the shore, leaping and scrabbling over large wet rocks as they neared the dam. They reached the edge of it just as the first of the wolves reached the bottom of the dirt road and caught sight of them.

"Down here!" a wolf called, his voice familiar. "Dolph, I have found them!"

Max looked back—and was surprised to see that the wolf who'd spotted them was none other than Wretch. His white fur was still matted in places with blood from the fight he and Max had had in Vet's lobby. And Wretch looked much too pleased to have caught up with his old foe.

"Hurry!" Max shouted to his companions. "Start across!"

"This is how we're getting to the other side?" Rocky barked. "This doesn't look too solid, big guy. And my legs aren't so long, you know?"

Gizmo leaped onto a bunch of piled logs near the shore and darted along the slick, smooth wood with ease. "Seems fine to me!" she barked behind her.

"We've got no choice," Max said. "Hurry up. If you fall in, I'll dive in for you. I promise."

Trembling, Rocky took one tentative step onto the wet log, then another. "This is not how I expected my day to end up," he said. "Maybe Dandyclaw and his Enclave had the right idea, hiding in a clearing."

"Hurry!" Max barked, then nipped at Rocky's heels.

"All right, all right, no need to bite!"

Rocky waddled over the debris just as easily as Gizmo, who was now a quarter of the way across the makeshift dam, teetering on an old kitchen door that was jammed between two rocks. Max looked back one more time—

and saw three wolves racing through the mud toward them, Wretch at the lead.

Max leaped onto the log—and it shifted beneath him, jerking to the side and almost tossing him into the rapids. He yelped but managed to lodge his back paw against a knot on the log's mossy, decaying surface.

Perhaps the log-and-trash dam wasn't as solid as he'd hoped.

No time to second-guess himself now. Max leaped from the log to the next pile of garbage, a half-dozen black plastic bags that bobbed together against a leafless treetop that had caught on something under the rapids. Again the debris shifted beneath him, threatening to spill him into the river. Icy cold water splashed up, getting into his eyes, blinding him. Sputtering, he stepped forward, more carefully this time, making sure he had his footing before taking the next leap.

"Look at him!" one of the wolves growled behind Max. "He is stumbling and will fall. We will, too."

"Then stay here and fail, coward," Wretch snarled. "If we lose these dogs because you worry about getting wet, it will be *your* haunches Dolph feasts on. Not mine."

Neither of the other wolves responded. A moment later, there came a wet squelching as Wretch and then the other two wolves tepidly stepped atop the first log of the jam.

"Max!" Rocky shouted from up ahead. "Come on, big guy! They're right behind you!"

Blinking through the water splashing onto his snout, Max managed to make out Gizmo and Rocky huddling on a large wooden crate that had caught itself in the jam. To Max's horror, he saw why the two dogs had stopped—whatever debris that had extended past the crate when they had started had now washed away.

The debris beneath Max's feet shifted. His heavy, plodding steps loosened the piles of branches and plastic bags. Two of the big black bags wobbled and were swept away.

The garbage bridge was falling apart, and any minute, Max would fall into the water, be sucked beneath the waves....

"You're almost here!" Gizmo cried. "Come on!"

A wolf howled, and then came a splash.

Max looked and saw the gray head of a wolf desperately trying to stay above the water as he was carried downstream. The river moved so fast that one moment the wolf was there, and the next he had disappeared beneath the gray and brown churnings of the river, far, far away.

"Stop!" Wretch growled, what felt like mere feet behind Max. "You will not get away from me this time, mongrel!"

Shivering, Max looked up. The crate and his two companions were only a few leaps away. If he walked as gingerly as he had been, he'd never make it before Wretch reached him. But if he jumped...

Rocky stared at Max, his big brown eyes forlorn.

Gizmo yipped and yipped, begging him to hurry. Wretch's roars filled his ears, the wolf so close that Max could feel his hot breath on his haunches.

With a deep breath, Max tensed his legs and leaped.

He came down hard on a pile of small logs that immediately separated, got caught in the waves, and vanished beneath the water. Before they could all disappear, Max scrambled atop the remaining logs and took in another steeling breath. He had only one shot at this, and there was no time to waste.

Bunching his legs again, Max leaped into the chilly air above the angry river.

There was a moment when he was in the air, aloft, when time seemed to slow down. The silver water went rippling past and the cool breeze blew in his fur, and he remembered that *this* was what Max was meant to do: to run, to leap, to chase. At times like these, he felt most like himself.

But the water beneath did not care what Max was meant to do. With one wrong leap, one bad step, the waves would devour him just as they had the wolf who had been swept downstream. Max held his breath as he flew forward, unable to hear but fully able to see his two small friends jumping up and down, barking at him with terrified eyes, hoping that his instincts wouldn't let him down, not now.

And Max landed belly-first atop the crate, his hind legs splashing into the icy water.

His weight made the crate tip, and Gizmo and Rocky slid down toward him, both yipping wildly. But then the crate righted itself and, shoved free from the debris, was immediately caught in the rushing waves. It spun in wide circles as it swirled downstream, and Max clinged to the wood with his front claws while his hind feet splashed helplessly in the water.

First one back foot, then the other, found purchase on the side of the crate, and Max pulled himself all the way aboard, panting and dripping wet, his heart racing.

"That was close, pal!" Rocky shouted. "You almost threw us all into the water!"

"That was amazing!" Gizmo barked. "It was like you *flew.*"

The crate, just wide enough to hold all three dogs, stopped spinning around so fast. Max stood up, shook himself dry, and then looked back just in time to see Wretch and the other wolf leap back to shore before the garbage dam gave way entirely and was swept downstream after Max, Rocky, and Gizmo.

Beneath the arching green steel of the bridge stood the line of wolves, Dolph in the center. He looked mad—madder than Max could have imagined. "You can run, but you cannot hide," Dolph barked with a growl that sent shivers down Max's spine.

"Ha-*ha!*" Rocky shouted. "Take that, Dolph, you dumb brute! You, too, Wretch! You stupid wolves will never get one over on us!"

Max wished he could join in the celebration. They'd managed to get the wolves away from the Enclave and saved the dogs there. But now the wolf pack had a renewed determination and a new trail to follow.

And Max had no doubt that trail would lead them back to him and his friends, sooner rather than later.

CHAPTER 15

GIZMO'S STORY

For a long while after the bridge and the wolves faded out of view, Max, Rocky, and Gizmo lay belly-down on the damp crate, watching the world lazily drift past them.

The rushing of the water had slowed, and so the roar of the river was no longer quite as deafening. Instead, the wooden crate bobbed gently on the waves as it slowly turned in circles, giving the dogs a full view of their surroundings.

The sun was just past the center of the sky, and under its warm rays, their fur quickly heated and dried. A few clouds drifted serenely across the bright blue sky. It all would have been relaxing, if it weren't for the fact that Max wasn't entirely sure how they were going to get back to shore.

Still, better here on the crate than in the bellies of a pack of wolves.

"Ohhh," Rocky wailed, rolling onto his back and staring up at the sky. "I ache all over. I've never run that much in my life. Never again! No more playing bait to a pack of wolves, all right, big guy?"

Groaning—for he ached all over, too—Max lifted his head to look down at his pal. "I promise to try to avoid wolves from now on."

"Where's the fun in that?" Gizmo sauntered around Max's haunches and came to sit near where Rocky lay splayed on his back. She peered over the edge of the crate, then swatted the water with a paw. "I can't believe we're riding the river! This is really a *lot* more fun than making beds."

Max turned his attention to the little Yorkshire Terrier. At the Enclave, he'd spent most of his time working with Brahms and Clearsight and a few of the other big dogs, so much so that when it came time to sleep, he wasn't really in the mood for chitchat with a chipper little dog.

But Rocky had certainly taken a shine to her. Even now, Max could see his sausage-shaped friend looking over at Gizmo with happy eyes.

Deciding he'd worry about getting ashore later, Max tilted his head at Gizmo. "So, Gizmo," he said, "you said your people were lost, too? Are you from around this area?"

Gizmo sat back on her haunches and darted her head back and forth, taking in the trees and sparse buildings on either side of the river. "Hmm," she said after a moment. "No. I don't think so, at least. But I lost my people long before everyone else left."

Rocky rolled over to flop back onto his belly. "You did?" he asked her. "I didn't know that."

Ducking her head, Gizmo let her pointed ears droop. "It was my fault, really," she said. "My people were taking us all on a trip to the woods. We were in a long, skinny home on wheels—RV, they kept calling it. Everything was just so new and exciting, so I ran all over the place, sniffed everywhere, pounced on the bed—it was just so fun! The man married to my pack leader—he was called Robert—got mad and told my pack leader, Ann, that she'd have to put me in my carrier."

Rocky growled. "A carrier, huh? Yech! I hate those. I wonder if the humans would like it if they got shoved into a tiny, cramped cage and carried around without knowing where they are. I bet they wouldn't like it *at all.*"

"What happened then?" Max asked Gizmo.

The little terrier gazed wistfully at the trees as the crate swirled to face her toward the shore.

"We were stopped for a long, long time, and Ann came and let me out of the carrier. So, I thought, *Oh! We're in the woods! Yay!* And I was excited to go explore! One of the windows was open, so when Ann was turned around, I jumped up on the counter beneath the window and looked outside. I saw trees, and then there was a squirrel! And it was running!"

Max nodded. "Running squirrels are irresistible."

"Aren't they, though?" Gizmo said, looking up at Max. "Well, I couldn't help myself. In those days, I was the most squirrel-crazy girl you'd ever meet. I dove out the window and ran into the woods. The squirrel took me for an amazing chase before it finally ran up a tree—I really just wanted to talk to it, since squirrels that get to know me just *love* me—but this one just threw some nuts at my head, chittered at me with raised fists, and ran inside a knothole. That's when I turned to run back to the RV and Ann, but I found a road instead. There were lots and lots of cars moving very slowly, but I couldn't see my RV."

"They just left you?" Rocky asked.

Gizmo shook her head. "I don't know," she said softly. "Ann cuddled and played with me all the time, and sometimes Robert did, too, when he wasn't busy. They loved me. They would have at least called out for me before leaving me behind. I think they just didn't notice I was gone until it was too late."

Max thought back to the TV at his old home, and the images of the cars moving slowly down the roads. "How long ago did this happen?" he asked.

"Would have been a few years ago," Gizmo said wistfully.

"Are you sure?" Max asked. "Are you sure it wasn't a few weeks ago? When all the other people disappeared?"

"I'm *pretty* sure," Gizmo said, thinking. "I mean, all the other dogs talked about being thrown out by their people, not being taken along in carriers. And I walked and walked for a long, long time, and there were still plenty of people around. Until recently, anyway. I wonder what happened to all of them...."

Max was about to ask Gizmo another question when a thud came from the side of the crate. The crate trembled, momentarily threatening to toss the three dogs into the waves below. Then the crate began spinning in the opposite direction—and slowly heading toward the eastern shore.

"What was that?" Rocky yelped, trembling as he clung to the top of the crate with his claws.

Max looked back down the river and saw a black, shiny boulder jutting up from the brown-and-gray water. Looking over the crate's edge, he saw a scuff mark on the crate's side. Thankfully, the rock hadn't cracked the wood.

"We just hit a rock," Max said, lying back down on top of the crate. "And looks like we solved the problem of how to get to the other side of the river!"

Gizmo's nub tail wagged in a blur, her sad memories of losing her people forgotten at seeing the eastern shore coming closer. "Yay! I like the water and all, but dry land is where the food is."

"Ohhh, food," Rocky moaned, flopping onto his back once more to reveal his pale belly. "I know why we had to leave our wagon behind, big guy, but oh, all the kibble we aren't going to be eating."

"Don't worry, Rocky," Gizmo said. "I lived off the land for years with no problem. I'm sure we can, too."

"How did you do that, exactly?" Max asked her.

"Sometimes it was handouts," Gizmo said, tilting her head as she remembered. "Some nice humans would see me, pat my head, and give me some of their food. All the humans just *loved* me. I'm pretty irresistible, too." She paused and licked at a paw. "And sometimes you just find dog food out in people's yards—though if you're not careful, the dog it belongs to may be around and take you on a chase." She giggled. "It's really funny when they get caught on their chains and get yanked back, though."

"What about after the people disappeared?" Max asked.

Scrunching her fuzzy brows, Gizmo thought and then said, "Hmm, I didn't realize the people had disappeared at first. I spent a lot of time in the woods, and I remember hearing lots of cars on the roads. And then one day, the cars just stopped coming. I went to investigate the roads, to make sure I hadn't gone deaf, when I met…" Her eyes went glassy and distant. "The Weimaraner."

"Weimaraner?" Max asked.

Gizmo nodded slowly. "Yes. The Weimaraner. Gunther was his name. I'd met other dogs during my travels,

174

but none with his charm or charisma. It was love at first sight. Or first sniff, anyway."

Rocky's head darted up at that. "Love, huh? You, uh...you *loved* this other dog?"

Sighing, Gizmo turned her gaze to the clouds. "He was bigger than me—"

"I don't see how that's a plus," Rocky grumbled.

"—and he had the softest gray fur I'd ever seen. Oh, and his accent! He told me he was brought over from *Europe*. Can you imagine?"

"Never heard of it," Rocky said.

"Rocky, let her talk," Max said, nudging his friend's side with his nose.

"Apparently, Europe is a whole other place across the ocean, and dogs there talk differently. Gunther had to learn a whole new way to bark in order to talk to dogs here, and he learned it all by himself." Gizmo sighed again. "He was so smart."

"'Was'?" Max asked. "What happened to him?"

Ears and tail drooping, Gizmo looked back down at the soft river waves that kept the crate bobbing forward. "He was like you and the other dogs," she said softly. "Abandoned by his people, only he was locked in his home with a bowl full of food. He had to bust himself out after his food ran out, and then he decided to search for his people, too. That's when he met me, and we decided to travel together.

"We had to resort to digging into garbage cans to

175

find food," she went on. "And there was lots of garbage, since no people trucks came to take it away. We managed to make some nice meals that way. Until the night we stumbled upon a wolf angling for the same trash can. We offered to share, but the wolf..." She swallowed a whimper. "Well, it decided it wanted to eat me. But Gunther defended me, and the two fought. Oh, how chivalrous Gunther was! A true friend, protecting my honor.

"They dragged each other into the woods. It was dark and I couldn't see, but they both grew quiet and when I went to investigate... they were gone."

"You don't think..." Max said softly.

Gizmo turned away from Max and Rocky. "I don't know. I never found out."

"That's a sad story," Rocky said. "I hate sad stories."

"A few days later, I stumbled upon the Enclave, and they had so much food and such nice places to sleep, and I was so sad about Gunther that I decided to join up with them. Those were the early days, before Pinky the Poodle went nuts, around the time his friend Precious left in a huff. I kept hoping Gunther would show up, but he never did. And when I smelled the wolf trail this morning, I'd hoped maybe, somehow..."

Her voice petered out, becoming small and silent. Rocky opened his snout as if to say something. Instead, he waddled across the crate and nuzzled her side.

"I hope I don't seem like I'm disrespecting Gunther," Max said softly, "but you mentioned Dandyclaw's friend leaving in a huff. That must have been when my friend Madame left, too. Do you know where they went?"

Gizmo tilted her head in thought. "Well, Dandyclaw was awful mad about the whole thing, so most of the other dogs wouldn't talk about it. But I heard that Precious wanted to go somewhere bigger and better than some clearing next to a small town. Someplace where there'd be more dogs. I don't know where, though."

"It's okay," Max said, trying not to sound frustrated. "I'm sure we'll figure something out."

Max laid his head back down on his paws—and that was when he realized that the crate had stopped spinning. In fact, it had stopped moving at all. Peering over the side, he saw that it had come to rest against the muddy shore.

"Hey," he said softly. "We hit land."

Gizmo looked up at Max. Then she let her tongue loll out and, in a convincingly cheerful voice, said, "Oh! Great! We made it!"

"Finally!" Rocky barked. He jumped down from the crate—and plopped onto shore, squelching into the soft mud nearly up to his belly. It covered almost the entirety of his legs. "Ugh, gross!"

Max leaped from the crate, followed by Gizmo. Both shoved off harder and landed farther away. Rocky tilted his head back and howled at the darkening sky, struggling to walk forward. "Help! I'm sinking, big guy! The ground is gonna swallow me whole!"

Chuckling, Max stepped forward, used his jaws to grab Rocky by the scruff of his neck, and yanked the little dog free from the mud. He dropped the Dachshund on the grass farther up the shore.

"Nature!" Rocky yowled between licks to clean his fur. "I can't stand it!"

"Where are we, do you think?" Gizmo asked Max.

Max studied their surroundings. The river flowed behind them, gentler than beneath the bridge where they'd found the crate but still fast enough to be dangerous. Farther north along the shore, back the way they'd come, all he could see were trees and brush. To the south, though, the trees gave way to clearings—and farther down, a bridge that crossed the river was covered with tracks, like the ones he'd stumbled over when fleeing from the abandoned car.

"I'm starving," Rocky said as he spat mud off his tongue. "I'd even eat garbage right about now. Though, of course, I'd prefer not to. Just so you know." As he looked around, his ears drooped. "But it looks like we're in the middle of nowhere."

Max sniffed the air. The wind was coming from the east, and with it came a stench of grime and murky air that Max had smelled only once before—when his pack leaders' parents had driven them through a place full of buildings that towered toward the sky, and where there was hardly any grass to be found. Just concrete and more concrete.

A human city. Someplace that was certainly much bigger and full of more dogs than the Enclave clearing.

"There's a city nearby," Max announced as he began to head down the shore toward the nearest clearing. "What do you want to bet Dandyclaw's old friend and Madame were heading there?" Unable to contain his excitement, his tail began to wag furiously. "And maybe they went there to find people!"

"Oh!" Gizmo said, her ears perking up. "A city! I bet there's lots of food and places to sleep around there."

"Food?" Rocky barked. "Sleep? People?! I'm sold!" Newly cleaned legs moving in a blur, the Dachshund bounded ahead of Max.

"And maybe it won't just be any people in the city," Gizmo said softly beside Max. "Maybe it will be *your* people, and your friend Madame found them, and maybe... if mine haven't given up on me..."

"Hey," Max said to her as they trotted side by side. "Don't worry. Even if we can't find your people, mine or Rocky's pack leaders would love to adopt you."

"You think?" she asked, her eyes earnest as she looked up at him.

"Definitely."

"Oh yeah!" Rocky said, looking over his shoulder at her eagerly. "I bet you my pack leader would love an outgoing dog like you. And we could cuddle on my doggy bed to keep warm at night!"

"Maybe!" Gizmo said. "Or maybe I could have my own bed. That would be nice."

"Yeah," Rocky said, ears drooping ever so slightly. "Your own bed could be nice, too. Certainly!" Looking ahead, he said, "Anyway, I say we find us some food and a place to sleep. I'm tired of all this *traveling*. I'd almost prefer to be in a carrier, and that's saying something."

The cool breeze bristled the fur along Max's back, and his eyes again went to the bridge up ahead. They'd made it to the opposite shore of the river, but with the bridge back at the town and the one here, the wolves could have, too.

The whole plan to save the Enclave had been to lead the wolves away, to set them on Max and his friends' tracks instead. Relaxing and chatting on the crate had let him think of other things, but now Max couldn't help but almost hear the howls of their pursuing foes.

"Actually, Rocky," Max said, "I don't think we're in the clear yet."

"Aw, we're not?"

Max shook his head. "Those wolves aren't going to stop chasing us now. We need to put as much distance between us and them as possible."

"Does that mean we get to run more?" Gizmo asked, wagging her tail excitedly.

"We have to run *more*?" Rocky whined. "Aww, man."

"I'm afraid so," Max said. "It's either that or—"

181

"End up like Gunther," Gizmo finished for him.

Rocky stopped, turned, and looked at his two companions. He seemed on the verge of whining in protest—but, seeing Gizmo's drooping ears and tail, only nodded his consent.

As the sun dipped behind the trees on the opposite side of the river, bringing with it the violet sky of night, Max watched over his two new friends lapping up river water. The journey so far had been a lot tougher than he'd ever imagined. And now he had more to worry about than just finding his people and Madame.

Now he had two new friends that he had vowed to keep safe, no matter what.

CHAPTER 16

THE FIRST HOUSE ON THE LEFT

The trio of dogs hiked through the night, first through the woods, and then across clearings and along dirt roads. They stopped every now and again to rest—because although they had their fill of water, their stomachs growled with an aching hunger—but Max wouldn't let them stay in one place too long.

Always he kept his ears perked, straining to listen for wolves stalking them through the trees. He sniffed at the air constantly, almost certain he could smell their dank, musky stench.

But as far as Max could tell, the wolves hadn't found them. He wondered if maybe they hadn't bothered to give chase at all. If maybe they'd gone back to the market for the kibble, or worse, to the Enclave.

Max tried not to think about it.

The dogs' pace had slowed almost to a crawl by the time the sun began to rise over the horizon in front of them. They'd reached a road twice as wide as the one that ran through the town near the Enclave, but this one rose up and up on a big hill. Max could barely keep his eyes open, and Rocky had taken to arguing with himself, so quietly that Max couldn't make out what the little dog was saying.

Only Gizmo seemed alert and awake. She jogged ahead of the other two dogs on her four short legs, head up and darting back and forth, ears pert atop her head, and small pink tongue hanging from her flat snout.

"Beef is good for dinner," Rocky grunted louder next to Max, almost as if unaware he was saying anything. "Chicken flavor, great snack. Maybe mix 'em. Mix 'em all up and have a new flavor. Maybe keep some crunchy, but soften some of it with water. Yeah. That'd be tasty, real tasty."

"What are you talking about?" Gizmo called back over her shoulder.

"I'm pretty sure it's kibble," Max said. "It's Rocky, after all."

"Hey!" Rocky said. "I resent that. I care about more than just food, big guy. I'm a complicated dog. Lots of emotions."

"Mm-hmm," Max said, his vision going blurry even as the bright morning light glared into his eyes.

"Oh, wow! Hey, boys! Come on and see!"

Max perked up slightly at Gizmo's chipper yips. He blinked to clear his eyes, then saw the little terrier jumping up and down at the top of the hill, where the road finally met level ground. Her short tail wagged.

Groaning, Max forced himself to walk faster, Rocky matching his stride. As he neared the top of the hill, he realized why Gizmo was so excited.

There, silhouetted on the horizon, was the city.

Max remembered driving through the city, but he'd never seen it from this view before—he hadn't been able to from the backseat of his people's car. It was one thing to be in the city and know you're surrounded by buildings climbing up into the clouds, but it was quite another to view it from this distance, to see the glittering, mirrored structures rise up to scrape the morning sky.

The orange light from the rising sun glinted and reflected off the giant buildings, making them sparkle above the smaller but still no doubt giant buildings surrounding their base. There were mazes of roads running between the buildings, and even some dots of green—trees, maybe. Perhaps a park or two?

Max stepped past Gizmo and a gaping Rocky, straining his eyes. It was hard to see, so he couldn't tell if there was movement. Walking people or cars or even birds, anything to show that the city was different from the isolated towns and countryside.

It was so early, and the sun made everything so

shadowy and misty, that Max couldn't be sure. He thought he saw movement, but it might have just been his imagination. And even if there wasn't movement yet, maybe there would be later in the day.

"So there it is, big guy," Rocky said as he sat down beside Max. "The city. You think there's an ocean near it, like where we saw the people on TV?"

"I don't know," Max said. "But there are a lot of buildings. We can definitely find some food while we search for our people and Madame."

"Ooh, kibble!" Rocky barked. Then, clearing his throat, he pointed his snout in the air. "I mean, and other things may be there, too, buddy. Many of the other things I care about in life."

Gizmo bounced ahead, facing Max and Rocky but running backward toward the skyline.

"Come on, boys!" she yipped. "I can't wait to get there!"

"I'm not sure we're all that close," Max said. "Those buildings are huge. We could be miles and miles away."

"So where do we go now?" Rocky yowled. "Can we at least rest in the trees? Haven't we lost the wolves yet?"

Max spun around, examining their surroundings. To the north was a big clearing that met up with the tree line. To the south was much the same, though there was a concrete ditch leading into a big concrete pipe that disappeared under the dirt and ran parallel to the road.

Farther east, down the main road, he saw the trees give way to smaller streets lined with—

Houses. Orange and yellow boxy homes built right up next to one another, looking sort of like the building blocks his pack leaders played with sometimes.

"People homes!" Max barked. "We can rest in one of those. But first..."

Max jaunted to the side of the road and stepped into the ditch, which was hard and rough beneath his paws. Sniffing the ground, he took a few steps forward, then peered through the concrete pipe. Water pooled in its bottom, and far down the other side, he could see light— an exit.

"Rocky!" he called, his bark echoing through the pipe. "Gizmo! Down here!"

Gizmo darted off the road, through the grass, and to Max's side. "What's this?" she asked.

"I think it's to drain water," Max said. "But more important, it's a way for us to keep the wolves off our trail."

"You want us to crawl through this murky water in a dark tunnel?" Rocky asked, poking dubiously at the stagnant water in the pipe. "I know it ain't such a big deal to you, big guy, but I'm going to be up to my neck in the stuff!"

Gizmo once again ran ahead, diving headfirst into the water. She leaped up and down, splashing around and laughing. "It's fun! You're not afraid of some water, are you, Rocky? After we braved that raging river?"

Max raised a brow and nudged Rocky with his nose.

"Yeah, Rocky. You aren't going to let Gizmo think you're a big fraidy-pup, are you?"

"Who?" Rocky asked, aghast. "Me? Afraid of water? Never! I *embrace* water! I live to crawl through muddy, leaf-covered, bug-infested water!" Head held high, Rocky marched up to the pipe, stepped one paw into the water—then leaped back. "Uh, but let me get used to the cold first."

"Actually," Max said, looking back across the road to the northern tree line. "Before we do anything, let's leave our wolf friends a false trail."

The three dogs stepped out of the shadow of the pipe, then ran south into the clearing on the side of the road. When they reached the trees down there, Max had them all stop, roll in the grass, and—if they had to go—do their business. Leaving a nice, easy-to-follow stench for a pack of angry wolves.

Then, backtracking through their own trail, they reached the ditch and the pipe once more. With Gizmo in the lead, followed by Rocky, and with Max crouching down to take up the rear, the three dogs splashed into the cold, stagnant water. The water seeped and squelched between Max's toes, the bottom of the pipe rough against the pads of his feet. The farther they walked, the deeper the water got, so much so that Rocky had to force his snout up high and even then he was sputtering for air.

Insects and spiders crawled in the muck coating the top of the pipe, but it soon became so dark that they couldn't see the bugs—they just heard their skittering legs. Water dripped and echoed through the pipe, broken up by the dogs' heavy splashes. Something slick and slimy stuck to Max's fur, and he felt so cramped, so trapped, that he started to wonder if this was really his best idea. Not even Gizmo seemed to be pleased to be playing in the water anymore.

Gizmo broke into a run, and Rocky followed, not needing to be asked. Still partially crouched, Max had to go slower than the two of them, but he forced himself to move as fast as he could.

And then, mercifully, he emerged from the pipe, running out of another concrete ditch, and finding himself on slightly overgrown but still wonderful bright green grass that was soft and warm beneath his paws.

Rocky and Gizmo shook their entire bodies, flinging disgusting drain water every which way. Max almost laughed taking them in—their fur was a puffed-out mess. Though with all the traveling, he doubted he looked much better.

"We made it!" Gizmo yipped. "That was...interesting."

"Yeah!" Rocky barked. "*Interesting* is the word for it. I'm just glad to be out in the sun, on the grass. *Hello, grass! Make room for Rocky!*"

The Dachshund fell on his side and flopped back and forth, rubbing his entire body on the grass. He closed his eyes, content, and let the sun warm his belly— which chose that moment to growl, loudly.

"Ohh," Rocky yowled. "Kibble! Sweet, glorious kibble! Why did we have to leave you?!"

Max peered up then to see where they'd come out—and found that they were in the yard of a large, three-story home. It was painted the colors of the rising sun, all buttery yellow and creamy orange, though the colors were peeling in the corners to reveal dark wood underneath. There were wispy, lacy curtains in the windows, but they were askew, the rooms behind them dark.

The house sat at the corner where the main road met the smaller side street, which was lined with a dozen or so identical homes crammed almost side by side. It was odd—the streets back in the country and town had a lot more space between houses, and they certainly didn't all look alike. But each one here stood tall, in the exact same shapes, with the same color bricks and paint, and the same small tract of lawn in front.

All the windows were dark, the yards empty. Just like back in the town, there were no cars, no signs of people. No morning birds sitting on the power lines or atop windowsills, calling to wake up irritable humans.

The identical, boxy buildings were abandoned.

"Well, we reached some houses," Max announced, trying to keep the sadness at finding yet another empty street out of his voice. "How about we see if we can find some food and some beds to sleep on?"

"Don't have to ask *me* twice!" Rocky barked as he rolled onto his feet.

"Wait," Gizmo said. She stood rigid, with her ears stiff atop her head and her eyes darting to take in the street. "Do you sense that?" she asked.

Max stopped and looked at the street again. "Sense what?"

"We're being...watched."

As soon as she said the words, Max's fur bristled and a shiver ran down his spine to his tail. He dared a glance behind him, back into the pipe, fearful that the wolves had figured out their trick and were going to come barreling down the road at any moment.

There was no one there. But still, someone or something was watching him—he could feel it now. As he turned back to the street lined with identical homes— he finally saw them.

There were dozens of them on the house directly across the street, lounging in the gutters and along the railings. They were peering through windows mostly covered with lace curtains and crouching in the flower beds. And Max wouldn't have noticed them at all, would have thought them to be statue figurines attached to the home, if one of the creatures hadn't snapped its tail.

Cats.

Now that he saw one move, he sensed the others also twitching ever so slightly, like hunters stalking prey. They were gray and black, white and brown, or spotted combinations of the colors. Most were large and sleek. Some young and wiry. A few fat, but still powerful. Their

almond eyes—glinting yellow and green and brown and blue—did not look away from the dog intruders.

"You see them?" Max growled in a low voice to Gizmo.

"I sure do," she yipped softly back.

"What?" Rocky barked, coming to Max's side and following his gaze. "I don't see any—oh. Wow. Never mind."

More of the cats began to move. One leaped from the top of the roof, where most had congregated, all the way to a porch railing down below, landing softly, sturdily. Eyes still on the dogs. Tail snapping, whipping at the air, daring the dogs to make a move.

"I'm not sure they want us here," Max said nervously.

"Normally I'd say who cares what cats want," Rocky said. "I chase 'em all the time!" Looking up at Max with wide eyes, he added, "But, uh, that sure is a lot of cats."

"Maybe we should find some other street," Max whispered down to his two companions. "With this many cats, they're bound to think they own this whole street, and we shouldn't try to get into trouble."

Gizmo rounded on her two friends. "Oh, you boys," she said. "If it isn't one problem you're worried about, it's another. They're just *cats*. And cats *love* me. I bet they might even share their food if we asked nicely, 'cause who knows how long it will take us to find some otherwise? We just need to introduce ourselves."

"Wait, Giz—" Max started.

But she was already marching across the street, head held high, ears perked up, tongue happily hanging from her snout.

"Hello!" Gizmo barked, her call echoing through the quiet neighborhood. "I'm Gizmo! I hope we aren't intruding."

None of the cats responded. They simply glared down at her, their tails snapping faster and faster. One on the roof—a slender yet large cat with gray fur and a white belly—rolled its eyes and sauntered out of view, apparently past caring.

Max and Rocky padded gingerly across the road, keeping a few feet back from Gizmo. She plopped to sit down at the grass at the edge of the lawn.

"Sorry to bother you all," she went on, "but we have been traveling all night and were hoping we might rest somewhere around here."

There came a hissing from the grass in front of Gizmo, then another cat joined in. Two smaller cats—one black save for white paws and a white splotch on its nose, the other a brownish gray with black stripes—stalked forward.

"You shouldn't be here," the black cat spat. It leaped at Gizmo, but stopped short—apparently trying to fake her out. Gizmo simply tilted her head, still panting happily.

"Yeah!" the striped cat said, swiping with her paw. "This place is cats only! We don't want your kind here!"

The other cats lounging on the house started to grow restless. Many stood, arching their backs to stretch. Some began to pace back and forth. Max swallowed, certain that they'd turn into an army of claws and teeth at any minute.

"Aw!" Gizmo yipped, darting her head back and forth to look at the two small cats. "You two are so cute! And so brave, being kittens and all."

"We're not kittens!" the black cat yowled. "Well, not for much longer."

"Of course not," Gizmo barked, nodding in agreement. "You're already almost bigger than me, and I haven't been a puppy for *ages*. What are your names?"

The two young cats looked at each other and blinked their wide eyes. The striped kitten looked back at Gizmo first. "I'm Phoenix," she said, her tone curious.

"Anubis," the black cat offered up, trying to sound gruffer than he was.

"I'm Gizmo," Gizmo said. "Nice to meet you."

The two cats blinked at Gizmo, clearly confused, then backed away into the grass.

"I think it's working," Max whispered down to Rocky. "Just sit here and look friendly."

Rocky shivered. "I'll try, buddy. But some of those bigger cats look like they'd take me in a fight, no problem. And you know what they say about cats. They go for the *eyes*."

Gizmo stood up and took a few more steps until she stood atop the concrete walkway leading to the porch.

An older, fat cat with black fur and a white belly who had been watching the dogs with a particularly mean look suddenly went wide-eyed as Gizmo approached. She jumped up and waddled a few feet away into the grass, then stopped to look back. Seeing Gizmo still coming, she ran and disappeared behind the house.

"Hey!" someone yipped. "Leave Panda alone!"

Not just someone, Max realized. A *dog*.

Catching sight of the speaker standing on the steps to the house, Gizmo sat down and raised her paw in greeting. "Hello! And who are you?"

The dog was half the size of Gizmo, slender and shivering. It had a narrow face and large, pointed ears much too big for its head. It reminded Max a bit of a rat.

"I've seen one of those before at Vet's place," Rocky whispered to Max. "That's a Chihuahua!"

The little Chihuahua took a menacing step forward and yowled at Gizmo, a guttural and twisted version of a cat's warning cry. "I told ya to step off, canine!" the dog barked. "Leave us cats alone!"

Gizmo arched her fluffy brows. "You...cats?"

All along the rafters and the railings, the remaining cats grew even more restless. They paced and meowed at the top of their lungs. Max and Rocky shrank back, slinking into the street. But Gizmo held her ground.

"Hey!" she yipped over their mewing. "Cats! Hi! I promise, I'm not here to chase you or cause trouble! I want to be friends!"

"Friends?" the Chihuahua who thought he was a cat yelped as he arched his back. "Dogs and cats will *never* be friends! It is unnatural!"

"Buddha! Inside. Now."

Immediately, the cats stopped pacing and yowling. As one, their heads darted to look toward the slightly open front door at the center of the porch. The Chihuahua—Buddha—bared his teeth at Gizmo, then followed their gaze.

"Aw, do I hafta?" Buddha whined, suddenly sounding much younger.

The speaker—authoritative, male—hissed, "Yes. Inside or you shall have half your portion of mouse for dinner tonight."

Ears and tiny tail drooping, Buddha glared once more at Gizmo, then bounded up the steps and disappeared into the shadowy house.

Gizmo stood once again on all fours, her nub tail wagging slowly as a figure emerged from the darkness of the doorway and into the sunlight on the porch. All the cats in the yard kept their eyes on him.

The cat was as large as Gizmo, and clearly one of the oldest of the bunch. His fur had patches of tan and black along his back, fading into white on his legs and his mouth. His eyes—narrowed, wary—were an iridescent green that seemed to bore directly into Gizmo's own.

"What do you want, mutt?" the cat said, its words spoken precisely, enunciated. "We have had others of your kind here before on my street. They have been nothing but trouble."

"Hi," Gizmo said. "I'm Gizmo. Can I know your name?"

The large cat sat at the top of the steps. He slowly, purposefully blinked his eyes.

"Raoul," he said at last.

Some of the cats near him began to mutter among themselves. In a flash, Raoul's head darted to face them. They fell silent and slunk into the shadows. The cat turned his attention back to Gizmo.

Gizmo bowed her head, then met him eye to eye. "Nice to meet you, Raoul. I promise we're not going to cause you any trouble. We're just hoping we can ask for your help. Even just directions to some place where we can get food would be helpful."

Raoul's tail flicked back and forth. He regarded Gizmo for a moment, then stretched his neck and peered across the lawn at Max and Rocky.

"He's looking at us," Rocky whispered. "Is he sizing me up? He's not gonna come over here and try to scratch me, is he, buddy?"

"Just stay calm," Max said. "Look friendly. Don't show your teeth."

Max and Rocky both bowed their heads and wagged their tails.

"Who," Raoul asked, "is *we*?"

"Oh!" Gizmo yipped. "How rude of me! These are my friends, Max and Rocky."

Max took a careful step forward, then another. All the cats were glaring at them. Taking a deep breath, Max sauntered quickly to stand behind Gizmo on the walkway, the smooth asphalt of the street giving way to rougher concrete beneath his feet. Rocky waddled beside him.

"I see," Raoul said, his feline expression unreadable. "And what brings you here?"

Gizmo related the story, fast and unrelenting. How all the people disappeared and how they had banded together to find them. How they were chased by wolves and ended up on a crate in a river, and then how they had to walk all night to find civilization. And how they were so terribly hungry and tired.

"And this is my problem *why*?" Raoul asked with an air of disdain.

Gizmo ducked her head. "Well, I suppose it isn't," she said softly. "We could always go somewhere else if you really don't want us. But we're all in the same situation now, aren't we? Left behind by our people and forced to fend for ourselves?"

From up above, a brown cat with tufted ears hissed. "We do not need people!" he spat. "We never needed them. We hunt mice, and we live happily."

A few other cats on the roof yowled their agreement.

"I miss my people," a soft, quiet voice said from beside Gizmo.

Raoul and the dogs looked as one to find the fat

black-and-white cat who had run off as Gizmo approached. The one Buddha had called Panda. She appeared between broken slats under the porch, emerging slowly from the darkness under the house.

There was no more meanness in the cat's eyes as she looked at the four of them. "I miss my man especially," she whispered. "He had a blanket, and he would put it on his lap. And I would lie on it, and he would pet my belly and let me nuzzle my head against his chin, and I would knead his belly in return. And he would feed me and give me water whenever I needed it, and at night I would sleep next to him." Blinking up at Raoul with forlorn eyes, she said, "I appreciate the home you've given us, but I do miss my man and his people. Terribly so."

Max lowered his head so that it lay in the grass, and ever so gently he nuzzled Panda's side. "I miss mine, too," he said.

The chubby cat jerked back. She met Max's eyes for just a moment, then, bowing her head, disappeared back underneath the house.

"See?" Gizmo said, taking a step toward Raoul, who watched Panda run off with a thoughtful look in his eye. "We aren't so different, us cats and dogs. We're all alone now, and the only help we're going to get is from other animals. So maybe…maybe we can help one another?"

"Besides," Rocky piped up, "you already got one dog hanging around. I mean, just 'cause he thinks he's a—"

Raoul hissed, leaped forward, and swatted at Rocky's

snout. Rocky yelped and darted backward, shouting, "Hey!"

"Rule number one," Raoul intoned as he stalked toward Rocky, carefully. "Never, *ever* imply Buddha is anything other than a cat."

"Rule one?" Gizmo asked.

"Yes," Raoul said, then sighed and turned to face her and Max. "If I am going to allow you to stay on my street, there are going to be some rules. Number two: Never chase any of us cats. And number three: You'll have to find your own food."

"You mean you're going to let us stay?" Max asked, rising to his full height, tail wagging.

"Not too quick on the uptake, are they?" Raoul said to Gizmo with a roll of his eyes.

"That's why I do all the talking," Gizmo yipped. Looking at Rocky and Max, she said, "Told you, boys: Cats just *love* me. Now let's find something to eat and finally go to sleep!"

CHAPTER 17

A CAT'S TALE

With Raoul's blessing to stay on his street, Max, Rocky, and Gizmo left the cat house to search the rest of the neighborhood for food. They'd only just padded onto the next lawn over—with many cat eyes still watching their backs—when the long grass ahead of them parted and the fat black-and-white cat named Panda appeared once more.

"Hello," she said softly.

The three dogs stopped and looked down at her. "Hello!" Gizmo said back.

For a moment, the cat crouched close to the ground, looking up at the three dogs warily. Rocky began to jump from leg to leg next to Max, growing restless.

"Uh, can we help you?" Max finally asked.

"Yes," Panda said. "I know where some kibble is. I thought I could show you."

"You'd do that?" Gizmo yipped, tail wagging. "Thank you!"

The cat jerked back at her excitement, as though ready to flee. Gizmo's tail slowed its intense wag.

"We'd sure appreciate it," Max said.

Panda took a deep breath, then turned her head and meowed. Another cat appeared, this one a skinnier version of Panda, only with gray fur in place of the white.

"This is my sister," Panda said. "Our humans called her Possum."

"Yes, Sister, enough with the introductions," Possum said, sauntering past her chubbier sibling with a sigh. "Come, dogs. We figured if we didn't feed you, you might go feral and try to eat us. Might as well share the kibble instead."

Possum slunk between Max's legs and strode to the front door of the house next to the cats' home. Blinking, Panda ducked her head and waddled to follow her sister.

"Oh, we would never try to eat you," Gizmo assured the cats as she, Max, and Rocky followed as well. "I like cats, but not like that!" She giggled, but was met with only kitty glares.

The home was a sprawling pink building, built exactly like the others on the street and so brightly colored that it almost hurt to look at it. It seemed in worse repair than any of the other houses in one specific way, however: Much of the siding on the bottom of the house had teeth marks in it, as though whatever animal had once lived here had taken to making the entire house one big chew toy.

Possum softly leaped up each of the concrete steps of the front porch, then nudged the door with her head. It opened, squeaking on its hinges.

Looking back at the dogs as they clambered up onto the porch, Possum rolled her eyes. "Yeah, I guess you three are some of the *good* ones. Just like that Doberman that came around."

Panda hissed at her sister and swatted her side. "Shush!"

"Doberman?" Max asked. "Did he live around here?"

"No," Panda said before Possum could get a word out. "Don't worry about it. If Raoul trusts you, then we do, too. Please, let's go eat."

"Yes," Rocky barked, his stomach audibly growling. "Please, big guy. I'm wasting away over here!"

Max nosed the door open all the way, then followed Panda and Possum through a dark, dusty foyer that smelled of long-gone people and dust and cats, then through a living room that was carpeted in wall-to-wall white shag—a deep, hairy rug that tickled to walk across. "Soft!" Gizmo said appreciatively. Finally, they paraded through a kitchen full of quiet silvery appliances and into a pantry at the far end.

Max's mouth filled with saliva as the beefy scent of kibble wafted from the pantry and met his nose, and he dove into the small room before he even knew what he was doing. Rocky and Gizmo were there in a flash, too, and all three dogs dug into the open bag on the floor, crunching on kibble until their bellies were full.

There was a leaky utility sink in the pantry, too. Its basin had been plugged and was brimming over. Water spilled over the sides and then trickled down a drain in the floor. Max stood up on his haunches and set his paws on the lip of the sink and drank his fill, while Rocky and Gizmo lapped up the overflow around the drain.

After the dogs' bellies were full, Panda and Possum led them to the living room, where they all curled up on the biggest, cushiest couch they had ever seen—a brown multisectioned couch that stretched from corner to corner and curved out into the middle of the room. As Max went to jump atop it, he caught sight of glowing kitty eyes peeking out from behind shelves and over cabinets, watching the dogs curiously. He hadn't heard them come in, or even noticed them if they were already there when he had first walked in. But cats were stealthy like that.

Max leaped onto the couch, turned once, and plopped down in exhaustion. Rocky and Gizmo jumped onto the lower glass coffee table in front of the couch before leaping onto the couch as well.

"This is some kind of bed!" Rocky said, before curling up against Max's back.

As Max drifted off to sleep, he sensed one cat, then another and another, emerging from their hiding spaces and curling up on the couch as well. He was surrounded by warmth and fur, his belly was full, and his legs were at long last getting rest.

Comfortable for the first time in weeks and weeks, Max fell into a deep sleep.

Max vaguely remembered waking up briefly throughout the day, but only long enough to blearily take in the living room before falling back asleep once more. He sensed more than saw dozens of cats lounging on the sofa and coffee table and fireplace, but exhaustion from two days of nonstop running kept him from caring, and he rolled over, curled around Rocky, and fell right back to sleep.

The light that streamed through the dusty curtains was dim by the time Max woke up fully, desperately needing to pee.

He yawned, then blinked in surprise as he realized that the entire cat population of the house next door had seemed to relocate to this one living room. Some, like Panda and Possum, were curled up and sleeping next to Rocky and Gizmo and Max himself, but many sat in high, hard-to-reach places, watching Max.

No two looked alike, though the two gray ones atop the mantel with their long necks and giant ears were close to being twins. Slinky brown-and-white cats with tufted ears hung over the sides of a tall bookshelf, and a squat orange cat hid in the recesses of the TV center. There were dozens and dozens of the creatures, some stretching paws, but most sitting silently, staring with wide eyes that shimmered reflectively in the low light.

"Uh, hello," Max whispered as he freed his legs from the cats on the couch and dropped to the carpet, only to find several kittens mounded amid the fluffy shag, sleeping softly in a fuzzy pile.

The cats who were awake merely blinked in response. Gingerly, Max picked his way among the snoring kittens and left the living room.

Max padded outside to find that the sun was setting, the sky rippling with all the colors of the garish homes on the cats' street. He quickly did his business in some bushes, then made his way back inside. As he came back into the living room, he saw Raoul sitting expectantly in the center of the coffee table in front of the couch. It was a wide glass panel and Raoul almost seemed to float above the white carpet.

Both Gizmo and Rocky were awake. Gizmo looked like she could barely contain her excitement. Rocky looked like he could barely contain his discomfort. "Big guy!" he barked, startling a fluffy white cat near him so that she darted down and seemed to disappear into the carpet. Not noticing, Rocky added, "So glad you came back!"

"I trust you had a good rest," Raoul said.

"I did," Max said as he sat in front of the couch, just behind the mound of kittens. The spot on the couch where he'd slept was now filled with curled-up, snoring cats who had relocated from their shelves to take advantage of the large warm spot Max had abandoned. "It's been a long time since we've slept somewhere so comfortable!"

"That's for sure!" Rocky said as he leaped down from his spot on the couch and came to sit next to Max. "We had to sleep in the *dirt* and in old blankets under pieces of wood. Like we were wild animals or something!"

Gizmo laughed. She lay with her head on her paws, the two kittens who'd hissed at her that morning now curled up on either side of her. "Don't listen to him. We had some great beds made out of those old blankets. I should know, I made them!"

Blinking his wide green eyes, Raoul looked at the three dogs silently. Then he said, "Hm. Yes. That's nice." Focusing on Max, he continued. "You said this morning that you seek your people, yes? That you do not know where they have gone?"

Max nodded. "That's right. We don't plan to stay here long. Just long enough to rest up before we head to the city. Even if the people aren't there, I think a friend of mine is who can help us in our search."

Raoul's tail snapped. "The city. Interesting."

"Why is that interesting?" Rocky asked. "You know something we don't?"

With a sigh, Raoul lowered his front paws and lay down on his belly. The other cats in the room watched him, as rapt as they had been on the porch next door—silent unmoving.

"I may," Raoul said.

"Can you tell us, please?" Gizmo asked. "Anything you can remember might help us."

"It can't hurt, Raoul," a soft voice said from the couch—Panda. "Maybe if these dogs find the people, then..."

Raoul nodded. "Yes," he said. "Maybe. I suppose I shall begin at the beginning. It started several weeks ago. Most of the cats here are from other houses around the neighborhood. We all noticed that our people started to leave and not come back—more and more of them each day. This wasn't strange, as humans leave us cats alone all the time—we don't need constant tending, like certain other pets do."

"Hey!" Rocky barked. "I don't *need* constant tending. I just appreciate it."

Raoul blinked his eyes slowly. "Mm-hmm. Myself and many of the other cats lived next door with an elderly woman named May. She would not leave, and in fact would go out each day to bring over the cats left behind so that they could be fed and watered. Of course we could hunt for mice if we wanted to, but she insisted on feeding us, and so we did not bother.

"I watched out the front windows each day. There were trucks parked in front of all the homes on the street, and the people would throw boxes and suitcases into them, then pile themselves into the truck bed and drive away. No one took furniture, just clothing and keepsakes and food. I suppose I thought they were going on vacation."

"But they weren't," yowled a frizzy white cat with a black patch of fur over his eye, glowering atop the fireplace.

"Yeah, they were running away!" another cat cried.

"Running away from what?" Max asked. Memories of the inky blackness from his dreams came back to him, and he shivered.

Raoul shook his head. "I couldn't say. They were panicked, clearly. They were rushed and reckless. All except for my old lady, May. She was the last human in the entire neighborhood."

"What happened?" Gizmo asked.

Closing his eyes, Raoul took in a breath, his fur bristling at the memories. "Mean people came," he whispered. "Men and women in green clothes and hats and plastic masks that covered their faces. They pounded on the front door, shouting and shouting, and—"

"They forced their way in," Possum said from the

couch, her voice icy with anger. "They *kicked* us away as we meowed and hissed at them."

Cats throughout the room began to hiss quietly, their tails slicing through the air.

"They dragged May away," Raoul continued, raising his voice. "I clawed at the humans in green, but they kept pushing me off. The last thing I remember seeing was my old woman, crying and screaming, as they took her into a big black car and drove away."

"That's horrible," Max said. He tried not to think of the same thing happening to Charlie and Emma and their parents. Hoped that their missing car and the lack of signs of a struggle at their home meant they'd driven away safely.

Raoul opened his eyes wide once more, then stood, arching his back. The cats stopped hissing and again fell silent, watching their leader in the dying daylight.

"It all happened over two days," Raoul said. "Once May was gone, the neighborhood was empty, and we were all left alone, wondering what to do. And so I brought the cats into my home, where at least we can look out for one another."

"What about dogs?" Rocky asked. "Aside from the Ch—"

Max nipped Rocky on the side. "Remember his rules, Rocky!"

Growling, Rocky jumped away from Max. "Fine, fine, yeah, nothing but cats here. I mean, surely someone who lived around here had a couple of dogs, though, especially since this house had kibble in it."

"There were dogs," Raoul said. "Three of them. But when the people and the trucks drove away, they chased after them. There was no way they would ever catch up to those trucks, but you know how dumb dogs can be." Clearing his throat, the spotted cat added, "Uh, present company excluded, of course. They're probably still following those trucks to this day."

"To where?" Gizmo asked. "Did you see where the trucks went?"

"To the city, I suppose," Raoul said. "That seems to be where all dogs who pass through here are headed."

"Just like the Doberman," Possum mewed from the couch.

Several of the cats near her hissed and swatted. She bared her fangs and swatted back. "What? That dog is long gone. Mentioning him won't bring him back."

"Excuse their behavior," Raoul said. "Before you three, a large Doberman stopped by on his own journey to the city. He was rather vicious, which is why we were so wary with you."

"A Doberman, huh?" Max asked. "Was he with another dog? One that looked like me, maybe, but with black fur and a sparkly collar?"

Raoul nodded. "He was. The other dog—the one who looked like you—came after the Doberman had had his fill of terrorizing us, and she nipped at him until

212

they both took the main road toward the city. I heard them arguing all the while. I'm surprised the Doberman put up with her. She seemed rather...frail."

"Frail?" Max whispered. He hadn't thought of it, but the journey had been tough for him, Rocky, and Gizmo, and they were all young. Madame, with her old bones... But at least she'd made it this far. And at least he was on her trail again.

"Thank you for sharing your story," Max said, trying to shove aside his worry for Madame. "Even if it wasn't the happiest one."

Raoul nodded. "Of course."

Night had fully fallen by then, and many of the cats had grown restless. They paced on the furniture or darted outside to hunt mice. Taking their cue, Max, Rocky, and Gizmo all padded through the dark, empty home to the pantry—where they found Buddha, the Chihuahua who thought he was a cat, chowing down on kibble.

The tiny dog stopped in his tracks midchew, eyes wide at being caught.

Gizmo giggled at the sight of Buddha's oversize ears perked at full attention. "It's okay, little kitten, we can wait till you're done eating."

"Yeah, no problem," Rocky grumbled. "Wouldn't want to interrupt a *cat* eating his dinner of *dog* food."

Buddha turned away from the bag of kibble and spat out the crumbs that were left in his mouth. "Blecch! Yuck!

I...I don't know what I was thinking!" He let out a sound that was somewhere between a yip and a meow, then wiped his tongue off on his paw. Before anyone could say anything, the cat-dog darted under Max's legs.

"Don't tell anyone," Buddha hissed as he disappeared out of the pantry. "Sometimes I'm just not into eating mice."

"We won't!" Gizmo called, but the Chihuahua was gone.

Laughing, Max, Rocky, and Gizmo dug into the kibble themselves. Going a whole day without manual labor and getting to eat when he was hungry made Max feel like he was almost back home again. Almost.

As they finished their evening meal, Max heard Raoul clear his throat behind him. Turning around, he saw the large spotted cat standing at the entrance to the pantry, his green eyes seeming to almost glow in the dark. The kitchen behind him, all blue linoleum and turquoise countertops, was mostly dark.

"I have a favor to ask you," Raoul said, his tone hushed.

"Anything," Max said. "I mean, we'd still be searching for food if it wasn't for you."

"Thanks for that, by the way!" Rocky said. "And don't think I say that lightly. Normally me and cats don't see eye to eye."

"Is that 'cause they're always looking down on you from above?" Gizmo asked with a giggle.

"Hey!" Rocky said. "Well … maybe, yeah. Fair enough."

"What's the favor?" Max asked.

Raoul padded closer, peering from side to side to make sure none of the other cats was nearby. Green lights blinked on appliances deeper in the room, and a clock on the wall *tick-tick-tick*ed. But none of the cats had come in here except Raoul.

"My fellow cats and I are comfortable here," the cat leader said once he was certain they were alone. "We fend for ourselves well. But I know that many of us do miss our humans, even if they won't admit it. I find it hard to even say this myself, but … I miss May. I miss my time on her lap being scratched behind the ears. I miss waking her up in the mornings by butting my head against her hand. I miss the way she'd stroke my fur when I'd lie beside her on the couch. I miss her." The cat stopped talking for a moment, suddenly intent on cleaning the pads of his front right paw. "I put on a brave face, but I know if I was able to, I would do just as you are— I'd go and find her."

"But you can't," Max said.

"No," Raoul said, "I can't. All of us wandering in the wild doesn't make sense. There are dangers."

"Like the wolves," Rocky said.

"Yes, like the wolves. And if I know anything, it's that trying to lead an army of cats is just going to lead to everyone trying to go their own way and getting into even more trouble."

"I understand," Max said. "But what is the favor?"

"Well," Raoul said, "I know it's a small chance. But it's a chance. If you do find the people, will you send word back to us? Then we would know where to go. And we could come join you."

"Of course we will," Gizmo said, stepping forward and nuzzling Raoul's side gently. "It would be horrible if you never got to see May again."

Clearing his throat uncomfortably, Raoul stepped away from Gizmo. "Thank you. And please, stay here as long as you need. There is plenty of room in this neighborhood."

"Thanks," Max said. "But we only need the night. Tomorrow morning, we'll be back on our way. Knowing that my friend was headed toward the city is a great help."

Raoul nodded. "Of course," he said, then turned and darted through the dark kitchen and out into the living room.

"Maybe we should stay a while longer," Rocky whined after the cat disappeared. "What's the big hurry?"

But Max turned and strode away, making a left out of the pantry and going through an archway into the dark dining room. Slick linoleum gave way to wood as he entered the room.

"Something has happened to our people," Max said as he walked underneath the long wooden dining table, toward a window facing the back of the house. "That's why we hurry. They may need us."

Rocky nodded sharply. "Right, right—I keep forgetting. I just get a bad feeling about that big city."

Gizmo stepped up beside him. "Why? It's pretty! Why would that give you a bad feeling?"

"It's not how the city *looks*," Rocky said. "It's how it smells. I mean, how it *doesn't* smell." He turned a tight circle. "I've been to big cities, and you can smell them for miles before you ever see them—there's that smoky stink the cars make, and other smells that choke the wind."

Rocky jumped onto a chair, resting his paws atop its high back and looking out the open window. Max followed his gaze. The neighborhoods behind the house sloped down, and the city could just be made out on the horizon, glittering in the dying light.

Rocky raised his snout to point toward the city. "But this city? I didn't want to say nothing earlier when we were all so tired, but I don't think it smells like *anything*. It's like there's no one there at all."

Gizmo jumped atop the chair next to Rocky. "Well, we're still far away," she said. "Maybe we're just too far to smell anything. I don't know about you, but I'm too busy smelling cats to smell much else." She tried to giggle, but it came out forced.

"Nothing smells right anymore," Max said with a sigh. "There's nothing anywhere."

"What could have made everything change?" Gizmo wondered aloud. "The farther we travel and the more stories we hear, the creepier it gets."

"Madame will know," Max said. "Like I told you, before she left Vet, she said something was coming. I bet she went to the city to find answers, just like us."

Rocky dropped his paws from the back of the chair, then curled up on its seat. "Well, even if she did find out what made all this happen, it can't be anything good."

"Probably not," Max said, staring defiantly out the window at the darkening city. "But I know one thing— no matter what caused all this, I'm not going to let some strange smells stop me. I don't know what is or isn't in that city." Turning to look over at his two forlorn friends, he added, "But I'm not stopping until I find out."

CHAPTER 18

DESOLATION ROAD

The early morning sunlight was a milky yellow. It cast a golden sheen on everything, making the dew on the lawn glitter and shimmer, and giving the world a beautiful glow that made the empty pink and orange houses look warm and inviting. But Max knew that was only an illusion. As he strolled out of the house, he sniffed the crisp air. It was going to be a hot day.

In the pantry, he and Rocky and Gizmo ate their fill once more and, at Max's urging, drank water until their bellies almost ached. With a good-bye to their new cat friends, they left the big, empty house and followed the street to one of the wide main roads that led into the city. All the cats they'd spent time with—Panda and Possum, the mewling kittens, the ones with the tufted ears, the Siamese twins—climbed onto the roof of May's house to watch them walk away, with Raoul perched upon the tallest point, standing still like a guardian statue.

All except one—the striped kitten named Phoenix. It took the dogs a moment to notice the little cat strolling confidently and quietly just behind Gizmo. It wasn't until the cats back at the house caught sight of her and yowled her name that the kitten spun on her heels and raced home.

"Aw, too bad," Gizmo said as they watched the blur that was the kitten leap into the overgrown front yard of the cats' home. "She could have been our mascot!"

"Well, we wouldn't want her to steal Rocky's job," Max said as he strolled down the center of the road, the sun beating against his golden fur. "Otherwise he'd have to do more work."

"Hey!" Rocky yipped. "I do plenty."

"Of course you do!" Gizmo said, then laughed. "Without you, we'd never get our daily reports about which kibble tastes best."

Max laughed as well, but Rocky's ears and tail drooped and he sauntered ahead, sullen and silent.

"We're only joking," Max said, nudging Rocky's side. "Of course you're helpful. You've had some great ideas."

"Yeah, yeah," Rocky muttered, but he didn't say anything else.

The three dogs marched silently for the rest of the morning. The sun baked the asphalt, so much so that eventually they had to leave the road and walk in the grass along it instead. Even with as much water as they'd drunk before they left, Max was already feeling his nose go dry and his mouth ache. Luckily, there were drainage ditches filled with water all along the road. They lapped up what they could before moving on.

For a while, it was house-lined street after house-lined street. The houses were all so similar and the roads all laid out the same way that it gave Max the bizarre feeling that they weren't moving forward at all. They all looked nearly identical to the cats' street, though some were painted in colors other than pink, purple, and yellow—Max caught sight of the occasional blue or green house, sticking out among the even, boxy rows like little Buddha the Chihuahua among the cats. Their small, square front lawns had started to overgrow with dandelions and tall grass, but otherwise the buildings looked as quiet and normal as they would even if the people hadn't left.

That was, until they reached one cul-de-sac where there'd been an accident. Two white trucks were crushed against each other, front bumpers having collided with what must have been an incredible force. The wind-shields were shattered. Behind the truck that had been heading out of the street to the main road, another truck lay on its side. Clothing must have been flung out of its bed, for the lawn of one home was covered with human blouses and pants and underclothes.

The next street was also crowded with cars—five of them, all different colors and sizes, huddled together and empty at the end of the street where the road turned into a circle. All the homes down this street had their doors wide open, with people belongings scattered on the porches and driveways. A kiddie pool, half deflated, lay baking on one of the lawns. Its plastic bottom was stomped over with muddy footprints.

There was graffiti on some of the houses, too, what looked like animal faces with giant red *X*s spray-painted over them. The symbols were all the same, and were usually on the front doors, but not every house had one. Max wondered what it meant—did someone just really dislike animals? Or did the dripping, painted symbols mean something else?

It was eerie—some roads were like the cats', pristine and quiet. Others looked as though everything had devolved into chaos when the humans left, with windows broken and curtains dangling from them, mangled; doors kicked in and splintered; lawns torn apart so that they had become muddy pits instead of pretty grass.

One street was both—all the big homes, copies of themselves, lying quiet and in good condition, save for one whose roof was half burned away and still smoldered. The stench of smoke and burned wood met Max's nostrils, reminding him of Vet's destroyed home, and he wondered if this had happened recently.

It wasn't just Rocky who was sullen by the time midday came around. The heat was getting to Max, even as he tried to stay in the cool grass and shadows alongside and behind the rows of homes, and even Gizmo had lost some of her good cheer at seeing the silent destruction they passed.

Eventually, the streets lined with abandoned homes gave way to other buildings. The main road the dogs walked down widened into more lanes, and as it did they caught sight of a corner store with its front windows busted out. Business buildings were separated by wide-open swaths of asphalt parking lots with plastic bags and crumpled, rancid garbage strewn across the black. Glass had been shattered from windows with empty displays now fallen through. Neon signs dangling, sparks flashing from where they'd been disconnected. And unlike the small town by the Enclave, there were abandoned cars everywhere—sitting alone in parking lots, or smashed along the streets, their doors open and leather seats baking in the sun.

Everything was broken, dark, decaying. Even the trees set in special plots along the sidewalk were dying, their leaves turning brown and crisp before falling into sad piles around the small iron fences that blocked them off from the concrete. And there were more crossed-out animal paintings here, in white and red and black, on the hoods of cars and on the sides of buildings.

Max didn't have the heart to investigate any of the ransacked buildings, at least not until they found a grocery store—that would be the best bet for kibble. He led Rocky and Gizmo farther down the main road, on concrete sidewalks now, past blinking stoplights and lit-up signs that shifted from a green walking man to a red raised hand. Signals that once controlled the cars and people who no longer existed in this silent city.

"What's that?" Gizmo asked quite suddenly.

Max leaped fully off the ground—all four feet in the air. The dogs hadn't said anything to one another in so long that Gizmo's voice completely shocked him.

Taking a breath to slow his heart, Max sat down on the heated concrete and asked, "What's what?"

The tiny terrier's ears were perked to attention. "I hear something," she said. "Come on!"

Max wasn't sure what Gizmo expected to find, exactly, but he got up and followed her anyway. With a groan, Rocky came after.

At the corner of the next intersection sat a brown-and-gray building that, strangely, still had all its windows intact. Max slowed as he neared it, unsure what to think. Because his ears were picking it up, too.

Music.

Not music like the stuff his pack leaders liked to

play—they preferred heavy beats and loud singing—but something softer, melodic, like what his pack leaders' parents listened to at night.

Gizmo reached the building first and pushed herself against the glass door, trying to shove it open. It moved a little bit, but she wasn't heavy enough.

"Here, let's help," Max said to Rocky.

Together, the three of them jammed against the glass. The door was heavy, but not locked, and it opened with a jangle of bells.

The music overtook Max's ears as hot air whooshed out of the building. It was blazingly hot inside, the sun heating the room through the glass all morning, and smelled as if someone had been roasting a familiar food all day. It smelled like something his pack leaders' parents drank.

Coffee?

The shelves behind the front counter were lined with mugs and shiny bags, and the counters themselves were crowded with bright silver machines. Round tables and cushy chairs sat beneath paintings of shapes colored brown and red; at one table sat a human's computer, open but with a blank screen.

The smell of the coffee beans and the gentle, wafting music and the plush chairs was enough to send a wash of memories over Max. He'd been in a place just like this, only there'd been the hum of human chatter over the sound of the music, and whooshing noises from the silver machines, and hisses of steam, and clangs of a cash register. And not just the smell of coffee beans, but the mingling aromas of hot drinks and pastries hidden behind glass cases.

His pack leaders' parents would sometimes take him running and stop at the shop, and he'd be let inside since he was such a good boy. He would sit at their feet beneath their table, and the other patrons would pet him while sipping their coffee, scratching him behind his ears while he panted a smile at them and thumped his tail happily.

Max's legs trembled at the sudden, distinct memories, and he dropped to his belly, still propping the door open with his body.

"Hey, buddy, you all right?" Rocky asked, nudging Max. "Don't pass out on me now, big guy!"

"It's nothing," Max whimpered. "It just…it's home." Daring to hope, for just a moment, he lifted his snout and let out a long, blaring, "Aroo!" He called again and again, desperation filling him.

But no one was there. His people weren't inside. It was just another empty building, left untouched for reasons he couldn't know. Maybe left behind to make him feel awful and alone all over again.

The three dogs went quiet, listening for a response.

From a dark hall past the counter covered with silver machines, there came a whispering doggy voice.

Max snapped to attention and jumped to his feet, so

fast that he almost let the door close, trapping them inside. He caught it just in time, then shoved forward, opening the door wider and letting the relatively cool outside air billow in.

"Hello?" Gizmo barked, taking a tentative step deeper into the coffee store. "Is someone there?"

Gleaming eyes down the hall, and a shadowy, shivering shape. A voice called out, quietly, "Shouldn't be here. Shouldn't show them where I am. Don't wanna eat 'em. Don't wanna get eaten."

"I have a bad feeling about this," Rocky whispered, backing out the door. "Giz, come out of there."

The terrier ignored him. With another step forward, she barked out, "We're friends. I promise. Do you need help? Are you trapped in here?"

The dog emerged from the hallway then. It was a mutt, so painfully thin that Max could see his ribs through matted fur. The dog's eyes were gaunt and open wide, manic. His tongue, black and pink, hung from jaws stained a deep yellow. The dog crept forward, almost limping.

And still it muttered. "Gotta stay away. Gotta keep 'em out. Don't wanna eat 'em. Don't wanna get eaten."

"Don't want to eat who?" Gizmo asked. "We can help you. You need water and food."

"Can't go out there. Can't win. Don't want to eat 'em."

"Gizmo," Max said, a low, warning growl in his voice. The fur on his back bristled and his body tensed, ready to move.

227

Gizmo took one more step forward. "We can protect you," she said softly. "It's okay, friend. It'll be okay."

The mutt's eyes darted to the counter, away from the other three dogs. "Don't want to eat 'em," he said, a whimper in his voice. Then, slowly, his large eyes turned back to Gizmo. "Wanna eat you."

With a terrifying bark, the dog lunged at Gizmo. She yelped and leaped away, the starving dog's teeth just barely missing her neck. Claws scrabbling over linoleum, she spun away from the mutt just as it got its bearings and she flew past Max, out of the coffee store.

As the scary mutt jumped forward, Max leaped back and let the door go. The frothing dog landed heavily against it, slamming it shut. It continued to bark and scrabble at the door, spittle from its angry shouts clouding the glass.

"We can't leave him in there!" Gizmo barked over the mutt's roars.

"He's gone crazy, Giz," Rocky said. "There's no helping him now."

Gizmo's tail and ears drooped as she watched the mad dog try to break through the door. Even as he stared at her with raging, insane eyes, she said, "But..."

"Rocky's right," Max said. "Come on, let's get away from here. Far away."

Gizmo nodded, silent. Max ran ahead, racing across the desolate road to the next sidewalk, keeping his eyes on the city looming ever closer, shutting out the sounds of insanity behind.

It took a few blocks of running before the mad dog's barks were lost for good. Max slowed down to conserve their energy. He longed for shade, but there were barely any trees on these roads—just more of the human buildings, quiet and locked up and useless.

As they walked on, Max caught sight of more dogs like the one back at the coffee shop: skinny, wild-eyed, unkempt. They were usually alone and watched the trio from the doorways of darkened buildings. Dogs, abandoned, but ones who hadn't found the Enclave or friends to travel with or a safe home like the cats'.

A pair inside one building, which looked like it once held racks upon racks of human clothing, fought viciously in the empty display windows, rolling around a couple of fallen mannequins. A street and a trash-strewn parking lot separated Max, Rocky, and Gizmo from this pair of dogs, but Max made sure to give the store a wide berth anyway. He tried not to listen, not wanting to hear either of the dogs' crazed barks.

After ten minutes more of running along, Rocky piped up.

"You know?" the little Dachshund said. "It pains me to admit, but I think I owe you two an apology."

"Why's that?" Max asked.

"Well, I got grumpy earlier when you said I never do anything," he said softly. "'Cause of course I do things. I'm the comic relief! I have ideas! But..." He ducked his head. "Well, truth is, Max, you do a lot of the hard work. You keep us running on track even when I'd rather be lazy. And Gizmo, you're always brave when I want to run and hide, and you always keep the mood happy when I want to wallow. I mean, I know I'm not much use and all...."

"Of course you are," Max said.

At the same time, Gizmo said, "Don't say that."

"So I guess what I'm saying is, thank you for dragging me along. I could have ended up as wolf food long ago, or worse, alone and starving like all the poor dogs out here." He stopped, sat down, and looked at Max and Gizmo with his big, watery eyes. "I know being outside and having to walk ain't ideal, but I can't imagine being anywhere else. I hope I can pull my slack when it counts."

"I seem to recall *somebody* jumping out of nowhere to knock a candy machine on a wolf to save me," Max said, sitting down as well.

"And you sure had lots of ideas back at the Enclave," Gizmo added. "And some of them were so smart they even impressed me!"

"They did?" Rocky asked eagerly, turning so that he and Gizmo were snout to snout.

Gizmo nodded. "They did," she said softly.

For a moment, the two small dogs' eyes met. The moment lasted longer...and longer. Max almost laughed.

Then Rocky's tongue darted out and licked Gizmo's nose.

"Oh!" Gizmo yipped, and jumped back, scrunching up her snout. "Why did you do that?"

Rocky ducked his head. "I dunno. Your nose looked like it needed to be...licked. It was just sitting there and...yeah."

Swiping her nose with her paw, Gizmo sneezed. She stood up and trotted ahead of Max and Rocky. "Do you think there's a grocery store in one of these buildings?" she asked, her voice nonchalant and chipper as always. "I don't know about you guys, but I think those cats spoiled me. I'm hungry already!"

"Good job," Max said to Rocky, nudging his side playfully. "That ought to get her attention."

"What? Huh?" Rocky sputtered. "I don't know what you mean, big guy. She's just a friend, is all."

"You boys coming?" Gizmo called from the corner ahead. Above her, a metal street sign creaked in the dry wind.

Despite the heat, despite the terrifying run-in with the abandoned dog and the wave of old memories at the coffee shop, Max felt—well, not happy, exactly, but hopeful. Rocky was right—who knew where any of them would be if they hadn't found one another? Max especially, only having barely escaped his cage—thanks to Rocky's help.

They'd made it farther on their own than he could have ever imagined. Maybe together they could make it all the way to their people's arms.

As evening set, they finally found a grocery store.

It was twice as large as the one back in the tiny town near where the Enclave lived—and twice as ransacked. All the windows were busted out, making the black tar of the parking lot glint and shimmer like a night sky full of stars. Empty shopping carts lay here and there like the shiny metal skeletons of long-dead beasts. The whole lot smelled foul, like rotting meat. The hot days had helped spoil the food the humans hadn't taken with them, and the first whiff of scent Max and his companions took outside the doors nearly turned their stomachs.

But hunger won out. They didn't care about the stench, so long as they could fill their bellies.

The three dogs wandered the aisles, all mostly empty except for the occasional box of dried food up high in the corner of a shelf, or rolls of the white paper the humans kept in the washing room. But that wasn't what was disturbing. Everywhere Max looked, there was evidence of fighting—and not between people. The damaged shelves were low to the ground. There were splatters of dried blood along the once-clean tiles. Max almost expected to find more wild dogs in here, waiting to attack...but strangely, the building was empty.

The pet aisle was much like the one at the other grocery store—untouched by humans. Wherever the people had gone, apparently they didn't think they'd need to stock up on pet supplies. Many of the bags of food had already been torn open and their contents eaten, leaving behind shredded paper sacks. But on a higher shelf was a shadow that Max thought might be an unopened bag.

He leaped up and sure enough it was. Another leap, and Max managed to tip the bag over. A third leap, and he tore open the corner with his sharp teeth. A shower of kibble poured from the opening and spilled down onto the floor, where he, Rocky, and Gizmo ate their evening meal.

Bellies full, they wandered back outside. Night was falling, bringing with it a mercifully cool breeze. All up and down the streets, as the light in the sky faded, the lights on the stores and streetlights flickered on.

"Where to now, buddy?" Rocky asked.

Max thought of the starving mutts from earlier in the day, the raging dog in the coffee shop, the bloodstains in the store, and he shuddered.

Max led Rocky and Gizmo to the center of the wide main road. The buildings along the road were now fewer and far away behind fences. Farther down the road, the buildings disappeared entirely and were replaced by wide-open gravel fields with big metal containers and strange machinery. Beyond that rose the shadowy towers of the city, seeming to fill the horizon from end to end.

"The city is so close!" Gizmo yipped happily. "We should run to it."

"I'm not so sure that's a good idea," Max said, eyeing the dark fields warily. Streetlamps had flickered on alongside the road, but their light didn't reach very far. Who knew what could be hiding in the shadows out there?

"So what do we do, then?" Rocky asked.

"I think we deserve a good night's sleep, don't you?" Max replied. Across the street from the grocery store, he saw rows of buildings several stories high. They were painted light blue, and stone and concrete walkways lined with iron railings ran in front of rows of identical doors and windows. He'd been taken to visit his pack leaders' friends in a place like this—apartments.

"Come on," Max said. "Let's climb high and see what we can see!"

He raced through the empty parking lot in front of the apartments, past an overflowing Dumpster behind a rickety fence and a bunch of mailboxes stacked atop one another. He led his friends up four flights of stairs—the steps were strange, a mixture of rough concrete mixed with large, smooth stones. Rocky and Gizmo followed as fast as they could on their stubby legs. Thankfully, the space between the steps wasn't too terribly high.

On the highest floor, Max padded to the end of the walkway and looked through the twisted iron railing, past the gravel fields, to get a better view of the city itself.

Like everywhere else they'd been, most of the city was shrouded in darkness. The skyscrapers were like immense, black obelisks now that they were this close. Fading sunlight glinted off windows, but there was no motion that Max could see, nothing human, anyway.

Another empty, humanless place. Max's heart sank. All that traveling, and still no people. Where had they gone? Why had they left? How would he ever find them? He was so tired. But at least now he could sleep. Maybe tomorrow would bring them closer.... Maybe at least they'd finally catch up with Madame....

"Hey, you see that?" Rocky asked, nudging Max's side. He pointed toward the center of the city with a paw.

Max stuck his snout through the railing and narrowed his eyes. At first he thought it was the setting sun tricking him, just more daylight reflecting off windows.

But it quickly grew dark enough that he knew for certain: One of the buildings was all lit up.

Bright white floodlights at its base illuminated a tall square building that looked familiar, like something he'd seen on his people's TV. But it wasn't just the floodlights—there were lights on in windows, and—could it be?—shadows moving behind the glass.

Movement.

"What do you see?" Gizmo asked, jumping up and

CHAPTER 19

THE UNTAMED CITY

On the second floor of the complex, the three dogs found an open apartment that didn't smell too bad. There, they filled up on water from the toilet and curled up on a stripped-down bed. Max drifted in and out of nightmares and dreams filled with angry wolves and swirling darkness and loving hugs and endless food.

But Max was so excited, he could barely sleep for long. He kept imagining what could be in that building. People, maybe, humans who were waiting for dogs like him and Rocky and Gizmo to show up so they could say, "Oh, how did we ever forget you? Come with us. We'll find your pack leaders right away!" And then he wouldn't have to worry about the vicious wolves thirsting for his blood or the seeping blackness after his people. It would just be him and Charlie and Emma, and Rocky and Gizmo with their people, and Madame laughing that her creaking bones hadn't meant anything bad after all, and this would all finally be over.

He was the first up when daylight came, pacing the floor in front of the bed until his two friends were "accidentally" woken up by the sound of his heavy, thudding walk.

"About time," he barked. "Let's go!"

After a quick return visit to the grocery store across the street for breakfast, the dogs were ready.

It was cooler this morning, a swift, fierce breeze chasing away the sun's heat. Max marched purposefully along the yellow lines down the center of the wide road. He kept an eye out for any predators lurking beneath the big machines parked in the fields or behind the stacked metal containers, but the landscape seemed to be as empty today as it had been in the week past.

As they walked, Rocky and Gizmo guessed what they would find in the building. Gizmo was positive that it would be the humans. Who else could keep the lights on?

"Well, it's probably not *all* the humans," Rocky said. "They couldn't all fit in that one building, I don't think. But hey, Giz, maybe if my people are there, they'd take you in!"

"Or you can stay with my pack. If my pack leaders are there," Max called as he sauntered confidently forward.

Rocky snorted. "You don't want them," he said to Gizmo. "One of them is a boy, and boys are rowdy. My pack leader is a girl, and she'd pamper you like nobody's business!"

"What if I like to play rowdy?" Gizmo asked, prancing and snapping her teeth.

"Well, she can do that, too!" Rocky said. "She's the best of both worlds!"

Max chuckled and focused on the first streets of the city. There was some sort of station up ahead, little glass shelters with signs in front of them. Several long white buses sat in the station, the advertisements on their sides torn and fading.

Beyond the station were more streets lined with more buildings. These were smaller than the skyscrapers at the heart of the city. Some had fanciful paintings on them of people playing with animals. Max narrowed his brows upon seeing that some rude human had sprayed red paint all over some of the animals on the murals. This wasn't like the eerie symbols he'd seen the day before—these Xs seemed angry, defacing artwork to show their rage. Max didn't like it at all.

Rocky and Gizmo fell silent as they passed the buses and turned down the street of the animal paintings. There were trees spaced evenly along the road. Wind rustled through the leaves, and aside from their own footsteps, it was all Max could hear.

He remembered the last time he was in the city, taken along with Emma and her mother to visit a friend who had moved here. The other little girl had a dog, too, a new, tiny white puppy who was so young that she barely knew how to talk. They'd gone to a park, where the adults had sat on the benches while the little girls used Max as an example to try to teach the puppy how to do tricks. But the puppy had been much more interested in sniffing anything and everything—trees, people feet, discarded trash, bird droppings. Not that Max could blame her.

Back then, the city was nothing like this. There had been constant noise. Hundreds and thousands of voices had filled the air, coming from buildings and the crowds of people walking up and down the sidewalks. Cars and other vehicles had belched and honked as they rode through the streets. There had been birds then, and other dogs like him, in the park and hiding inside apartments, barking playfully.

Now it was silent, just like everywhere else.

But it didn't matter, Max reminded himself. There was the building in the middle of the city. There were people there—there just had to be. That was all that mattered.

They passed through an intersection and walked around another abandoned bus. Max looked up and kept his eyes on the towering structures. Those were their goal. The center of the city. If they kept heading due east, they'd get there before long.

It wasn't until Max reached the next intersection that he heard the growls.

He stopped in his tracks, and Rocky and Gizmo each bumped into his backside with an "Oof!" The two smaller dogs came to stand on either side of Max—then went just as stiff and still. They were at the base of several brick apartment buildings. In front of one were scaffolds that rose several stories up, ragged plastic hanging loose from the edges and drifting in the wind.

The growls came again, and this time Rocky and Gizmo heard them, too.

"Oh no," Rocky whispered. "I knew this was too easy. I just knew it."

"Maybe they won't see us," Gizmo whispered back hopefully.

But it was too late.

Max saw them now—dozens of them. Large dogs like himself, though so thin, so dirty, so mad in the eyes that he couldn't tell what breed they once were. They appeared from the shadows in the streets in front and on either side of him, stalking forward and baring their teeth.

For a moment, Max thought he saw Madame among them, starved and angry, but he was relieved to realize that it was some other poor, starved dog. He couldn't imagine her like these creatures. Wouldn't allow himself to consider that that had been her fate in the city.

Darting his head to the side, Max saw more of the wild dogs wind around a fire hydrant and appear from the darkened doorways. Coming slowly forward.

Cornering them.

None of the dogs approached as the leader. They just growled, muttering to themselves, talking over one another.

"Where do they think they're going?"

"Not their territory."

"They fancy. Looking fancy, like the dogs downtown. Downtown fancy dogs."

"—Well fed. Where did they get food? I must have it. *I must!*"

"They hid the food!"

"Hid it, they hid all the food. They stole it for themselves like the fancy dogs."

"—Took my humans. They took them away from me!"

The voices were growing louder, as were the growls. The mongrels, neither together as a pack nor separate individuals, seemed ruled only by starvation and fear.

And hatred for Max, Rocky, and Gizmo.

"Run," Max whispered.

"Maybe they can tell us—" Gizmo started to say.

"Run!" Max bellowed.

He grabbed Gizmo by the scruff of her neck and gently flung her away from the dogs onto the road west out of the city. She landed lightly, then took off without looking back. Max and Rocky raced behind her—and immediately they heard the sound of dozens of paws galloping over asphalt as the mad dogs gave chase.

They'd have to find another route to get downtown.

Max glanced back over his shoulder. Max, Rocky, and Gizmo were definitely outrunning the starving dogs—they were so weak they'd never have a chance to catch up.

Only they had one advantage Max did not: They knew these streets.

Max and Rocky caught up to Gizmo just as they reached the next intersection back the way they had come near the animal murals and bus stations. They veered right down a small street between a high fence and the back of a long building and kept racing forward, without any aim other than to get away.

"Did we lose 'em, big guy?" Rocky panted.

Max was almost about to say he thought they had, when half the feral pack appeared around the corner of the intersection in front of them. Teeth bared, the wild dogs barreled forward.

Max turned to run the opposite way—but it was too late. The dogs chasing them had caught up now and blocked the far end of the street.

The two groups of wild dogs came forward slowly, growling incessantly even as they barked more accusations at the three companions. Max backed his friends toward the center of the alley, not knowing what to do, not knowing how to escape. They were so *close*; they couldn't lose now. They just couldn't!

That was when Max spotted the big hole in the ground. There was a green metal covering over it, but as Max moved farther down the street, he saw a set of stairs descend into darkness. It was their only hope.

"Follow me!" he barked to his friends.

At full gallop, Max raced to the steps. He bounded down them, almost stumbling over the cool concrete, but he managed to catch himself before he slipped and fell. In the cool dark at the foot of the stairs, he looked back up to the bright square of sky where the stairway met the street. Had his friends made it?

He was relieved to see Rocky and Gizmo side by side, hopping from step to step as well as they could on their short legs.

And Max also saw that although the wild dogs had chased them to the top of the steps, they were not trying to follow them down.

"What is it?" Rocky asked between gulps for air as he reached Max's side. "Why did you stop running?"

"Why did *they* stop running?" Gizmo asked, noticing what Max was looking at. Though the wild dogs still glared at them with angry eyes, they made no move forward.

Chest heaving for air and heart thudding, Max looked behind him: The stairs went down another flight into an inky darkness. He couldn't see very far. Whatever was down there, it scared these dogs. And if they were scared, maybe he should be, too.

"I don't know if we should go any farther," he said. "If they won't go down, maybe there's something dangerous."

Someone laughed in the darkness. A low, wheezing laugh. Max stiffened and Rocky whimpered. Gizmo cleared her throat and called out, "Who's there?"

"Oh, just the big scary monster," the speaker said, his voice old, strained. "And if you ain't mad like those ones up top on the street, maybe I won't eat you." He chuckled drily. "Or maybe I will."

"You don't *sound* like a monster," Gizmo said. "In fact, you sound like a dog."

The speaker laughed again. "A-heh-heh. Why don't you come down and see, little one?"

"Gizmo!" Rocky hissed.

With one look behind her at the snarling, wild dogs on the surface streets, Gizmo held her head high and marched down the steps into the dark. Max held his breath, waiting. Her footsteps stopped, and for a long moment, there was silence.

Then Gizmo burst into giggles.

"Come on, boys!" she yipped. "Unless you're afraid of an old Shepherd."

The speaker, it turned out, was an old Shepherd indeed—a German Shepherd, in fact. The old dog led the three companions deeper down the stairs, so far into the darkness that Max was surprised when the darkness gave way to an intermittent flickering fluorescent light. They ducked beneath turnstiles and walked carefully over chilly steel gratings set into the concrete.

The Shepherd was the same size as Max, though a bit stockier, with brown fur on his bottom and black on top. One of his eyes was a cloudy blue, pupil and all; the other was a deep brown. There were scratches on his side, fresh ones, but the old-timer didn't seem to pay much mind.

"Thank you for letting us come down here and get away from those crazy dogs," Max said as they walked.

"Eh, don't worry about it, pup," the German Shepherd said. "Didn't want to leave you up there against all those crazies. You'd either fight 'em or join 'em, but ain't no reason to join dogs like that. No need to go hungry. They's plenty of rats down here for all of us."

"Rats?" Rocky asked.

The old dog smacked his lips. "Rats."

As Max's eyes got used to the dim light, he saw that they were standing on a platform. To their left, the platform came to an abrupt edge, leading into a pit lined with tracks. In the flickering light, Max saw fading posters plastered to big square pillars that rose to the ceiling, glass-enclosed ticket counters, and doors with bright red signs on them built into the concrete walls.

"What should we call you?" Gizmo asked after introducing herself, Max, and Rocky.

"Eh, Rex is fine," the dog said, leading them down a flight of steps to the tracks below. Max's paws stepped from cool concrete to jagged stone, broken up by two thin metal rails that ran parallel to the walls.

Rex stopped suddenly, sniffed at the dank wall next to the tracks, then raised his hind leg and proceeded to do his business without a care in the world.

Gizmo met Max's and Rocky's eyes and stifled a giggle. Rex was still marking his territory.

"Ahhh," he said as he finished. "Anyway, others of us are ahead. I'm supposed to take you to them."

"Why?" Max asked as Rex led the way down the tracks.

"Gotta make sure you aren't Corporation spies, of course," he said as though it were perfectly obvious. "And here we are, pups."

They rounded a corner and bounded up another set of concrete steps to find themselves in a wide-open station, bigger than the one they'd just come from. There were yellow pillars down the center of the room, between which were benches for people to sit on. There were glass-faced cases on the walls with posters behind them, and machines with yellowing newspapers trapped inside. On either side of the room, beyond more turnstiles, stairs led up to street level.

And the tracks off the edge of the platform weren't empty. A vehicle that looked like a bus mixed with a train sat there, its windows shattered. There was black graffiti on the seats inside, and on the outside of the train, and on the yellow pillars. Graffiti everywhere.

At first, the place seemed empty. Then Rex let out a sharp bark. A Collie who looked a lot like Clearsight back at the Enclave, only with matted fur, wandered out from one of the ticket counters. A fat, dead rat hung from its jaws.

The Collie spat the dead rat to the floor. "What we got here?" the dog called—male. Definitely not Clearsight.

"Found some not-crazy pups, Bailey," Rex grumbled. "You wanna ask them if they part of the Corporation?"

Rustling came from the train car, and Max turned to see a dozen doggy heads pop up to look out the window. They blinked lazily. Many were as small as Gizmo and Rocky, though there were a few larger dogs, too. A dog who looked very much like Max, except with fur the color of tree bark, stepped out of an open door on the side of the train, yawning.

The dirty Collie, Bailey, came up to Max, Rocky, and Gizmo and sniffed them one by one.

"You Corporation?" he asked, glaring into their eyes.

Max blinked. "Um, no?" he said. "At least, I don't think so. What's the Corporation?"

Bailey nodded, satisfied. "Nah, they ain't Corporation." Turning away, he wandered back toward his dropped rat. "Plenty of room to sleep in the subway, lots of rats down here, make yourself at home."

"Rats is good eats," one of the small dogs called from the nearest window. "They're not so bad, at least. Until the people come back."

"Yeah, just till the people come back," another yipped.

Most of the dogs had lost interest and had dropped beneath the windows to resume sleeping. The chocolate Lab plopped to the platform and snorted loudly. Rex, meanwhile, sniffed at Bailey's dead rat until the younger dog sighed and slid half of it over to him.

"Uh, I'm not entirely sure these dogs are any more sane than the ones upstairs," Rocky whispered to Max and Gizmo. "Corporation? Eating *rats*?"

"Well, they're not trying to eat *us*, so that's a plus, right?" Gizmo said. "I think it's a good thing, anyway."

Max cleared his throat and took a few steps toward the German Shepherd and the Collie, both digging into their rat lunch. "Actually, we aren't really looking for a place to stay," he called out. "Though, of course, thank you for offering. We're actually looking for our people."

"Looking for the people?" a gruff voice barked from the subway car.

"Can't look for them," the Lab mumbled, his voice strained. "They long, long gone."

Smacking his jaws, Rex looked over at Max. "Can't really look for the people without going up top," he said with a full mouth. "Not a good idea to go up there. Not with the Corporation."

Max took another step forward. "We actually saw this building in the center of town. It's the only one with lights. And I think there are people there."

Both Rex and Bailey went rigid. The dogs in the subway car popped up to stare at Max, growling among themselves.

"But, pup," Rex said, swallowing his mouthful of rat, "that building *is* the Corporation. There's nothing but bad things to be found there. And no people anywhere."

No people.

Max's ears drooped at the news, and his legs threatened to break beneath him, sending him collapsing to the ground. He'd hoped so much that there would be people there, that this was the end of their journey. Shivering, he had to swallow the whine that threatened to escape his throat.

But just because the people weren't here didn't mean another friend wasn't.

"I . . . I don't care if there are no people there," Max said. "Are there dogs, then, at least? A Doberman and . . . and a Lab named Madame. Do they sound familiar? Have they come through here?"

"Not one of us," Rex said. "Any Doberman I know is gonna be with the Corporation. If that Madame is with one of 'em, that would be where you'd find her."

"So then the building is where we want to go after all," Max said.

"You saying you're Corporation, then?" Bailey barked.

Max looked back at Rocky and Gizmo, who looked as defeated as he was by the news of no people. Then he took in the frightened eyes of the small dogs in the subway car, refugees from the apartments in the city, no doubt.

"Yeah," Max said softly. "I suppose I'm Corporation."

The other Lab yelped, leaped up, and darted back to hide inside the subway car.

"You know what we do to Corporation dogs?" Bailey growled menacingly.

Max shook his head.

Bailey laughed, wild. "We lead 'em back home so they'll leave us alone. Come on."

For a while, Max, Rocky, and Gizmo were led through the dark tunnels of the subway by a full procession of dogs.

Bailey and old Rex were in front, followed by the three companions. The rest of the dogs filed out of the subway and followed, talking among themselves, apparently excited by the unexpected trip. Rocky listed the breeds he recognized: the Chinese Crested, with long tufts of dingy white wispy fur dangling from its big pointed ears and from its brows. The Papillon, who had a tan face with a white stripe down its middle, and two wide, fluffy ears that looked like furry butterfly wings. The wide-faced Pomeranian, and the Pug with the flat snout, wrinkled forehead, and baleful eyes.

All the dogs walked carefully over the craggy stone and metal tracks. It was cold down in the track pit, and the air was damp and smelled of mold and rotting things and tar. It was so dark that Max could barely see in front of him, and all he could hear were the panting breaths of the procession, the distant pinging of water dripping from high above, and the low voices of some of the dogs as they spoke to one another.

"Saw me a big rat other day," one said. "I got it cornered and it said, 'Please don't eat me, mister! I have a mate—I missed her!'"

"What did you do?" another dog asked.

"Well, I ate him up, of course. I hate bad rhymes."

But the parade of dogs dwindled the farther the group traveled. Some darted off after rats they saw trying to sneak by in the shadows. Others just got bored and wandered back toward home.

And others seemed to lose their nerve. Fur bristling, they yipped and howled as though being chased by wolves and raced back to their subway. Before long, it was just the three companions, Bailey, and Rex.

"I'd love to take you Corporation dogs farther," Bailey said, backing away from the darkness ahead. "But I know better than to mess with the ones up top."

And then the Collie was gone.

Rex silently took the dogs the few dozen feet to the steps leading up to the edge of the next station. Max could only sense the cavernous station platform, not see it—there were no lights here. Just darkness.

"Well, this is where I'm off, too, pups," Rex barked softly. "It was nice meeting you all. You seem like you got good heads. I wish you'd reconsider going to the Corporation. If you had any sense, you'd be as afraid of it as we are."

"What's so bad about this Corporation?" Gizmo asked. "What could possibly be scarier than those feral dogs?"

"I wish I could explain," he said, his voice growing distant in the darkness. "But I don't want to stay too long." His footsteps faded. "Good luck, pups!"

"Well," Rocky grumbled. "That was pretty unhelpful."

"I'm sure he tried," Gizmo said. "He's old and probably not all there in the head. Especially after living down here all this time and eating rats."

Max sighed. "At least they took us *somewhere*. Let's see if we're near the building."

Max bounded up the steps and sensed the darkness open outward into the pitch black of this new subway station. He could barely make out dim daylight streaming down the stairs on either side of the vast open room.

Before Max could lead his friends across and up the stairs, however, a noise made him stop.

His ears perked up: claws. Skittering claws. Hundreds of them—maybe thousands, he couldn't tell. Not dog or cat.

Much smaller.

That was when he saw the piercing red eyes glowing in the dark. Pair after pair, as many as the stars in the sky.

Getting to the stairs wouldn't be so easy after all.

They were surrounded by a swarm of rats.

CHAPTER 20

OUT OF THE DARK

As Max's eyes adjusted to the scant daylight from the stairwells, he could more clearly make out the rats.

Immediately, he wished it had stayed dark.

They were like a living, seething, greasy black carpet covering the entirety of the abandoned subway station. Unlike the few rats Max had seen scrambling in the shadows on the trip here, these were bigger, fatter. They undulated, their crimson eyes piercing into him as they surged forward.

And as they drew closer, they opened their mouths and twitched their whiskers and began to chitter and chant, low and menacing.

"There are dogs here," several of the voices said at once, the words overlapping one another and seeming to echo.

"They'd dare come near?" another chorus of voices said in response.

"They think they'll eat rat."

"Now, we can't have *that*."

The squeaky, overlapping voices rose into vicious laughter and terrifying chants, a shrill chorus of hundreds and hundreds, becoming a din that echoed throughout the cavernous station until Max could no longer tell what they were saying and had to fight the urge to lie down and cover his ears.

Max started to back up, and beside him, Rocky and Gizmo did the same. But Max's back paw hit something hot, damp, and furry, and he yipped and spun around.

And saw that the rats had circled behind them, too, covering the tracks at the base of the steps. Their beady eyes and long, curving teeth glittered in the darkness between the silvery subway tracks.

Max's heart thudded, a deafening drumbeat to the rats' cacophonous chanting. It was so dark, and there were so many of them. There was nowhere to run, nowhere to go. They were trapped.

But he had to protect his friends.

"Gizmo, Rocky—stay behind me," he whispered. The line of rats in front of them was edging closer. "I'm going to try to fight my way through and make a path. You two run."

"Maybe..." Gizmo whispered, her tone unsure, "maybe I can try to talk to them, like the cats?"

"*Gonna get the mutts,*" the voices chanted. "*Gonna gnaw their butts.*" More laughter.

"I don't think that will work this time, Gizmo," Max said softly.

"Hey," Rocky said, forcing himself past Max. He looked at Max and Gizmo, then took in a deep breath, swelling his chest. "I told ya two, it's my turn to prove myself. Let me handle this."

The rats were so close now that Max could smell their rancid breath coming from all sides. "But, Rocky, what can you do?" Max asked. "You'll get hurt."

Rocky shook his head so that his ears flopped. "You have to think like a small animal, big guy. And I'm the smallest here."

Before Max or Gizmo could protest, Rocky sauntered forward, cleared his throat, and barked as loud as he could, "Attention, rats! Rats, can I have your attention, please!"

The seething mass of rodents stopped moving, their voices lowered. Some began to squeak to themselves.

"You got us, rats!" Rocky continued. "You scared us three dogs good! We're only three, after all. You are a *legion*. We are trembling and humbled before you!" As he spoke, Rocky turned tight circles, addressing every rat in the chamber. "We have never before encountered such...might! Such overwhelming power! We humbly request we be allowed to bow down before the leader, who has proven once and for all that dogs are no match for the might of rats!"

The rats went completely silent. For a moment, nothing seemed to happen. Max held his breath, straining his eyes in the dim light.

Then a narrow path opened in the sea of rats just in front of Rocky. One large rat split away from the shadows and scampered through, its long tail dragging behind it. The rats closed ranks after it waddled past.

The big rat plopped itself in front of Rocky and reared up on its haunches.

Max was stunned by the size of the creature. It was almost as big as Rocky—definitely the biggest rodent he'd ever seen. It looked down its long snout at the Dachshund, its whiskers twitching.

Rocky bowed his head and lowered his ears and tail. "You must be the great leader of these rats," Rocky said.

The giant rat raised a claw and stroked the sleek black fur on its chin. "I am," it squeaked.

"I have never seen such a pack of rats this mighty. All of them are fat, their fur glistening—obviously you feast well. And you are so well organized. Rats who can control a whole human subway station like this are rats who can do *anything*. I'm surprised that your glorious feats are not talked about far and wide."

The rat nodded along with every word Rocky spoke, its movements seeming almost involuntary. "It is true," it said. "I am Longtooth, and to this pod I am king. I raised my fellows from the depths, and we are a mighty thing!"

Rocky dared a glance up at Longtooth. "You definitely are, Your Highness!" Rocky yipped. "No wonder all the subway dogs ran away in terror. They knew they could never face you and hope to survive!"

All the rats in the subway raised their voices again, in scratchy hisses that to Max sounded like pleased cheers. Longtooth raised another paw, and the pod of rats fell silent.

"It is rare we come across dogs as smart as you," Longtooth said. "What to do, what to do..."

"Well, that's why we have come down here," Rocky said. "There are dogs up above who *laugh* about you—can you believe it? My friends and I said, Nooo, never question rats, especially rats in groups. But they laughed and laughed and said they would kill you all without even working up a sweat."

Longtooth darted forward, shoving himself snout to snout with Rocky. Rocky flinched but did not back away.

"The mad dogs above?" Longtooth hissed. "About us, they say this of?"

Rocky nodded. "Just ask my friends."

Hundreds of red eyes snapped from Rocky to Max and Gizmo. Max nodded vigorously, and Gizmo yipped, "Yup, they said all that!"

"It's worse than that, King Longtooth!" Rocky howled. "Oh, the things they said! They said you only *exist* because they allow you to! That you're not even worth fighting because you're so…so…" He wrenched his head away, eyes closed. "I can't even bear to say it."

Gripping Rocky's ears in both front claws, Longtooth shoved himself even closer to the little Dachshund. "What did they say? Tell me! They must pay!"

Rocky swallowed, then opened one eye. "They said you weren't fighting because you're not only stupid, you're also so insignificantly *small*."

That riled up the rats. Their chittering voices rose once again, a rush of noise about the idiocy of dogs and how they would form an army to destroy the mongrels. Longtooth let go of Rocky and backed away, one claw raised in the air and the other pressed against his chest as though he were mortally wounded by the words.

"No!" Longtooth squealed above the roars of his rats. "Quiet!" As the rats fell silent, Longtooth once again regarded the dogs with quivering whiskers.

"I have made a decision," he said at long last. "To prove that I am not stupid and that I wield my power with *precision*, I will grant you three mercy for trespassing in my subway. Tell me"—he staggered forward again—"is it a small animal who grants mercy in such a big way?"

"No!" Rocky said. "Only the largest and most powerful can take pity on three misguided dogs."

"Exactly!" Longtooth said, clearly pleased. "We are large and powerful! So large and powerful that we shall let you go back up above, where you will share what you

261

learned here with them all. You will let those mad dogs know: We are anything but *small*."

"Your wisdom and mercy overwhelm me, Your Highness," Rocky said, bowing his head and backing up to stand once more beside Max and Gizmo. "We will tell of your might and glory to every dog we meet."

Longtooth turned to his legion of rodents and raised his claws again. "Leave us!" he shrieked. "This your king commands!" Blinking and with a shake of his head, Longtooth added a quick, "Uh, commands-us!" With a deafening rush of squeals and clatterings, the mass of rats separated, racing in all directions and disappearing into the shadows once more. Where once had been a hairy carpet of thousands of terrifying rats now was only plain concrete and train ties.

The rat king turned back to the three dogs and raised its snout high. "Good timing. I was running low on rhymes. And where are you dogs heading, anyway?" he asked, looking at Max as though he towered over him instead of the other way around.

Max cleared his throat. "Uh, well, we were told that up above is where the Corporation is located. That is where we are headed."

Longtooth *tsk*ed and shook his head. "I wouldn't advise going there, dog. Better to go up farther downtown. Last thing you want is to run into the Corporation."

"But why?" Gizmo asked, stepping forward and tilting her head. "The subway dogs wouldn't tell us."

Dropping to all fours, Longtooth shook his head once more. "The Corporation is more dogs, only they're...organized. Obviously my rats and I don't fear dogs, but these aren't like other dogs I've faced. They're something else. Something very strange and disturbing."

So not only weren't there people in the lit building, Max realized. But it was some force of dogs. *Strange* dogs. Madame was many things, but Max would never call her strange—would she really be with dogs like that?

But could he really take a rat's word for it? What might be strange to Longtooth could be normal to Max and Rocky and Gizmo. And they'd come so far....

"We thank you for the warning," Max said, stepping forward to take charge once more. "But we're willing to risk it. Our journey is too important. We're searching for our lost people, and not even some strange dogs are going to stop us."

Longtooth let out a low whistle. "You're on a journey, huh? Looking for the missing people? That's pretty brave for a bunch of dogs." Looking around to make sure no rats were around, the rat king added, "Just between you and me, I don't think you mutts are all bad. Tell you what, if you want to go face the Corporation, do it with my well wishes. I'll send word to some other rats I know about your mission. Maybe we can help each other in the future."

Max panted a smile. "Thanks. I'd appreciate that."

Longtooth waved a paw. "Yeah, it's nothing. Now get

along, you three. And good luck." With that, the giant rat king skittered away, disappearing once more into the darkness.

"Yay!" Gizmo whispered at the sight of the disappearing rat. "You did it, Rocky!"

Rocky ducked his head but couldn't hide his wagging tail. "Aw, it was nothing, really," he said. "You just gotta think like they think, then you can get 'em to do whatever you want. Mostly."

"You did good," Max said. "That went much better than a fight. We may even have made a new friend."

"You guys, you guys, you're embarrassing me!" Unable to control his wagging tail, Rocky waddled up onto the dark subway station platform and toward the stairs. "Now how about we go back up? I don't know how bad this Corporation is, but I do know I'm awful tired of tunnels!"

The midday light burned their eyes as Max, Rocky, and Gizmo emerged from the subway station and found themselves on the city streets once more.

Blinking, Max cleared his vision and took in their surroundings. They were in some sort of square, where there were benches and trees planted in islands of soil in the concrete. Surrounding the square were buildings—tall ones glittering black and steel that rose so high they seemed to disappear into misty gray clouds.

All around the square, empty cars and buses sat askew, half on the sidewalks and half on the roads. One car had run into a utility pole, which had fallen to smash through a window of a nearby building.

Cool wind rushed through the streets, carrying with it newspapers and empty paper cups and fallen leaves, which swirled past and collected in the gutters and mounded in dirty drifts against the sides of the buildings. Everything seemed shrouded in gray. And everything was terribly quiet.

But Max by now knew better than to think that meant they were alone.

"We're by the large buildings," Gizmo said, breaking the silence. "So we're downtown, right?"

Max nodded, spinning in circles to find his bearings. The buildings were so tall—brick and glass and stone—that he couldn't see past them. "This Corporation building has to be close," he said, softly so that his barks didn't carry in the wind.

Shivering, Rocky whimpered and came to stand close to Max, so close he almost disappeared beneath his legs. "Something feels weird," the little dog whispered. "It feels bad in a *different* way from before, worse even than when we saw those mad dogs."

Max couldn't explain why, but he had to agree. Perhaps it was the eerie whistling of the wind as it blew down the streets and between the tall buildings. Or the silence after the noise of all the animals down below.

And then someone laughed.

Deep, guttural, wild laughter.

All three dogs spun around. Max expected to see the wild dogs who had chased them below and was prepared to run back down into the subway system if necessary. Or maybe it would turn out to be one of the Corporation dogs, and Max could talk to it.

But the creature who emerged from behind an overturned bus was someone Max had hoped he'd never see again.

The scarred gray wolf, Dolph.

The wolf leader stalked forward, teeth bared. Max couldn't help but notice the scorch mark along his side, the fury in his eyes. And as Dolph came closer, more wolves emerged from behind cars and from side streets, loosely surrounding Max and his friends. The white wolf Wretch trembled with rage as he slunk in front of the subway entrance, blocking their one escape route.

Max cast a glance down at his two friends. Rocky was a tremor of black fur, so terrified that he couldn't move. Gizmo glared down the approaching foes, but Max knew she wouldn't stand a chance against the wolves, no matter how brave she was.

He'd made a promise that he wouldn't let any harm come to his friends. And though it might mean he wouldn't be able to finish this journey he had started... well, at least he'd know Rocky and Gizmo were safe.

"If you see a chance," Max whispered to his two friends, "run."

Swallowing down his fear, Max bared his teeth, lowered his head, and marched forward to face Dolph head on.

"How did you find us?" Max growled, trying to keep the feral wolf talking. Buy himself some time.

Dolph reared back his head and laughed, the evil sound echoing between towers. "You think you are smart, mutt?" Dolph barked another laugh. "Your false trail was laughable. It was easy enough to find where you'd really gone. And, well..."

The wolf twitched his head and a skinny coal-black member of his pack darted forward. There was something in the other wolf's mouth, some animal whose spotted fur was coated in blood. A hollow opened in Max's gut, and his limbs trembled as the wolf unceremoniously spat the poor creature to the ground and Max saw who it was.

Raoul.

The cat lay there in an unnatural heap, his legs askew, his chest rising and falling slowly. One green eye was scratched shut. The other distantly met Max's horrified stare.

"Tried to stop them..." Raoul wheezed. "Others got away...others...safe...run..."

Max couldn't help himself. He dove toward the cat

and licked his matted, bloodstained fur, trying desperately to find the source of the wounds, to stop the bleeding.

"Raoul," Max whimpered. "Don't go to sleep, Raoul. We're going to find your old lady, May. And we're supposed to lead you to her. Remember? Raoul?"

With a soft sigh, the cat's chest stopped moving. His open eye looked past Max, unfocused, seeing nothing at all.

"We found these felines easily enough," Dolph growled. "We smelled you on them. Most ran away. Some like your stupid friend here tried to fight me. But one caught was all too pleased to tell us where you were headed in exchange for being let go." Again Dolph laughed, the sound digging into Max's ears, his brain. "We ate him anyway."

A fire surged through Max's limbs. He roared and leaped forward, his vision red, his sights on Dolph's sneering, scarred face.

The wolf leader reared up, and the two met chest to chest. But Max was better fed, better rested, and driven by his sorrow and his anger at this horrible beast.

The impact of his body against Dolph's sent the wolf tumbling heavily onto his back. The coal-black wolf who had mauled Raoul snarled and prepared to leap.

"No!" Dolph bellowed as he rolled back onto his feet. "This one is *mine!*"

Max and Dolph circled each other, their expressions mirror images—gums pulled back, eyes narrowed, ears laid flat.

"This would have been so much easier if you'd just given us the kibble," Dolph snarled.

Max didn't respond. He darted a glance at Rocky and Gizmo. The wolves had made no move for them yet. But behind them, Wretch laughed.

"Enjoy the show," Wretch snarled. "You're next in the ring, little dog."

Eyes back to Dolph, Max watched as the wolf started another taunt, more words meant to throw Max off balance, give the wolf a way in.

Instead, Max leaped again.

This time, Dolph was ready. Max lunged for the wolf's throat, but he barely grazed the fur before he felt Dolph's sharp claws tearing at his side. Howling, Max twisted to break free, but Dolph lunged and snapped, and a searing pain lanced through Max's head.

And the wolf shoved Max away, slamming the dog on his side against the asphalt with such force that his insides seemed to rattle. His head smacked hard against the street.

Max lay there, stunned, a ringing in his ears. The world around him had gone slow and blurry. Blood dripped from a cut above his eyes, staining his fur, obscuring half his vision in red.

Dolph laughed a mocking howl. "A smart dog would

have given up to me long ago," the wolf sneered. "You may be better fed than me, mutt, but you were raised to be a *pet*. You never had to fight with your own siblings to eat. You can never win against me."

Groaning, Max forced himself to stand on his four wobbly legs. Dizziness rushed over him, but he didn't care. He wouldn't give up now. He would not!

"I'd rather die fighting you than give up," Max spat, his words slurred but the intent in his voice strong. "I wouldn't be able to live with myself if I didn't fight for my friends."

Max darted forward, hoping these rallying words would bolster him, but he was too weak. The world spun around him and he stumbled.

Dolph dove in, claws to Max's chest, and easily flipped him over onto his back. Max squirmed and struggled, but Dolph towered over him, dominated him.

From the square, Rocky and Gizmo both cried out. But there was nothing they could do.

"You want to die?" Dolph snarled. "So be it."

And then Dolph bared his teeth and dove his head down to tear out Max's throat.

CHAPTER 21

THE CORPORATION

A bark echoed through the city.

A chorus of canine cries responded, hundreds and hundreds of different barks calling out together, as one.

Max waited. He waited to feel the teeth rip through his fur and into his skin, then wondered if it had already happened. If he was dead like poor Raoul, and these barks were the sounds of all the other dogs in the place dogs went to after they died—golden fields where daylight never ended and the running was endless, where the only thing that interrupted play was the promise of sleep.

But no, Max wasn't dead.

Dolph was still hovering over Max, pinning him to the ground. But from what Max could tell, the wolf had grown still, stunned.

Around them, the barks increased in volume. They seemed to come from everywhere and nowhere. They echoed off the buildings around them and came from the streets, calling and answering one another.

Max could barely make out the dozens upon dozens of dogs who surged from around the street corners, barking and barking so loud that it made Max's aching head feel as if it would explode. There were so many dark shapes that Max wondered if maybe these weren't dogs at all, but the swarm of rats from below now grown dog-sized. They'd been nearly as big as dogs anyway, those rats.

Through his bleary, bloodstained eyes, Max did see two familiar shapes: Rocky and Gizmo.

"Run," Max wheezed. "Run!"

But the sound of the barks became all Max could hear, and the world spun so fast that the black swarm of rats—or was it dogs?—became like the surging darkness in his nightmares, consuming everything it touched.

Max's world went black.

Soft, lilting music. Max's ears twitched.

It was the same music from the coffee shop. The one with the crazed dog trapped behind its glass doors.

But had any of that been real? Perhaps it was all a dream. He was certainly not outdoors. No, his bed was too comfortably soft, too warm.

Max rolled on his side and let out a soft "Aroo." The sound of his own voice was enough to make him blink open one eye, and then the other.

Bright fluorescent light surrounded him. He thought fearfully back to being caged at Vet's, but then he blinked once, twice—and through clearer eyes saw that he was lying in a large, plush doggy bed, which in turn was resting on a carpeted floor.

Max tried to lift his head, then winced—he was sore all over. His head ached, and his sides hurt. More gently, he twisted his head to take in his surroundings.

He wasn't home. Somehow, he was inside a human store, one lined with rows and rows of tall shelves filled with books.

Stretching, Max's hind legs escaped the doggy bed and kicked something plastic. That was when he noticed the bowl of kibble. Beside it was a twin bowl filled with water. A hose snaked between the shelves and ended there, water dripping from its end and soaking into the carpet.

With a groan, Max forced himself to flop up. He ate a bite of kibble, then washed it down with water, trying to remember how he'd ended up here.

The mad dogs in the city. The rat-eaters in the subway. The big rats led by Longtooth. The wolves and... Raoul. Poor Raoul, who would never see his old lady ever again.

Max whimpered, no longer hungry. Pulling himself

back into the doggy bed, he remembered one last thing—the surging blackness, the echoing barks.

And Rocky and Gizmo at the center of it all.

Adrenaline rushed through Max's limbs, and he jumped to all fours, not caring about the pain from his fight with Dolph. "Rocky!" he barked. "Gizmo!"

Panic threatened to overwhelm him—he couldn't have lost them to the wolves or the darkness. With the people gone and Madame who knew where, they were all he had. He had vowed to protect them and—

"Hey, you're awake! About time, big guy."

Relief washed over Max, and he sat back hard onto the doggy bed as Rocky and Gizmo sauntered around a shelf and rushed to his side.

"Yay!" Gizmo yipped as she dove to nuzzle his belly. "I was so worried, Max! But you were so brave!"

"I'm just glad you two are safe," Max said. "What happened?"

Rocky jumped back and forth, his tail a blur of excitement. "Oh, it was like nothing I'd ever seen, buddy!" he said. "And I've seen a lot of things."

"We thought the wolves had us for good," Gizmo added. "But then all these dogs came from nowhere and chased them off. They saved us, Max, and took us here."

"And where's here?"

Plopping to sit down, Rocky waved a paw. "Well, this is some human store at the very base of that building we were heading toward. You know, *the* building."

Max's ears perked up. "The building with the lights? The Corporation?"

"Yup!" Gizmo said. "I don't know what those sewer dogs and rats were going on about. These dogs seem perfectly nice to me."

From across the store came a whooshing sound, then padded footsteps. Moments later, two burly beige dogs with drooping faces rounded the bookshelves and sat down on either side of Max, Rocky, and Gizmo.

"You're awake," the dog on the right said.

"The Chairman wants to see you," the other said.

With that, the two dogs rose, turned to face back the way they came, and waited expectantly.

"The Chairman?" Max asked.

"No questions," the first dog barked.

"Just come with us."

Rocky and Gizmo offered Max reassuring looks. Figuring any dog who saved his life, gave him a bed, and fed him couldn't be all bad, he forced himself up again. His legs were wobbly for the first two steps, but the rest had done him good and his strength was coming back.

The two Corporation dogs marched in unison through the shelves of books as Max, Rocky, and Gizmo followed. They passed the checkout counters and then headed straight toward a glass door.

Max almost barked to ask how they'd get past the door, but to his surprise, it whooshed open as the dogs neared. He'd never seen anything like it.

"How did it do that?" he asked, incredulous.

"No questions."

"Keep following."

The bookstore led out to a square open area inside the building that rose several stories above them. There were shops in every direction. Their lights were on, and Max could see dogs lounging inside—some near a store filled with sports equipment, others beneath tables at a restaurant.

The Corporation dogs led them across the tiled floor to a big glass tube that ran from the ground up into the ceiling. Standing in front of the tube was a dog bigger than Max himself. It had the sleek shape of the Greyhound back at the Enclave, but its tan fur was shaggier, its head even narrower.

"Three for the Chairman," one of the burly dogs said as they neared.

"Three for Chairman," the large dog said, her voice high, her tone mechanical. "Right away."

Standing on her hind legs and resting one paw against the front of the tube, the large dog nosed a button Max hadn't seen before. Seconds later, with another whoosh, the glass doors on the front of the tube opened.

"In you go."

Max sniffed the ground of the tube. More carpet. He wasn't entirely sure what this thing was, but if they wanted him inside...At the urging of another of the burly dogs, he walked in, Rocky and Gizmo right behind.

The large dog climbed inside past the glass doors, then rose up once again to press one button out of the many that were on the inside wall. Moments later, the glass doors wheezed shut.

With a hum that reverberated through the glass walls, the floor began to rise.

"Whoa!" Max barked. "What is this?"

The large dog yawned and sat down. "It's just an elevator," she said. "You get used to it."

"Oh, wow!" Gizmo yipped. "Look!"

Max followed her gaze to look out the clear tube. It turned out that they were in a small enclosure inside the tube, and now they were rising up through the building. The floors below grew smaller and smaller as the dogs were carried up into the sky.

Rocky yipped after one look, then backed away into the center of the elevator, squatted onto his belly, and covered his eyes with his paws. The large dog laughed. "Don't worry," she said. "You can't fall."

"Well, better safe here in the middle, okay?" Rocky yipped, his voice muffled.

They reached the ceiling of the promenade and lifted through it. They rose through floor after floor of hallways lined with doors, and through the glass Max could see dogs stalking the halls, making themselves at home. They walked stiff, focused. Max had seen dogs like this at Vet's from time to time—the trained dogs. They often talked about being taken to shows and winning ribbons, as though ribbons were especially useful.

The humming quieted as the elevator began to slow. Max looked up at the door and saw that the button the large dog had pressed had lit up. The floor stopped rising, and the doors whooshed open.

"All right, everyone out," the large dog said. "The Chairman expects you."

Rocky darted from the elevator in a blur. Chuckling, Gizmo followed. Max padded softly behind, nodding his thanks to the large dog. She ignored him.

The elevator had taken them to a wide-open floor. Unlike the floors below, this one was not divided into hallways and rooms. Three sides were covered entirely with windows that looked out over the now-dark city— and from what Max could tell from the shadowy buildings below, they were *awfully* high up.

The fourth wall had a stage of some sort surrounded by folding chairs, some still in neat rows, others collapsed. It was on this side of the room where several dogs lay curled up, sleeping in doggy beds. Only one lay on the stage itself, its head propped up, waiting.

The dog was large, larger than Max, and seemed to be made up of sharp angles. Its paws and bits of its snout were a woodsy brown, but the rest of its fur was as black as the midnight sky. Its knifepoint ears were at attention, and it watched them from across the room with dark, unreadable eyes. Its tail, like Gizmo's, was cut short into a nub. The tail did not flinch, gave no indication of the creature's mood.

"Oh," Gizmo whispered, catching sight of the dog. "I know him. That Doberman was at the Enclave. That's Dandyclaw's friend!"

"The Doberman," Max whispered. "If he's here, then Madame must be, too!"

"It's about time you're awake," the Doberman barked across the room. "Come closer."

The words were cool, calm. But Max felt the command in them, could smell the dog's dominance in the air of the wide-open room. Not wanting to anger the dog who'd helped save him, Max walked forward with Gizmo and Rocky behind him, stepping carefully past and over the folding chairs in front of the stage.

The Doberman lifted his snout as they approached. "Ugh, the stench of you creatures," he sniffed.

"I know you!" Gizmo yipped excitedly. "You were with Dandyclaw. You're—"

The Doberman snapped his jaws. At the sound, the dogs sleeping on either side of the stage rustled, but did not move. Only they weren't sleeping at all, Max realized— like their leader, they were Dobermans, though smaller in size and different colors. They watched Max and his friends silently.

"Hey!" Rocky barked. "Don't snap at her!"

The Doberman closed his eyes. When he opened them again, he was glaring directly at Rocky.

Tucking his tail between his legs, Rocky backed away. "I mean, uh, please. Big guy."

"I was in the Enclave, yes," the Doberman drawled. "With that simpering Poodle Dandyclaw and his grand plans to make a new society in a pit of mud." He let out a sharp bark. "He thought too small, that one. He was also much too consumed with being a *savior.* Which is why I left to do his idea *right.* The humans are gone, and so we shall have a new society in their stead—one run by dogs, for dogs."

"You're the Chairman, right?" Max asked. "You sent your dogs to save me?"

The Doberman's ears twitched. "Yes, I am the Chairman," he said. "But saving you was incidental. I sent my dogs to get rid of some wolves."

"Well, thanks all the same," Max said, bowing his head. "But I'm glad to have a chance to meet you. A friend of mine left the Enclave with you. An older dog named Madame Curie. We've heard stories of you two traveling together, and I really must talk to her."

First one brow, then another, on the Chairman's face rose. He looked Max up and down, considering him carefully.

"Madame," the Chairman finally said. "Yes, of course I know her. We did indeed come to this city together."

"Oh, yay!" Gizmo barked. "Max, your friend! We found her!"

The Chairman held up a paw. "She's here, yes. But

she's ... not taking visitors at the moment. She is doing very important work."

Max took a step forward and was met with the glares of the other lounging Dobermans. Warning him.

"Please tell her that Max is here and would like to speak with her," he said. "Please tell her it's very important."

"Max," the Chairman drawled. Waving his paw, he said, "All right. Done. I'm not sure when she'll be available, but I suppose while you wait, I can put you to use."

"Put us to ... use?" Max asked, his time at the Enclave coming back to him.

"Here in my tower," the Chairman intoned, "I am creating a true new society. One where I—where *we*—can live in luxury, as I am accustomed. We will not *scavenge* like the mad dogs on the streets or the filthy mutts in Dandyclaw's woods. We will not eat *rats* and hide in the dark like the subway mongrels."

"Luxury?" Rocky asked. "No eating rats? Sounds good to me!"

"Of course it does," the Chairman snapped. "But I have expectations of my Corporation. We work to gather the things we need to live our lives to the fullest. I expect obedience. There are no individuals here. There is only me—your Chairman and your leader—and there is the rest of you." Leaning forward, the Doberman put himself snout to snout with Max. "How does that sound to you?"

It sounded to Max like the Enclave all over again.

Only on a scale far grander than Dandyclaw could have ever imagined. Dogs running a whole building—a whole *city*? Hundreds or maybe thousands working as an army to survive?

Max looked at Rocky and Gizmo. This place, this Corporation, had been their only real hope to find the humans. They'd traveled so far, had faced so much. Maybe it wouldn't hurt to rest again for a little bit while waiting to speak with Madame. To talk to all the many dogs inside the Corporation and gather more leads about where the people had gone before setting out again, hopefully with a clearer path toward finding their pack leaders once and for all.

Besides, if those wolves came back, Max knew he'd need help fighting them off.

Rocky seemed absorbed with the idea of living luxuriously, but Gizmo's eyes were wary, worried. Max knew how she felt. He knew better than to trust the Chairman, especially not with his grandiose boasts and after hearing how he'd treated Raoul's cats—poor Raoul!

But maybe they could use the Doberman just as he intended to use them.

"I think we would like to join your Corporation, Chairman," Max said, bowing his head. "I'm sure Madame, as busy as she is, would want us here as well."

"Excellent," the Chairman said with a slight wag of his nub tail. "It is much better to be willing workers than to be…unwilling." The Chairman laughed. The other

Dobermans lying in their beds joined in, the sudden chorus of voices making Max's insides feel wobbly, off balance.

"Your interview is over," the Chairman announced, and the other Dobermans' laughter abruptly stopped. "Find a place to sleep below. You will be assigned duties in the morning."

CHAPTER 22

SHADY BUSINESS

Max almost laughed the next morning when he learned what his first job as a member of the Corporation would be: dragging a wagon to stores within the city, filling it with bags of kibble, and dragging it back to the doggy fortress.

"Apparently great minds think alike," he'd muttered to Rocky.

"I'm not convinced he didn't somehow steal the idea from me!" Rocky had yipped back.

Though Max had laughed on the outside, inside he still smarted from his wounds, his near loss of his friends, the death of Raoul. He knew deep down that something was very wrong here in the Corporation.

But Max was tired.

He felt so helpless after coming so far for nothing. And then suffering the beating from Dolph and his pack. But Max reassured himself that this was only temporary. Max would finally speak to Madame and learn what she knew about why the people left. And when the time was right, they would move on. Just like always.

That first day, Rocky and Gizmo were allowed to accompany Max to the nearby pet store supercenter to help stock up on food. They were overseen by a stoic German Shepherd who amusingly enough was named Rex, though he didn't seem to get why Max, Rocky, and Gizmo found that so funny.

The pet store was on the lowest floor of one of the nearby high-rises. Like the Corporation building, the store's electricity was still on, though he wouldn't have been able to see the store from the apartments where he first saw the Corporation building. A dog had to only walk up to a door and it would whoosh open like magic. Many of the Corporation's dogs paced the streets between the Corporation and the pet store, guarding it from the wild dogs who would try to break through and get at the supplies. Even the doors to get in were protected by Corporation-approved mutts who spent their days inside approving who came and went.

The dogs were different breeds, but they were all large and carried their heads high, stiff. Trained. Their eyes were focused, and it seemed to Max that none of them had ever played a day in their lives. Not that he'd ask to make sure—he didn't exactly want to make small talk with them, and based on their glares as he walked by, the feeling was mutual.

They passed by glowing blue fish tanks as they entered the store, the fish inside floating atop the water, still. The light in their tanks flickered, and green algae grew upon the glass. Beyond them, there was a room with a broken glass window and a bunch of cages where animals had once sat—*for sale?* Max wondered. How strange. But the cages were empty and open now.

Rex led them past boxes picturing tubes and ferrets, towering scratching posts, cages for small animals. The dog section of the superstore was half ransacked by now, many of the amenities like dog beds and food dishes already dragged off the shelves and back to the Corporation headquarters.

Strangely, none of the toys had been taken. There were ropes and bones and squeaky toys dangling from pegs, and Gizmo was so beside herself at seeing them that she ran forward, leaped up, and bit into a toy shaped like a pig. It let out a loud, wheezing squeal that echoed through the cavernous store.

Rex started, then immediately dove at Gizmo, barking in rage, spittle flying from his teeth. Gizmo yelped, dropped the toy, and leaped away.

"Hey, what's the deal?" Rocky asked, stepping in front of Gizmo, who shivered as she gathered her bearings.

Growling, Rex looked at Max, Rocky, and Gizmo, one by one. "I am your escort for a reason. The Chairman will not have us playing with toys."

"But why?" Gizmo asked, swallowing the tremor in her voice and stepping forward with her head held high. "He won't even let you play at night after work is done?"

Rex grunted. "There is no time for play, runt. We must sleep and work. That's the only way to keep our new way of life from collapsing. Now come."

Rex turned and continued his march through the aisles, to the wire racks where the kibble lay stacked. As they got to work loading Max's wagon with a bag of kibble, Gizmo sidled up to Rocky.

"Not having any toys doesn't exactly sound luxurious to me," Gizmo said. "I wonder what the Chairman is thinking. Especially having his dogs yell at me like that." Her fur bristled as she looked over at Rex, who watched over the work, now bored.

"Hey, Giz," Rocky said, spitting out the corner of the bag he'd been dragging. "We've only been here a day. Maybe we only get toys after we prove ourselves. Right, Rex?"

Rex yawned and looked away, staring forlornly at the concrete walls of the storeroom. "Sure. Whatever you want to believe. Just do not touch them on my watch." He bared his teeth once more. "Got it?"

All three dogs nodded.

Max didn't join in the conversation. Of course the

Chairman wouldn't want distractions. He could argue, but the last thing they needed was more scoldings from Rex. Even with all his sleep, he still ached from his fight with Dolph, still felt so sad remembering how Raoul had looked lying there on the street. All he wanted to do was finish his assigned work for the day and then go lie down and wait to speak with Madame.

The three companions and their escort went back and forth several times that day, passing other dogs carrying wagons back and forth between the superstore and the Corporation. Occasionally, Max thought he caught sight of some of the mad mongrels lingering near the buildings beyond the patrolling guards, but every time he darted to look, they disappeared into the shadows behind abandoned cars, or mailboxes, or a pile of knocked-over garbage cans.

In the Corporation building, they were directed down a hallway between a sporting goods store and a restaurant, just off the promenade. It led to a bunch of blank, white rooms filled with metal tables, file cabinets, and corkboards on the walls. It was here that they unloaded and piled up the kibble. There was a young female Greyhound there, leading a procession of smaller dogs into each room. Each little dog carted a small wagon behind them, which they filled with kibble before darting off to go fill the empty bowls throughout the building.

Max had to admit, it was quite an efficient system.

As the day drew on, Max tried to make small talk with Rex and some of the other dogs they passed, to get their take on the human disappearance. But they all refused to even offer any sort of greeting, let alone any theories or clues. Soon Max gave up on attempting to chat with anyone other than Rocky or Gizmo. By the time evening came and the three dogs were released to collapse in their beds in the bookstore, they were too exhausted to do much more than go to sleep, even as Max idly wondered why Madame still hadn't come for him.

The week after was much the same: They'd rise, eat, and set to work until exhaustion took them into sleep at day's end. Despite what he'd told himself, Max found it easy to fall in line, to keep putting off looking for his people. He was just so tired, and he never had any energy to spare. He'd figure it all out tomorrow, he told himself.

And then tomorrow would come, and he'd forget about everything but doing his assigned work.

The other dogs were as sad and worn out as he was, and everyone fell into place with complete obedience. It wasn't hard for Max to understand why: There was work to be done to fill their days, to keep them from worrying about their lost pack leaders. There was a comfortable bed to go to each night and rise from each morning. There were three meals a day and endless, fresh, cool water. There was no threat of starvation, or attacks by wild animals, or shivering in the dark as chilly rain soaked their fur.

Living in the Corporation was a lot like being back at home.

But without any of the things that made home *home*.

After several days, the Chairman came down to the bottom floor of the Corporation building and circled the promenade with his entourage of Dobermans. Max, Rocky, and Gizmo watched from the doorway between the bookstore and the promenade as the Chairman barked out his evaluations. All the dogs sat obediently in the stores they'd made homes, and the endless music echoed throughout the hall, jaunty and upbeat.

"Lady!" the Chairman barked at the store with the pink walls, its shelves stocked with headbands and metal jewelry.

The Greyhound who oversaw the doling out of kibble stepped forward and bowed her head. As she did, one of the Chairman's Doberman companions whispered in his ear. He nodded, then turned his attention back to the dog, and her small helpers lined up behind her.

"Well, I'm glad to say that all your little assistants have been as silent and efficient as I commanded," the Chairman drawled. "Kudos to you."

Lady panted a smile, then turned back to her helpers. All of them wagged their tails.

"But I'm afraid, Lady, that you've been mixing up the flavors again," he said.

The Greyhound's ears drooped. "I...I did?"

"Those on the second level get the *pedigree* formula. It's the fourth level that gets lamb and rice."

"Oh," Lady said softly. "But I thought..."

"To training!" the Chairman bellowed.

One of his Dobermans stepped forward, growling, and nipped at Lady's side. Sighing, she got onto all fours and followed the Chairman's guard to the glass elevator. Max watched her as she passed the empty, dusty tables where humans once ate food from the restaurants and the big potted plants with the wide leaves to the glass elevator. All the while, the music played on, so happy and joyful that Lady's drooping tail and broken spirit seemed entirely out of place.

And then the Greyhound disappeared into the elevator and was whisked up above.

That done, the Chairman and his entourage sauntered across the promenade to the bookstore.

"He's coming this way," Rocky hissed.

"Act natural," Gizmo whispered. "I'm sure we did fine."

The Chairman's commanding scent was overwhelming as he approached—musky, almost like the wolves, but with some sort of aroma in it that whispered to Max's brain: *Obey.* Max went stiff as the Doberman stopped in front of the three dogs and looked over them appraisingly.

"You seem to have fit in well," the Chairman drawled at last. "Surprising."

"We do our best!" Gizmo said.

Walking to stand snout to snout with Max, the Chairman regarded the Lab with judgmental eyes. "You have scars," the Doberman said after a while. "You've been in fights. Not common for many of the domesticated dogs we take in here."

"I've had to fight," Max said, swallowing the growl in his throat. "It hasn't been an easy road for us."

The Chairman barked a laugh. "I can imagine. I have a new job for you, then. Our strength is in numbers, and so though I am loath to invite too many mongrels into our society, there are some in the streets who can benefit from what we offer."

"What do you offer, exactly?" Rocky asked.

"Safety," the Chairman said without looking at the Dachshund. "So, Max—your name is Max, yes?"

Max nodded.

"Max, you will be joining our scouting missions. These fall outside the guarded grounds. But I trust you can handle yourself."

"What do these...missions...involve?" Max asked, wary.

"You'll see." To Gizmo and Rocky, he said, "And you two have had enough time playing at carrying kibble. I'll send someone down with new assignments shortly."

Not waiting for any further questions, the Chairman turned and exited the bookstore with his entourage in tow.

"Wait!" Max barked.

The Chairman halted, then slowly turned to glare back at Max. "What is it?"

"It's Madame," Max said. "You told her I'm here, right? I still haven't heard from her, and it just seems strange that she wouldn't come talk to me."

The Chairman flicked his tail nub. "I told you already, Max, that Madame has an important role within the Corporation and is incredibly busy. She knows you are here. In fact, it was her high regard of you that led me to consider you for the scouting missions."

"It was?" Max asked.

The Chairman nodded. "Just keep to your tasks, Max. You'll see Madame when the time is right."

Not waiting for any further response, the Chairman and his entourage quickly walked away. Max watched them go, unease in his chest. It just didn't feel right that Madame would be here, would be so close, and it would take a whole week to even hear that she knew he'd arrived.

The scents in the air muddled Max's brain, as they always did. He was still too exhausted. He didn't want to think too much. Work would be fine. Work would keep him occupied.

But his family...

"Aw!" Rocky whined, plopping himself onto the carpeted floor after the Chairman's evaluation. "I thought as long as we were here, at least we'd be able to spend our days together."

"It'll be all right," Gizmo said. "We'll be doing something new! Hauling food gets boring fast."

The endless, looping music filled the store, and Max looked around. The lights were always on here, their beds always fluffed, their bellies always full. And there were thousands of books lying around just waiting to be chewed on if the mood hit. It wasn't *home*, but it was enough that if they weren't careful they could stay comfortable. *Too* comfortable.

"Are you two happy here?" Max asked softly.

"In the Corporation?" Rocky asked. His ears drooped. "After all we've gone through, it's a nice break, ya know? But . . . I wouldn't want to stay here forever."

"So you still want to find your people, right?" Max asked.

"Don't you?" Gizmo asked with a tilt of her head.

"Of course!" Max barked, much too loudly. "I mean, of course I do. That's the whole reason we came this far in the first place. But there's something about this place. . . ."

Rocky paced back and forth, looking around the store as well. "I know what ya mean, big guy," he said. "It's like, even with all the work, we get to be like *dogs* again. No making tough decisions. No fleeing from wolves. No fighting to eat. Just doing what we're told and living the simple life, with the Chairman as our pack leader."

Gizmo yipped angrily. "But there's more to life than this, Rocky. There's more to being a dog."

Max shuddered. "She's right. Not many of the other dogs here seem all that happy."

Gizmo lowered her head to rest it on her paws. "I bet if they had toys, they'd at least be a little happier. That would make it more like home. Maybe we can talk to the Chairman about it and he'd reconsider."

"Maybe," Rocky said, not sounding convinced.

"I still want to find our people," Max announced. "So we need to ask questions of any new dogs we work with, okay? Maybe we can find out where Madame is working, and we can go to her instead of waiting for her to come to us. She'll be able to tell us where to go next— I'm sure of it. Her bones will tell her the way."

Gizmo stood up, her tail wagging for the first time in days. "We're going to find our families, right, Max?"

"If the big guy says we're going to find them," Rocky said, "then we are going to find them. You can count on him. Me. *Both* of us."

Max smiled at them as best he could. They had faith in him. Now he just had to find the faith in himself again so that he could know for sure he could keep his friends safe.

Later that morning, two of the Chairman's Dobermans marched into the bookstore to collect Max. They were slightly smaller than the Chairman, but almost identical in appearance—sharp, dangerous features, and black-and-tan fur.

"I am Daisy," the female said. "This is Creature."

"Hi, I'm—" Max started to say.

Creature let out a sharp bark. "Atten*tion*."

Max went stiff all over.

The male Doberman nodded appreciatively. Turning, he commanded simply, "Come."

They walked through the promenade toward the front entrance. As they walked, Daisy chatted easily with Creature. "Hear we spotted a decent one from the fifth floor. Just a few roads over, too. Gonna be an easy bag-and-tag."

Creature snorted. "*Easy*. Who wants easy?"

"Excuse me?" Max asked. "Sorry to interrupt, but what's a bag—"

Daisy turned, abrupt, and snapped at him. "Just follow. No talking."

Swallowing back a growl, Max did as he was told.

The two brutish mutts who had escorted Max to the Chairman on his first day in the Corporation stood guard at the front doors. It was only then that Max realized that much like in the pet store, these dogs opened *and* guarded the doors. No one got in *or out* without their help. He watched as they pressed recessed buttons that turned the doors on with a hum, allowing the doors to slide open with a whoosh when the three dogs crossed their threshold.

The Chairman wasn't just using the electricity to keep everyone inside the Corporation comfortable. He was using it to keep them trapped.

This wasn't like the Enclave at all. Dandyclaw had nothing but his pitiful growl to try to keep people from leaving. The Chairman had learned from that—no one was going to get out unless he said so.

Max wasn't happy with that idea at all.

Max was escorted outside and to the front of the Corporation building, to an area that he hadn't seen before. There was a big open square here, much like the one where he, Gizmo, and Rocky had come up from the subway tunnels before the wolves attacked. In the center of this square was a concrete fountain sputtering streams of water that sparkled in the morning light, and dozens and dozens of leafy green trees grew from designated plots at each corner.

"Oh, how wonderful," Max barked. "It's like a giant bath!" Turning to Daisy, he asked, "Do you think I can—"

"No," Daisy barked back. Sharp. Commanding. "The Chairman's fountain is to be left alone."

"But the Chairman was the one who said I smelled, so—"

Creature sighed. "Let it go, mutt. We're not here to splash around in water. We have a mission."

Before, Max would have argued with the dogs. Told them he could do whatever he wanted. But something in him felt like it was Charlie or Emma reprimanding him instead. "No," they would have said. "Bad boy. Down from the fountain." It was no different, really. Was it?

The two Dobermans walked in perfect, matching strides to the narrow street just past the fountain. Max shook his head, then raced to keep up. "I'm still not sure what the mission is, exactly," he said.

"Just keep in line," Daisy commanded without looking back. "You'll pick it up."

The Dobermans led Max down an alley where a green Dumpster had somehow been tipped over, its contents strewn all across the small street. Many animals must have been here, Max thought while looking at the torn-open garbage sacks. Foraging for food, while the Chairman hoarded all the pet store's food for himself.

Daisy sniffed at the garbage, then nodded at Creature. Silently, they picked their way through the refuse and continued on their way. Max bounded over the torn trash bags and almost barreled into his two escorts, who'd stopped short at the end of the alley.

"Quiet," Creature hissed. "Look."

Max peered past the two Dobermans and saw a dog about his size sniffing at another Dumpster in an alley across the road. Its breed was hard to guess, since its fur was a matted mess and the poor dog had grown so skinny. But unlike the mad dogs who had chased Max, Rocky, and Gizmo before they'd gone underground, Max could tell that this dog still had an alertness in its eyes that seemed smart.

"That's the one," Daisy said. To Max, she whispered,

"This is your training lesson, got it? Watch and help if we need you. Otherwise stay quiet."

Max only nodded, unsure what to say.

"Don't move!" Creature bellowed as he and Daisy crept up on the mongrel.

The mongrel stiffened and yelped, dropping from where she had set her paws against the Dumpster and backing against the alley wall.

"N-no!" she cried out. "Please, no! I can't go there!"

"You are being claimed by the Corporation," Daisy announced as the two Dobermans came to tower over the shivering mongrel. "You can either come with us voluntarily, or as our prisoner."

"But either way," Creature growled, "you're coming with us."

The mutt cowered down low to the ground, her back against the wall. "I don't know what the Chairman does in there, but I'm not going," she howled. "I'd rather be free and starve than be his slave!"

"Not an option," Daisy barked. "Max! Come! Now!"

Swallowing back his disgust, Max darted across the road and came up beside the two Dobermans.

Daisy glared at Max and jerked her head toward the mutt. "Go around behind her and force her to stand. She is not to get away."

"But why are you forcing her?" Max asked. To the mutt, he said, "It's not so bad at the Corporation, is it? You'll have food and water—"

The mongrel bared her teeth and narrowed her eyes. "You don't know what you're talking about. I've seen friends go in there. They're not the same when they get marched through the streets, dragging wagons and guarding buildings like they were trained for it. They'd never follow orders from anyone unless something was done to them!"

"Don't talk to her," Creature commanded. "Nip her until she stands."

"But—" Max started to protest.

"Do it."

Max did as he was told—snapping behind the dog until she yelped and jumped to four trembling feet. The Dobermans growled at her and snapped their teeth as well and, cowed, she began to walk.

"Please don't make me," she whimpered as she was forced across the road and into the alley filled with garbage.

Max bit back the urge to turn and run, taking the mongrel with him. He couldn't leave Rocky and Gizmo behind, for one. And this dog would be better off after being fed. She didn't know what she was talking about. The Corporation was an easier life. A safer life.

It took a while, but the two Dobermans and Max managed to force the mongrel to march all the way past the fountain to the front doors of the Corporation. She sat there, shivering and whining, while the two burly dogs unlocked the door and let it whoosh open.

"I won't go in," she whimpered, glaring defiantly up at the two big, dangerous Dobermans.

Daisy met Creature's eyes and nodded. As one, they lunged toward the mongrel, Daisy biting into her shoulder and Creature her haunches. The mongrel screamed in pain, but the Dobermans didn't care. They carried her inside even as she squirmed, trying to break free.

Stunned, Max could only wander aimlessly past the threshold, into the Corporation building. The sliding doors behind him whooshed shut, landing heavily together with a resounding *click*.

Max watched as the Dobermans dropped the mongrel inside the glass elevator. They nodded to the big dog who operated the control panel, and a moment later the mongrel's anguished cries were muffled by glass.

Daisy and Creature sauntered back across the promenade to Max, their expressions pleased. "Ready for another?" Creature asked Max.

Max knew that if he tried to speak, he'd be unable to keep himself from roaring and attacking these Dobermans in his anger. Instead, he kept his mouth shut and nodded.

Deep inside, though, Max knew that what he'd just taken part in was something horrible. Dog turning against dog—it was even worse than wolves versus dogs. He would refuse to be involved with a Corporation that would do such things. Worrying about the wolves prowling the streets, or never finding his people, or feeling guilt over Raoul—none of it mattered when the alternative to continuing his journey was *this*.

Resolved, Max decided that he was going to need to save his strength for later—when he, Rocky, and Gizmo would find Madame, learn where the people were, and then get out of this terrible place and leave it far, far behind.

CHAPTER 23

THE SEARCH

Max's anger boiled deep within him all day long. He had to watch and *help* the two Dobermans bring in three more scrounging mutts from outside. All were terrified. All ended up complying.

Worse, as they combed through the city, Max saw that they weren't the only hunting parties. Other roving Corporation dog gangs—Dobermans and Pit Bulls and Rottweilers, the Chairman's biggest and baddest trained beasts—darted through alleys, seeking out new conscripts for the Chairman's growing army.

By early evening, Daisy and Creature decided they'd filled their quota for the day. Now all that remained was to prepare the captured dogs for their "training."

"It is not required, but you are welcome to come and

observe," Daisy told Max. "I'm sure the Chairman would take note of your willingness to serve, especially after the excellent job you did today."

Max swallowed back the bile in his throat. Thinking of Rocky's expert lies to the rats in the subway, he tried to mimic the smaller dog's convincing tone. "I think I should rest so I can be in even better shape tomorrow. Maybe then I can learn more about the training."

Both Daisy and Creature glared into Max's eyes, their gazes dark and unreadable. Finally, Daisy dismissed Max with a flick of her sharp ears, saying, "Fine."

Relieved, Max padded through the sliding glass door back into the bookstore that was his temporary home. He ate a few tasteless mouthfuls of kibble, drank his fill of water, then plopped into his bed, waiting, trying to keep his anger in check.

He needed to get out of this place.

Rocky and Gizmo weren't back yet. The lilting human music was soft in the air, and Max felt his heart beat softly to match its calming beats. The room was so warm. And the Chairman's commanding scent was everywhere—subtle, but there. Telling Max instinctively to fall in line. To live here in the luxury of the Corporation.

Eyes drooping, Max almost forgot the horrible day. Almost fell asleep.

The bookstore's doors opened and shut, and doggy

paws padded over the carpet between the bookshelves. Blinking, Max looked up to find a grumpy Rocky and a disgruntled Gizmo marching to their respective beds.

"What happened?" Max asked.

Rocky took a giant bite of kibble and, mouth full, wailed, "Oh, buddy, it was horrible!"

Gizmo dropped to her belly, ears drooping as she rested her head on her paws. "It really was. And I don't say that often."

Swallowing, Rocky gulped up some water, then flopped onto his back. "They made us go into a room with a bunch of other dogs. And all day long, they kept making us go through the same exercises over and over and over."

"Sit," Gizmo said. "Stand. Roll over. Play dead."

Max tilted his head. "Like pet tricks? My pack leaders taught me those. They aren't so bad."

Rocky flopped a paw over his head. "Those weren't the bad ones," he said. "They also told us to attack. And we had to be in perfect formation or they wouldn't give us even a pebble of kibble."

"They made me beg," Gizmo said softly. "Over and over, and everyone laughed."

"But why?" Max asked.

Rolling over, Rocky got to his feet and waddled over to his bed. "The Chairman wants us all trained," he said. "He wants us all *perfect*." Opening his jaws wide, Rocky yawned and then plopped onto his bed. "But at least we're here now. Where it's so warm, and there's so much food."

Moaning comfortably, Gizmo said, "And there's such pretty music."

Both of the smaller dogs closed their eyes. Max almost did the same. Sleep would be nice. Especially with a full belly, and in such a nice place...

A voice in the back of Max's mind bellowed at him. Begged him to remember the screaming of the dogs they'd captured. The horrible things they'd all faced that day.

And so, struggling against all his instincts, Max forced himself to wake up and stand.

"Rocky!" he barked. "Gizmo! Wake up!"

Both dogs awoke with a start. "What is it, big guy?" Rocky asked. "I'm getting my beauty sleep over here."

With his jaws, Max grabbed Rocky by the nape of his neck and lifted the small dog off his bed, then set him next to Gizmo.

"Hey, I got legs!"

"Whoa!" Gizmo said, darting up as Rocky fell beside her. "Wow, what's going on?"

Max shook his head. "There's something bad going on here," he said. "Don't you see? Everything we're asked to do, everything about the other dogs here, is wrong. Why are we being forced to do the tasks we're doing? Why can't we see Madame for even a minute? But we come back here each night exhausted, and something about this building is just so comfortable that we forget ourselves and fall in behind the Chairman. We need to snap out of it!"

Blinking, Gizmo tilted her head and said, "You're right. Of course, you're right! Wow, I can't believe I almost just fell asleep."

"I can," Rocky grumbled. "My bed is so comfy."

Max paced, studying the shelves around them as though they might hold the answer. "I smelled it earlier, I think," he said. "The Chairman's scent. It's everywhere, this is his territory, and because of that, I feel like I should listen to him. But we can't, guys. We need to escape before we become mindless slaves like the rest of the dogs here—or worse, mean dogs like the Chairman's special Dobermans."

Rocky took in a long, deep drag of air, then, scrunching his nose, backed away as though he could escape the smell. "You're right, buddy," he said. "The Chairman is *everywhere* in here. But not like he marked his territory—more like it's in the air! How could he have done that? Did he leave his scent in all the air vents or something?"

"I don't know," Max said. "But that seems like a good explanation to me."

"Oh, I knew I didn't like him," Gizmo growled, her eyes narrowed. "I remember watching him and Dandyclaw at the Enclave. He acted like he was Dandyclaw's sidekick, but one day they went into the woods, we all heard fighting, and Dandyclaw came back alone. Limping. I'd never seen Pinky the Poodle look so scared. But that was when Dandyclaw started acting strange about letting us leave the Enclave, too."

"I'm glad we missed the Chairman," Max said.

"Wanna know the best part?" Gizmo asked, then giggled. "Back then, he wasn't called the Chairman. His name was *Precious*."

"Ha!" Rocky said. "More like *Vicious*."

Max wasn't really in a laughing mood. Already he could feel his resolve starting to go fuzzy around the edges, to begin to fade. He marched past Rocky and Gizmo, heading toward the bookstore exit.

"Come on, guys," he called behind him. "Let's get out of here while it's dark. We need to find Madame. She could be as trapped as us by the Chairman; we need to get her out of here, too."

"Yay!" Gizmo yipped. "Okay! I'm so glad we have our *real* leader back. I'm tired of Precious the Chairman."

The two small dogs at his heels, Max reached the sliding doors that opened into the promenade. Only, when he stood in front, they didn't open. He tried nudging the crack between the door with his nose to find some way to force the door open, but nothing happened.

"Is it locked?" Rocky asked. "How could they just lock us in here?"

Max thought for a moment, then remembered what he'd seen earlier in the day—the burly dogs at the front exit and the buttons they pressed to make the doors work. Maybe . . .

"Hey, Gizmo," Max said. "Check in the corner of the doors and see if there's a little button."

Gizmo darted to the side of the door and sniffed. "Oh, there is!" she said. "It's hidden by these shelves, but I think I can just reach it."

Stretching out with her paw, she grasped behind a bookshelf that was pressed right up to the wall. For a moment, all Max could hear were their doggy breaths, the endless store music, and the scratching of Gizmo's claws against wood.

And then, with a click and a whoosh, the doors slid apart.

"Come on!" Max said, his voice hushed. "We need to get to the elevator and go upstairs. I bet you we'll find Madame on the floors we haven't been to."

The promenade was dark, the lights off. But it wasn't pitch-black—low evening light from the stores all around it sent long shadows over the tiles. And the floodlights out front lit up the exit.

With Rocky and Gizmo following him, Max crouched down behind the planters and benches that lined the walkway and led them as quietly as he could toward the elevator. His heart pounded as he crawled—he saw no guards, but it couldn't be so easy to escape, could it?

Trying not to question his luck, he jumped up to examine the control panel. The dog who usually stood watch over the elevator had made it seem simple enough— just press the button with your nose, and the doors opened. Max shoved his snout against the cool steel button, and a moment later, the glass doors opened.

As Max and his friends crowded into the elevator, he asked them, "What floor should we try first?"

"Well," Rocky said, "we've been to the very top. That button toward the bottom must be for here, since it's the button they always click to bring us back to the bookstore. I'm pretty sure it's not the middle buttons; Giz and I have been to all those, and I never saw anyone who looked like your friend."

"What about the button right beneath the very top one?" Gizmo asked. "I don't think even the little dogs who fill the food dishes go there!"

"It's worth a shot," Max said. Leaping up, he pressed the button with his nose.

It lit up, and a moment later the car was rising through the dark promenade, the stores below cast in deep shadows. Max didn't see a single dog—most were probably sleeping, and the Chairman probably expected the locked doors to keep everyone inside.

No one spoke as the elevator took them past floor after darkened, empty floor. The Corporation building was eerily silent; Max remembered his time in the kennels, when there was barking at all times of the day.

The Chairman had trained his dogs well.

Finally, the elevator hummed to a stop, and the doors slid open.

Max, Rocky, and Gizmo emptied out into a hallway

lit dimly with pale lights set in the ceiling. The floor could have been like any of the others above the promenade and shops—hallways with seating and potted plants, and artwork hung on the walls between doors that opened into bigger rooms.

But unlike those floors, it was surprisingly cold, as though the Chairman had turned the temperature down to freezing even while he let the other dogs live in perfect warmth.

The air was stale, as if no one had breathed it in a while. As Max sniffed, he realized he didn't sense the Chairman's overwhelming scent. But he did smell something else.

Something familiar.

Madame.

"She's here," Max whispered. "She's here! I smell her! Come on!"

Following his nose, Max dashed down the carpeted hallway. She was through a darkened doorway at the very end, he could tell.

And as he grew near, other smells met his nose. Waste. Blood.

"Madame?" Max called out, not caring if anyone could hear him. His heart began to thud as he realized something was very wrong in that room. "Madame!"

He burst through the doorway, blinking his eyes as he looked around the black room, trying to find her in the dim light that shone in from the hallway. He could see the shadowy form of a dog lying in the center of the room, but he couldn't tell if it was her or not.

"Maxie?" a familiar voice croaked. "Oh, Maxie, is that you?"

"It's me," Max whispered, taking a step forward. He sensed Rocky and Gizmo galloping up behind him.

As he moved deeper into the room, Madame became clearer. Same smiling, wise eyes. Same black fur, studded with white like the stars in the night sky. Same collar with the three golden connected rings that glittered against her dark fur.

Only her legs were twisted at odd angles. And she was skinnier than she'd been when last he saw her. Much too skinny.

"Oh, Maxie," she sighed, resting her weary head on her front paws. "We have so much to discuss."

CHAPTER 24

YES, MADAME

◆

"Oh my!" Gizmo yipped upon seeing the poor old Lab lying there, broken. "You're hurt!" She darted forward and immediately began licking at Madame's legs, their fur matted and stained.

Madame winced but did not shout. Softly, she said, "It's okay, little terrier. There's nothing you can do. My legs have been broken and will never heal."

"Never...?" Max whispered. "Madame, what happened? Did you fall?"

"No," the old dog wheezed. "Precious did this to me. The moment he had his lackeys, they set upon me. They broke me and left me here to die. I never should have trusted him, but...I was desperate."

By now, Max could almost see the room in its entirety.

It might have been a people meeting room—it was long and rectangular, and a big table took up most of the space in the center. Chairs were stacked in the corners, and one wall was all windows looking out over the dark, abandoned city.

Madame lay beneath the table, curled on a pile of paper scraps. Next to her were two empty dishes, both bone-dry. Neither had been filled in ages.

And it was so cold. Max couldn't imagine how Madame could stand it, with her fur falling away and ribs showing through her skin. He trembled at the sight of her, despaired and angry all at once. But mostly, he was confused.

"I don't understand," he whimpered. "Madame, why did you leave Vet's? Why did you travel with the Chairman? What did your warnings mean?"

"Maxie, my boy, it's a long story." Madame chuckled, but the laughter quickly gave way to coughing.

Gizmo grabbed one of the bowls in her jaws, then ran up to Rocky, who watched with wide eyes. "Here," the little dog said. "I'll get the other one. Let's find her some water. There has to be a people bathroom around here."

When both dogs had disappeared down the hallway, Max slowly nuzzled Madame. "May I lie next to you?" he said. "You must be so cold."

"Am I?" Madame mused. "I suppose I must be. I've been beyond feeling cold for a while now, pup. But please do. I would love the company."

Max lay down behind her and curled up close, careful not to jostle her. Guilt threatened to overtake him—all this time he'd worried more about finding out her secrets than how she'd been faring. He'd spent a whole week in the Corporation, just waiting around to speak to her. A week! If he'd come for her sooner...

He was whimpering despite himself, and Madame shushed him. "It's all right, Maxie," she said softly. "I've lived a long, long time. I'm just glad you found me before I passed on."

"Passed on?" Max whispered. "No..."

"It's all right," she said again. "But listen to me, Maxie. There is much you should know."

Rocky and Gizmo appeared in the doorway, both shoving dishes with their noses over the carpet. Water sloshed over the edges, but most stayed in the bowls. Madame gave them her thanks, lapped up her fill, and began her story.

"My pack leader is a scientist," she began. "I spent years and years by her side in her labs, both at places she worked and at her home. She named me after her idol, a fact I always took pride in, let me tell you. We both grew old, and soon we never went to the big labs anymore. We just stayed at her home.

"In the days before she took me to stay with Vet, she'd started receiving frantic phone calls, about what, I don't know. But it was enough to raise my hackles and get my old bones creaking in worry. My pack leader

317

worked a lot with animals, you see. Not just dogs, but all kinds. And if she was getting phone calls when she was so old, well—that meant that something was happening with us. With us animals."

"That makes sense," Max said. "We've seen so much coming here, heard so many stories. People being dragged away from their pets. *X*s painted over animal pictures."

"I never found out for sure what was going on. She seemed worried when she dropped me off at Vet's, but not so much that she didn't trust me to be there for my usual checkup. I do remember my pack leader and Vet having quite the nervous conversation, but I didn't pay it as much mind as I should have.

"All I know is, the night before the people all left, I felt a dread inside me, Maxie. Deep inside. When Vet came to open our cages that next morning, I couldn't bear the thought of you out on the streets with the panic I could sense in the air. So I shut your cage before I ran out. I hated to do it, but I didn't want you getting hurt, and I thought maybe I could come back for you when it was safe, or that you'd be able to get out on your own...." She sighed. "I felt horrible when I couldn't go back. I'm so glad you did find a way out."

"So that's how you got locked in!" Rocky exclaimed. "See, I told you Vet would never have left you trapped. You gotta trust me on these things, big guy."

Max didn't respond. He shifted so that he could hug Madame closer, with one paw over her narrow, sickly chest. He could feel her heart beat softly and slowly, and he closed his eyes.

"I ended up in the Enclave," Madame went on. "Though it wasn't called that at first. When I showed up, it was just the Poodle, the Doberman, and a Collie they'd rescued from some men in special white suits."

"Special suits?" Gizmo asked.

"These big, baggy white suits humans wear to protect them from getting sick," she explained. "That's what my pack leader said when we were together in the labs.

"Anyway, it didn't take me long to realize that Pinky the Poodle wasn't all well in the head after his owners kicked him out. He was territorial but also never wanted to be alone. He decided that the Enclave's clearing was his, and he was going to fill it with dogs who would be with him forever. I didn't much like the idea of sitting around doing nothing, not when my pack leader was out there somewhere, trying to fix whatever was happening, so when Precious decided to leave, I went with him."

She hacked a cough, and Max almost jumped. His eyes snapped back open, and he met his old friend's gaze. "You need to rest," he said. "And drink some water. We can talk more later."

"We won't have time, Maxie," she said. "Just listen."

Max gazed out the windows at the other end of the room, focusing on the brilliant stars in the night sky as he did as he was asked and listened.

"We were headed to the city," Madame went on. "I

knew from here I could find my way, and Precious could find other dogs to help. Only Precious kept getting more and more vicious. I figured it was irritation at our situation, just a young dog acting out, and so I agreed to help him set up his Corporation. I showed him how to use the buttons to open the doors and use the elevator. But then he started asking how he could keep all the other dogs we'd invited in line with what he wanted....

"I tried to head things off and help the other dogs escape—and that was when he had his new sidekicks attack me and trap me here." She sighed. "Silly, silly me. I should have just gone on by myself. Luckily, I have you now, Maxie. You can go on for me."

"Go on where?" Gizmo asked. "Max said you might know where all the people went. Do you?"

"I have ideas," Madame said. "I heard my pack leader on the phone. The people needed to go to the coasts, to the oceans. It's not just a safe haven, but she believed something about the ocean was the answer. And the easiest way to find an ocean is to follow a river."

"A river?" Rocky asked. "We came from one of those. We rode on a raft."

"Sounds exciting!"

"Eh," Rocky said with a shake of his body, "I could have done without it."

Madame chuckled raspily.

"So the people can be found by following a river," Max said.

"And wouldn't you know it, Maxie, but the river you were riding on curves down below the city before heading south again. You'll just need to escape the Corporation and get there, and then you'll be on your way."

"*Our* way," Max said forcefully. "We'll find a way to get you out of here, too, Madame. We'll take you to your pack leader, too."

For a moment, Madame didn't say anything. Max watched as her long, pink tongue darted out of her black snout to lap up more water. As she drank, his eyes drifted to the spots on the back of her neck where fur had fallen out. He winced at the sight—then blinked when he noticed something tattooed in her now-exposed skin, just above where the collar rested.

Three connected rings in a row. The same symbol on her collar, only represented in fading black ink.

"Madame?" Max asked. "That symbol on your collar. It's on your neck, too. Does it mean something?"

Her thirst slaked, Madame responded, "It's a symbol that was important to my pack leader. If you see it, she could be around."

"That's great!" Max said. "That means it will be easy to find her and reunite the two of you."

For a long moment, Madame did not say anything.

"Madame?" Max asked softly.

The older dog sighed. "I'd love to go with you, Maxie. And oh, how I'd love to see my pack leader again." Her voice almost cracked. "But I can't risk what happened to me happening to you. You're too young to end up crippled and starving."

"That won't happen!" Max barked. He got up onto all fours and began to pace back and forth beside the long table. "We'll go downstairs, and we'll get one of the wagons they use to carry kibble around. We'll put you in it and take you with us. It'll be easy!"

"Listen to him," Rocky said. "We're expert wagon carriers. You'll love the ride!"

"I know I would," Madame said, her sad brown eyes on Max's own. "But Maxie, the Chairman is even worse than you've seen. Any dog who gets out of line he locks up to die. There are others besides me. I just got the special privilege of dying alone because he was worried about what I know. If you try to take me with you, there's no way you'll escape. You have to go alone."

"I won't," Max said, growling stubbornly.

"You *must*," she said. "Your family needs you. My pack leader will help save the other dogs—all the animals. I know it. You must leave here and get to the river. Follow it to the ocean, and only stop if you see the three circles. This is the only way you'll be safe. Promise me, Maxie."

"I—" Max started to say, still defiant, still refusing to see another friend sacrifice herself to help him.

"Promise me!" Madame bellowed, louder than Max would have thought possible. Her bark echoed through the cold, dark, empty room.

Limbs trembling, Max lowered his head. "Yes, Madame."

"And you two, you're his friends," she said, turning her gaze to Gizmo and Rocky. "You keep an eye out for him just as much as he does for you. All right?"

The two small dogs nodded. "Yes, Madame," they responded in unison.

"Good pups," she said warmly, closing her eyes and lowering her head. She let out a long, contented sigh. "I thought I'd have to go alone," she said softly. "Unfulfilled. Thank you for finding me."

"You're not alone," Max whispered back, laying his head next to hers. Wordlessly, Rocky and Gizmo joined him, and all four dogs cuddled together, sharing their warmth.

"I so liked knowing you," Madame wheezed. "I liked the sun. But I liked the moon, too. I liked the fireplace, and the radiator in the den. There was that one chew toy that made the best squeak. And I liked..."

She trailed off, and her breathing slowed until it stopped altogether. A moment later, Max could no longer hear her heartbeat.

For a long moment, Max, Rocky, and Gizmo stayed there, eyes closed, sharing Madame's final bed.

One by one, Rocky, then Gizmo, and finally Max left Madame's side. There was nothing they could do for her now—and they'd made a promise. They needed to escape and reach the river.

As they walked down the dim hallway back toward the elevator, they heard its doors open with a hiss and a whoosh.

Max, Rocky, and Gizmo stopped in their tracks as a small army of dogs surged down the hall toward them. They were the Chairman's fierce, focused, perfectly trained dogs: several Rottweilers and Pit Bulls, a Malamute, and a Chow. At the lead were four of the Chairman's Dobermans—including Daisy and Creature.

Max was filled with sadness at leaving Madame behind, but he had to set it aside now. Otherwise, her death would mean nothing.

And Max was determined that it would mean something.

So he held his head high, confident, as the Chairman's troops came near.

Daisy shook her head and sighed as all the dogs stopped and sat in unison. "I had hoped better of you, Max," she said. "You did good work today, and for a domesticated dog, you know how to fight. You could have been useful. But here we find you sneaking around in forbidden areas."

"I guess I'm no more use to the Chairman, after all," Max said, taking a step forward. "So I suppose me and my friends here should go on our way and live with the wild dogs you want nothing to do with."

"I'm afraid," Creature growled, "that it doesn't work that way." Looking back over his shoulder, the Doberman let out a harsh, guttural bark.

The dozens of trained dogs surged around them. Half went left, the other half right. In a flash, they'd surrounded Max, Gizmo, and Rocky, their teeth bared, growls in their throats.

"Move!" Daisy commanded. "To the elevator. On your own, or we can drag you there."

Yipping in anger, Gizmo darted forward. "Not on your life, lady!"

"Giz!" Rocky cried out. "Don't! You'll get hurt!"

Daisy leaped, jaws open wide to grab the little terrier around her middle.

"Wait!" Max shouted.

Daisy stopped just short of biting. Gizmo did not move, did not let her angry expression drop.

Ducking his head, Max stepped over Gizmo, forcing Daisy to back away. "We'll go," he said. "Just don't hurt us."

Laughing, Daisy backed up to stand next to Creature. "The choice of whether or not anyone gets hurt is up to you."

Max looked down at Gizmo, then at Rocky. He nodded, trying to wordlessly reassure them. Then he marched to the glass elevator. He heard Rocky and Gizmo follow.

At the elevator, Creature leaped up to press the button to open the door. As the trained army of dogs continued to watch, endlessly growling, Daisy and Creature nipped at the three dogs' backsides until they were fully inside the elevator. Then Creature came inside, jumped up to press another button, and quickly leaped out of the elevator before the door could close and trap him inside.

"Nothing can ever be easy," Rocky moaned as the doors clapped shut. "First poor old Madame, and now this. The world has always gotta make everything so difficult!"

"It'll be okay," Gizmo said, gently nuzzling Rocky's side. "Max has got a plan. Don't you, Max?"

Max opened his jaws to answer, but before he could, the elevator started to move down. They descended through the shadowy floors of the building and into the promenade.

But instead of stopping at the main floor, the elevator kept going down.

"Whoa, what's happening?" Rocky asked, leaping up to stand at full attention.

"I think we're going below," Max said, watching as the floor of the promenade seemed to rise, enveloping the elevator in darkness.

"To the subways again?" Gizmo asked as they were completely enshrouded in black. "Why would we go there?"

"I don't think so," Max said.

A brief moment later, the elevator stopped. It was

still dark when the glass door whooshed open to reveal another door—this one cool metal. Max wondered if they were going to be trapped in this elevator—until the metal door slid open with a hiss. Weak yellow light flooded over them.

Standing just outside the elevator door was the Chairman. Behind him were more of the stiff trained dogs, sitting obediently, listening quietly.

The Chairman sniffed, then rolled his dark eyes. "What a waste. Come, Max. Your friends, too."

The large Doberman turned on his heels and marched into a dark open area that seemed to be made entirely of concrete. Here and there were large pillars that rose to hold up the roof, and Max could see the shadows of abandoned human cars. It was some sort of underground parking lot.

Max hesitated, eyes darting to see if there was an exit they could run to.

"*Come!*" the Chairman bellowed.

Immediately, six of his dogs blocked the entrance to the elevator, teeth bared. Silently, Max bowed his head and marched out onto the cool concrete, his friends behind him. He hated acting cowed like this. But he had to, at least for now.

The six dogs circled Max and his companions as they marched to where the Chairman stood waiting near a chain-link fence that spanned the entire parking lot. Once there, the dogs pulled back to block the trio's escape—and to let the Chairman pace.

The Doberman shook his head in disgust as he walked back and forth in front of Max. "I gave you a chance to be a part of something," the Chairman said. "But rather than join my new society, you chose to try to defy me."

"You're just like Dandyclaw, you know that, Precious?" Gizmo suddenly yipped. "So insecure that you can't risk letting anyone do as they please!"

Max stiffened, prepared for the Chairman to leap at her as Daisy had done above. Instead, the Chairman met her eyes and chuckled.

"Yes, you would think that," he drawled. "But this isn't about insecurities, my dear pup. This is about how a civilized canine society *should* be. One in charge, the rest obedient at my feet. Otherwise we will fall into chaos like the dogs on the street, and really, who of us wants to live in chaos? It's so..." He shivered.

"Civilized, huh?" Rocky growled. "We saw what you did to Madame! What's so civilized about breaking a dog's legs and leaving her to die?"

"She didn't listen to my philosophy, runt," the Chairman snapped. Pacing once more, he continued, "You see, I envision a world where all dogs are part of the solution instead of causing endless problems. And so, once you are part of my Corporation, you are to fall in line or…" This time, the Doberman met Max's eyes. "You are to be broken until you have no choice but to be a good soldier. Madame made her choice when she tried to spark a mutiny. It seems you've made your choice as well."

Turning from the three dogs, the Chairman bellowed sharp commands. The tall tan dog who operated the elevator walked up to a door in the fence, near which a control panel of some sort sat atop a pole. Nudging the buttons on the control panel with her nose, the chain-link door slid open with squeaks of wheels and a tinny clang of metal hitting metal.

The dogs behind Max, Rocky, and Gizmo leaped forward, barking and nipping at their haunches, forcing them forward until they were past the threshold of the open door. They turned and watched, unable to do anything as the tall dog once again pressed buttons and the fence door clanged closed, locking them in.

The Chairman peered through the fence at them, his entire self a shadow because of the dim yellow light behind him. "Enjoy your stay," he said. "I'm sure you'll find your fellow problem dogs to be *interesting* company."

With another laugh, the Chairman sauntered away, his obedient soldiers following behind, leaving Max and his friends trapped.

CHAPTER 25

PRISONERS

The underground parking lot was silent until the Chairman and his guard dogs disappeared into the elevator. The doors clicked shut, a motor hummed, and they were gone.

That was when the other "problem" dogs emerged. The dogs Madame said had been locked up to die, just like her.

Max smelled the other dogs long before he could see them: damp, sweaty fur and festering sores and sickly breath. It was dark beyond the fence—none of the lights were on in this section, and Max strained to see from the low lights behind them.

They huffed and snarled, their footsteps heavy against the concrete. Ahead was a rickety wooden shack of some sort, and from behind it Max could see the shadows of the nearest dogs.

"Hello?" Gizmo called out. "Hi! We've been put here by the Chairman, too. We're friends!"

Her genial words were met with wheezing, mocking laughter. The nearest shadows came closer, revealing skinny dogs with tangled fur and scratches covered in dried blood. There were more than Max had thought, dozens and dozens of them, all different sizes, though most were as big as Max—clearly, the bigger dogs were considered more of a threat by the Chairman.

"You hear that, Hog?" an old female called from the darkness. "We got us some new friends."

Another dog snorted. "Friends, huh?" he belched, his voice rubbed raw. "Real friends keep you fed. You got us some food, sweetie? Got us some bones to gnaw?"

"'Course she does, Hog," the female called again, emerging into the pool of dim light to reveal herself as a woolly dog so covered in gray fur that her eyes were hidden. "All dogs got bones with 'em. Some you just gotta dig into a bit first."

The woolly dog cackled, and the shadowy dogs behind her joined in, their mad laughter echoing through the pillars of the garage.

"Oh, they're crazy," Rocky grumbled. "Great. Are we the only sane dogs left in the world? We can't be, can we?"

"Sure seems like it," Max muttered.

Ears drooping, Gizmo backed away from the woolly dog to stand beside Max. So far, the old female was the only dog to show herself. The rest seemed to enjoy the darkness.

Max cleared his throat. "We aren't here to cause trouble," he called. "We're here for the same reason you are—we don't want to follow the Chairman."

The old woolly dog cackled again. "Oh, you're a sweet one, ain't you," she barked. "Thinking you know why we here. Hog! Hog, you show these new ones what happens to most of us. Scare us up some of the *real* crazies—the first ones."

Roaring barks boomed through the parking lot, and Max jumped, surprised by the sudden vicious noise. A moment later, a massive muscled brown dog with a drooping face raced forward, chasing four smaller dogs into the light.

The four dogs were so skinny that Max could see their entire skeletons through their loose flesh. Fur had fallen away to reveal pink skin. The dogs, riled up from being chased by Hog, pulled back their lips to bare their teeth—but many of their teeth were missing. They barked, but the sounds were desperate wheezes.

"You see now?" the woolly dog said. "This is what we are or will be, you stupid pups. We ain't friends. We're dead dogs walking." Cackling, she and Hog disappeared into the shadows. The hissing, emaciated dogs limped after them.

"Ohhh," Rocky moaned. "Max, this is bad, buddy. This is real bad."

"I hate the Chairman so much," Gizmo whispered. "And I don't hate *anybody*. The Chairman is just...he's a bad dog. A bad, bad dog!"

Max tried to control his trembling limbs as he looked at the dogs watching them from the shadows. First poor Madame, now this. Some dogs still snarled; others had grown silent. None of them made a move toward them.

"Okay," Max said after a moment. "Any ideas from the idea dog? Rocky?"

Rocky tilted his head. "I'm still stuck on the whole trapped with wild dogs part," he yipped. "But, uh... well, actually, how come none of the dogs are coming at us? Why are they all hiding?"

"You think they can't handle the light?" Gizmo wondered aloud. Then, stepping forward, she shouted into the darkness. "Hey! Are you dogs afraid of the light or something?"

More than one canine broke into boisterous laughter at that. "You got us!" one called. "We're afraid of the light! It's just so spooky."

Gizmo shook her head up at Max. "Guess it's not that."

"What other reason could they have to hide in the dark?" Max asked.

"Maybe they were told to stay in the shadows and scare us," Rocky said. "Yeah, that's probably it. I bet the

Chairman told them to in order to spook us." Lowering his voice, he said, "And I gotta say, big guy, they're doing a good job."

"Isn't the whole reason they're down here because they *didn't* listen to the Chairman, though?" Gizmo asked.

"Good point," Max said. "Both of you. Maybe it's just that these dogs have their own leader, like every pack we've come across. He or she must be trying to put us in line, just like the Chairman and Dandyclaw and Dolph. They're trying to act all tough and in charge, even though they're trapped."

"Maybe if they had a new leader to follow, they'd help him try to escape," Rocky said, his tail beginning to wag slowly.

Her tail joining in a happy blur, Gizmo looked up at Max with her tongue happily hanging out. "A leader like Max, maybe?"

Max laughed. "If you insist." He shook his head. "It feels really good to be able to think things through again, doesn't it? I'm so glad to be away from the Chairman's stupid controlling scent."

"But Max," Rocky said, "what if you can't take down the old leader?"

"I think I might have an advantage," Max said, already padding forward with his snout held up proudly. "I just had a full meal a little while ago, after all. When do you think is the last time anyone here ate well?"

Halfway between the fence and the wooden shack, Max let out a long, challenging howl. A moment later, the woolly dog and her giant sidekick, Hog, appeared from the shadows.

"What you making noise about," the woolly dog croaked.

"I want to see the leader," Max announced. "Would that be you?"

The woolly dog laughed until she wheezed, Hog bellowing in laughter beside her.

"Oh, honey, I ain't the leader of nobody," she said. "Hog! Hog, are you the leader?"

Hog chuckled. Drool dripped from his snout and splashed on the concrete. "I just do what you say."

The woolly dog tilted her head. "Well, I s'pose I lead him." She laughed again.

Annoyance flared in Max's gut. After all he'd been through, after seeing two friends die right in front of him, he was tired of being laughed at. Baring his teeth, Max lunged forward and snapped his jaws. The two dogs immediately went silent.

"Stop wasting my time," Max growled. "I want to see the alpha of this place. Now."

A deep, guttural growl emanated from the shadows. The woolly dog and Hog fell silent, and the dogs who were in the shadows went still. As Max watched, the dogs behind the shed parted to let a broad, muscular dog walk between them. The woolly dog and Hog ducked their heads and skittered to the side as the new dog emerged.

The dog could have been the Chairman's rounded cousin. His fur was patterned the same, black with a spatter of brown. But where the Doberman was all angles, this dog's snout was wide and drooping, his ears hanging flaps much like Max's own.

"He's a Rottweiler," Max heard Rocky whisper to Gizmo behind him. "I met a few working for the Chairman. They weren't too friendly."

The Rottweiler stopped a few feet in front of Max. He growled, then snapped his jaws. "What you want?"

Max nodded but did not take his eyes off the Rottweiler's. "My name is Max," he said. "Yours?"

The fearsome dog considered Max a moment, then said, "Fester."

"You're the alpha?" Max asked.

Again Fester growled. "You questioning that?" He barked a vicious laugh. "Out there, the Chairman rules. But I didn't like that none, so he put me here." The Rottweiler took a menacing step forward and bared his teeth. "And now in here, *I* rule."

Max chuckled to himself. "So you're an alpha, locked in a giant kennel, ruling a bunch of starving misfits?" He rolled his eyes. "Yeah, you're some alpha, all right."

Fester lowered his front end and bellowed a bark. Max stood his ground.

"You question me?" Fester roared. "You come here and challenge me?"

Clearing his throat once more, Max raised his voice. "Who we *should* be challenging is the true alpha of this building: the Chairman. But I suppose you, Fester, would just like to sit here and waste away. Because you're too *scared* to go for a real fight."

In the shadows, Max could hear the other dogs murmuring as if the ideas of escaping and fighting the Chairman were new to them.

"We could get out of here?"

"Do you think?...Nah, it can't be. But what if...?"

"So hungry...so thirsty..."

Fester didn't seem to care, ignoring the voices that muttered behind him. The beast of a dog's whole body trembled in anger. "You challenging me?" he bellowed. "Huh, golden puppy? You challenging me?"

Max nodded and showed his teeth. "Yes," he said. "I am."

With a howl, Fester leaped, teeth and claws flying wildly. Max stepped to the side easily, then spun around to see the Rottweiler scramble to a stop, surprised at having missed his foe. Max stood tall, muscles tensed, ready for the next pass.

Chest heaving, Fester turned to face Max once more. He snarled, waiting...and then he bounded forward. Max's heart thudded as the slobbering beast rushed toward him, but he held his ground.

The two dogs met chest to chest, Fester's eyes wide as his head darted back and forth, spittle flying everywhere. The dog's limbs fumbled over Max's chest, and Max's own front legs flailed until, finally, he got a grip on the other dog. Forcing himself forward with his hind legs, Max flipped the Rottweiler onto his back, then wrapped his jaws around the dog's throat.

Fester lay there, stunned by the quick turn of events, and all the other dogs at the fence took in sharp, surprised breaths. Max's chest heaved as he towered over the half-starved alpha of the "problem" dogs, pride swelling within him. He'd won. At long last, he'd won one.

"All right," Fester muttered after a long moment of silence. "Let me go, already. You win. You're the leader."

"Yay!" Gizmo cried from the fence, leaping up and spinning around. "Max, that was great!"

"Good job, buddy!" Rocky whooped.

Max stepped back from Fester and let the Rottweiler stand up. The dog lowered his head and tucked his tail between his legs, fully yielding to Max.

Holding himself high, Max stepped farther into the darkness. "I don't know about you dogs," he called out, "but I'm awful tired of the Chairman and being trapped here. Anyone want to help us escape?"

There was a hushed silence, then the murmuring of voices as the dogs muttered among themselves.

Then, one by one, they emerged into the light: the woolly dog, big Hog, all sorts of other dogs of various breeds and in various states of neglect. The one thing they all had in common, the one thing that made Max's stomach fill up with sadness, was the obvious despair in each of the dogs' eyes.

Several weeks ago, these dogs had homes. They had families. Just like Max and Rocky, Gizmo and Madame.

Now, they were worse than just abandoned. They were starving prisoners.

Max had made a promise to Madame: to escape the Corporation and find help. And now he made a promise to himself: He would leave only if he could help these poor dogs escape, too. Save them like he couldn't save poor Madame.

Rocky and Gizmo waddled up to Max's side. As they did, Fester looked up at Max and asked, "So, boss, what's your plan to break us out of here?"

Max looked to the rickety wooden shack that the dogs surrounded. He had no idea what it was for, but there was a window on the side facing him that showed a folding chair inside. Looking back over his shoulder, Max saw the fence—too tall to jump over, but about the same height as the shack.

"Have you ever tried to break out before?" Max asked Fester. "I mean, none of you can be happy to just stay in here, right?"

Fester bristled. "Of course we have. We tried climbing the fence, but it's too high. We tried climbing on each other, but that didn't work out too well. We even tried running out when the Chairman opened the gate, but his guard dogs are too fast. We tried everything."

"What about that shack?" Max asked. "Have you tried moving it?"

Looking back over his shoulder, Fester regarded the shack as if for the first time. "Uh, not that I know of. We've tried climbing it, but it's too far from the fence to make a good leap over. Now that you mention it, it don't look nailed down."

Max looked down to Rocky, who was also looking between the shack and the fence. "You thinking what I'm thinking, pal?"

Rocky's tail wagged. "I'm thinking we're going to need to find a way to move that shed."

CHAPTER 26

BREAKING FREE

Max strode to stand tall in front of his newfound followers. They watched him with rapt attention.

"So, you guys ready to bust out of here?" he barked.

Several of the dogs yipped their excitement.

"Good!" he barked. "A friend of mine didn't make it out of the Corporation, but I promised her that we would. And I intend to keep that promise. Let's get out of here!"

Dozens of voices rose in a hoarse cheer. Only one called out, cranky as always: the woolly dog.

"What's your plan, then?" she asked.

Max trotted up to her. "What's your name?"

Blinking up at Max, she croaked, "Liza."

"Well, Liza," Max said, "a bunch of us bigger dogs

are going to shove that shed over there to the fence and make a ramp. You think once I do, you can help herd everyone up over it? You're pretty. You look like you'd be good at keeping people in line."

Liza let out a girlish titter. "Oh, you bet I can, sweet cheeks," she said. Then, turning behind her, she shouted, "Hey, Hog, you hear that? The new boss thinks I'm *pretty*. You ever heard such a thing?"

"I called you pretty just yesterday," Hog grumbled.

Liza laughed. "Oh, Hog, you don't count."

Max quickly rounded up the bigger and stronger dogs: Fester, Hog, the young Boxer, and a Saint Bernard who'd been napping and missed the whole kerfuffle that led to Max being in charge. Together with Max, the four dogs put their shoulders against the back of the old shack and forced it to slowly scrape across the floor. Wooden timbers creaked and groaned, and some of the less sane dogs howled and cried, distracting Max from the task. But he was determined to get out of this prison.

At long last, with one final shove, the entire shack tipped forward. The front wall crunched against the center of the fence, and the front tip of the roof met the top of the fence with a resounding clang. The entire shack leaned forward, forming a perfect—if not entirely sturdy—ramp.

The dogs whooped and cheered until Max shushed them, reminding them: They might be being watched.

Max had Gizmo test the ramp first, to make sure it

would at least hold a small dog's weight. She took one tentative step, then another—and realizing it was solid footing, raced to the top and leaped. She landed easily on the concrete floor on the other side.

"Oh!" she called out. "That was easy! And so much fun!"

Tail wagging, Max went to the fence. "Good job!" he barked. "You think you can keep the others organized as we send them over?"

"Of course!" Gizmo said. "But why? What are we doing after we're all over?"

"I'm not sure yet," Max said. "But try to keep the group together."

Turning back, Max nodded at the woolly dog, Liza.

"Liza," he said, "I need you and Hog to start sending dogs over one by one. Start with the smaller ones, then the big guys."

"What if they don't wanna cross?" she croaked, tossing her head in the direction of a few dogs huddling in the corner, muttering to themselves and avoiding the crowd.

"Then they don't have to," Max said. "But I think they'll change their minds."

"Hog!" Liza called, circling until she spotted her giant sidekick. "Hog, you heard all that, you dumb mutt? Help me round up the little dogs!"

"I heard," Hog grumbled. "Don't gotta always call me names, you know."

As Liza and Hog nudged dogs from the crowd and escorted them to the makeshift ramp, Fester approached Max, just as Rocky came to Max's side. The Rottweiler still ducked his head and tail in compliance.

"So, Fleetfoot," Fester muttered, "you need me for anything special?"

"Huh?" Rocky asked with a tilted head. "Fleetfoot?"

Behind Max, Liza barked, and he heard a dog scramble up the ramp and land on the other side. The waiting dogs cheered.

Fester lifted his head and let out a halfhearted "Aroo." Then, looking at Rocky, he said, "That's what some dogs are calling Max here now. After he darted me so fast. Fleetfoot."

Max's tail wagged. "I've never had a nickname before," he said. "I think I like it."

"Yeah," Fester said, then sat down. "Anyway. You need me once we get over the fence?"

"Oh," Max said, peering through the chain-link fence to see Gizmo standing in the dim yellow light, talking amiably with the two dogs who had gone over. Already another was climbing cautiously over the fallen shack. It wavered at the top of the fence, then gingerly jumped, whining when it landed.

Turning back to Fester, Max said, "Well, what do you think, Fester? You're a leader. Me, I figure there's two things we can do once we get over," he said. "Either we can try to take the Chairman by surprise, storming the

Corporation and freeing the other dogs, or we can just try to escape, quickly and quietly."

Rocky peered past Fester at the dogs milling near Liza and Hog, waiting to be sent over. "I'm not sure these guys are in any shape to be fighting anybody, big guy," he said. "Especially not the Chairman's army."

"I could try to protect 'em," Fester offered. "I'm not always so weak, you know. I may not be so smart as you, but I can fight when I've eaten."

Max nodded. "I bet you can," he said. "I never even would have tried to take you on if I hadn't known you'd gone hungry, to be honest."

Fester laughed. Another cheer rose from the dogs as yet another prisoner leaped to freedom.

"So how do we get out?" Fester asked. "We take that elevator up?"

"Nah, big guy," Rocky said, turning to look through the fence. "See those people cars down here? They had to come through some door that leads outside, right? I bet we can run out from there."

"And then you can lead as many of the dogs as you can to someplace outside the Chairman's domain," Max said to Fester. "Maybe head into the subways, if you want to stay in the city."

Fester nodded. "I could do that. But what about you guys, Fleetfoot?"

Max looked wistfully past Fester at the ramp again.

All the small dogs were over, and now the bigger ones were climbing up. The fallen shack creaked but held.

"The whole reason my friends and I came here was to find our people," he said. "I had a friend here named Madame who told us where to go. She said that all the humans, all our families, went to the oceans. And that the best way to get to the oceans is for us to follow the river."

"The river," Fester muttered. "That big one that rushes under the bridges?"

"That's the one," Rocky said.

"Well, I never had much of a human family myself," Fester said. "Most of my friends were dogs on the street. A lot are still out there and probably need help. But I'll tell anyone who asks which way to go if they need to find their people."

"Thanks, Fester," Max said, tail wagging. "And you're wrong, by the way. You're plenty smart."

Fester's tail wagged back, but all he did was nod, then go to wait his turn at the ramp.

After another hour or so, all the dogs whom they could persuade to move had climbed up the fallen shack and leaped to freedom on the other side. They milled between the broad concrete pillars, Gizmo circling the restless pack as they waited to hear what would happen next.

Some dogs wouldn't budge no matter how much Max and the others pleaded with them, though: The skinny, wild-eyed dogs with the missing teeth skittishly ran deeper into the shadows. And a quartet of large dogs refused to even acknowledge that anything was going on at all.

Max wouldn't be able to save everyone, and if they stayed here much longer, they would all be caught again. So Max let Rocky, Liza, Fester, and Hog barrel up the ramp one by one. The great big hound knocked a piece of wood loose as he leaped over the fence, and the whole shack groaned—but it only wobbled in place. Holding his breath, Max scrambled up the wood and leaped, landing heavily on the other side.

As he did, Hog's deep voice called out, "Hey, Liza? What's this green circle do?"

Max looked over to see Hog hit the same button on the control panel that the elevator operator had hit at the Chairman's beckoning hours earlier. In response, the chain-link door clinked as it rolled open.

Max stared. Gizmo laughed so hard that she fell onto her back, her little legs punching at the air.

Rocky snorted. "You know, buddy?" he said, looking up at Max, who was gaping. "Sometimes I wonder if we're as smart as we think we are."

Shaking his head, Max chuckled to himself. "Well, let's leave it open," he said. "That way, the others can leave when they're ready."

Max, Rocky, Gizmo, and Fester went to the front of the pack. On Max's command, the group of freed dogs padded forward through the underground parking lot, past the concrete alcove where the elevator waited, past the empty cars. Row after row of fat, round pillars rose to the ceiling, yellow stripes painted around them and human numbers stenciled on, big and black. At first, the only light came from the dingy orange bulbs above, and the dogs seemed perfectly content to follow Max's lead—until, up ahead, they saw dim, early morning daylight.

The exit.

There were two large doors, big enough for giant human trucks to fit through, and they were wide open. Before Max could say a single thing, Liza called out, "Oh, Hog! Daylight! We're free!"

The other dogs barked and yipped and howled, some so happy to see true light that they seemed on the verge of collapsing in happy tears. The dogs surged around Max and his friends, a chaotic mess of canines who rushed to run out the doors without any regard for stealth.

"Well, guess this is where we part," Fester said, already galloping toward the exit himself. "I'll look after 'em best I can. Good luck, Fleetfoot!"

"You, too!" Max called. Then, looking down at Rocky and Gizmo, he said, "You two ready to get out of here?"

"You know, Max?" Gizmo said. "I love me a good

adventure. And this has certainly been a grand one. But I've been ready to get out of here for ages!"

Rocky laughed. "Now you're sounding like me!"

"Let's go!" Max barked.

The three ran at full speed, bursting onto the abandoned street just behind the surge of Corporation prisoners. They stopped momentarily to catch their bearings and let their eyes get used to the morning light.

"Which way do we go, big guy?" Rocky asked.

Before Max could answer, there came a long, loud howl from the left. All three dogs turned—and saw a pair of Dobermans standing silhouetted at the end of the road.

"The prisoners!" one bellowed. "They're escaping! *They're escaping!*"

The speaker turned and ran toward the front of the Corporation building. The other Doberman, however, merely bared its teeth and roared in fury.

Then ran full tilt toward Max, Rocky, and Gizmo.

"We go right!" Max barked. "Run, run, *run!*"

The three dogs' legs were a blur as they raced down the street, their paws kicking up old human trash that littered the road, their breaths ragged in their throats. They were scared, sure, but Max also realized he was happier than he'd been in days. He was *running*, free.

"Where *are* we going?" Gizmo panted as they galloped across an intersection.

Max ducked beneath a fallen streetlamp, then

leaped over an abandoned bicycle. Rocky and Gizmo ran around.

Behind them, the Doberman's barks doubled, then doubled again. Max had to look behind now—and immediately wished he hadn't. The Doberman had been joined by six of the Chairman's trained dogs.

And in the lead was the Chairman himself, his eyes a cold fury.

"Right!" Max bellowed. "Go right!"

As they hit the next street, the three dogs skidded on the pads of their feet and took a sharp turn. The surroundings were a blur now—tan stone sidewalks that curled around once-tended trees, fancy black streetlights, brick buildings with arched windows that showed dusty shelves of books and paintings and old furniture. Max kept his eyes focused ahead and forced himself to run harder than he'd ever run before.

The howls and barks of the Chairman's approaching army echoed through the streets. As Max ran, he realized they weren't alone. He saw a rat dart out from beneath a pile of newspaper and disappear into a sewer drain; a mangy dog cowered behind a mailbox on a corner; three cats watched the chase from a second-story window. But the city seemed otherwise empty—just Max and his companions pursued by the Chairman's brainwashed, vicious soldiers.

Max veered around a corner, then another, trying

desperately to lose their tail—and then skidded to a stop, finding himself blocked off from the next street by a high wooden fence.

"Oh no!" Rocky wailed. "Oh, buddy, this ain't good! We came so far!"

"Hey!" Gizmo shouted. "Don't give up, Rocky. Now is not the time to give up."

Chest heaving and tongue lolling from his mouth as he panted, Max turned, intending to run back the way they'd come. But the Chairman was already there, his army at his heels. They eclipsed the sun behind them, their long shadows stretching toward the three dogs.

The Chairman jerked his head at his army, and they all stopped as one, then sat, waiting. Satisfied at their obedience, the Chairman snapped his jaws at Max. Chuckling, the deadly Doberman stalked forward.

"Max, Max, Max," he said, shaking his head. "I must admit, I'm impressed. A little golden Labrador such as yourself, besting foes at every turn. If I had hands, I'd give you a round of applause."

"Thanks," Max growled, stepping forward to block his friends. "I just do what I must."

Still sauntering forward, the Chairman tilted his head. "It's a shame I'll have to break you," he said. "You're lucky that's all I'm planning for you, however. Your little friends..." He bared his teeth. "I think they shall take the brunt of the punishment for setting my prisoners loose. I'm thinking broken legs, cold empty rooms, no food or water...." Glaring at Max, he said, "Sound familiar?"

Max's heart thudded hard in his chest, fueled by anger and fear all at once. His eyes darted every which way, looking for some escape. But the only way out was through the Chairman. And there was no way he could take on that army of dogs in a fight.

They'd only just escaped, and already they'd lost.

Max opened his jaws, intending to say something, to find some words to at least taunt the snotty Doberman. But Gizmo spoke instead.

"Precious!" she commanded, her voice high and sharp. "Halt!"

The Chairman blinked, his eyes going blank. Immediately, he stopped in his tracks.

"Precious!" Gizmo shouted. "Sit!"

The Chairman plopped to the ground obediently. Behind him, his army of dogs looked at one another, clearly confused.

"What..." Max shook his head and looked down at the little terrier. "How did you do that?"

Tail wagging, Gizmo met his eyes. "Remember how paranoid Pinky the Poodle was at the Enclave? How if someone knew our real name they could command us?" She giggled. "Well, someone all about training and order like Precious here probably follows more commands than all of us combined."

Rocky laughed. "Ha! I guess there was something to that Dandyclaw after all."

Tail wagging, Max stood to his full height. All three dogs started to walk toward the Chairman. Just then, the light came back on in his eyes and the Chairman shook his fur, as though trying to dry himself after getting wet.

"What?" he sputtered, his eyes narrowed. "What did you do to me?"

"Oh, nothing, big guy," Rocky said. "But how about—Precious! Play dead!"

Again the Chairman blinked, his vision went glassy. Rolling his eyes up into his head, he let his tongue loll free, then collapsed to the ground in a dramatic fashion.

"Boss?" one of the dogs who had followed him said. "You okay?"

Max looked over the other dogs—an even ten of them now, Dobermans and Pit Bulls and Rottweilers, the Chairman's usual fighting crew—expecting them to rear up and attack. Instead, they sat perfectly in formation, awaiting orders like the good trained dogs they were.

"Let's go!" Max barked to his companions.

As the army of Corporation dogs watched helplessly, Max, Rocky, and Gizmo raced past them, out into the street, and then rounded a corner.

"Ha-*ha*!" Rocky bellowed. "Stupid Chairman. Stupid Corporation!"

"Don't get too comfy," Max called over his shoulder

as they rounded a car parked in the middle of the road. "I don't think he'll play dead for too long."

As if on cue, an angry, vicious howl rose up from the alley. "After them!" they heard the Chairman cry. "You stupid mutts! Go! Now!"

"Keep running!" Max shouted over the barking of the pursuing dogs. "Don't stop until we find the river!"

CHAPTER 27

OVER THE EDGE

◆———◆

The barks and yelps from their pursuers were joined by even more voices the farther Max, Rocky, and Gizmo ran through the city.

But the three dogs had enough of a lead, and had made enough twists and turns, that the Corporation dogs hadn't managed to catch them.

Yet.

Max had no idea how long they'd been running, except that the sun had moved higher into the sky. His joints and muscles burned, and his stomach ached for food and water. He couldn't stop, though. Not until he and his friends were out of this chaotic city and back on their true journey.

Rocky and Gizmo matched Max's great strides, their

short legs blurs beneath them. But Max could tell their energy was draining, even Gizmo, who never seemed to lack for energy at all.

"Just a little bit farther," Max urged between heaving pants. "The big buildings are behind us."

His friends didn't have the energy to respond.

Max got the feeling the Chairman was too smart to fall for their command trick again. Max almost considered finding a subway tunnel and trying his luck in the dark against the Chairman and his Corporation dogs. But something told him they wouldn't be as skittish below as the tunnel dogs—or nearly as afraid of Longtooth and his rats.

Strength waning, Max was ready to collapse in an alley, to hope the Chairman had given up, even though the barks of his army still echoed behind them, growing ever closer.

And then they crossed an intersection, and Max saw it.

A bridge.

The street they were on gave way to a broad blue steel bridge, which hung low over the water. As Max and his friends grew close, he saw that unlike the bridge back in the little town near the Enclave, there was no visible path to run to the water below.

"Oh, it's so pretty," Gizmo said softly as they slowed near the foot of the bridge. "Look at the water, how it glitters in the sun."

The water *did* look nice—and more important, calm. All they'd need was a way down, and maybe they could hide near its banks and follow it toward the ocean.

"There's no way down, buddy," Rocky said, peering through the guardrails as they stepped onto the bridge.

"Well, maybe there is on the other side," Max said. The barks behind them started up again, even louder. "Let's hope the Chairman will forget about us once we're out of his city."

"They're still coming?" Rocky asked, then whined deep in his throat. "How come everyone we meet is so relentless?"

"We're just lucky," Gizmo said, wagging her tail. Looking up at Max, she said, "Back to running?"

Max nodded, even though he ached all over. "Back to running. We're almost free."

Taking a deep breath, Max forced his legs to move. He couldn't run as fast as they had in the city, not any-more, but he could at least jog fast enough to hopefully get across the bridge and find a way down to the river.

The trio darted ahead silently, panting and unable to talk. The barks behind them drew closer and closer, but the sound of the water below drowned them out, almost letting Max believe that the barks were fading away instead of coming near.

And then he saw shadows ahead.

A dozen figures. Canine size, but huge. Gray and white fur. Vicious snarls.

Wolves.

"Oh no," Rocky whimpered, slowing to a standstill. Max and Gizmo did the same.

Max couldn't take it anymore. He didn't want to give up, but he was so exhausted. Heaving a deep sigh, he collapsed to the ground, resting on his belly.

"Max!" Gizmo yipped, nudging his head. "Are you okay?"

Ears twitching, Max listened to the growls as the wolves came closer. He thumped his tail back and forth, just twice. He didn't have energy for a full wag.

"I'm conserving my energy," Max said. "You two do the same."

"But Max!" Rocky barked, darting back and forth, frantic. "You see the wolves, right, big guy? The big, mean wolves led by Dolph, coming right for us?"

"I do," he said. "But I also hear the Corporation still chasing us."

Rocky stopped in place and cocked his head, listening. And he could hear it, too, the padding of dozens of feet, the yips and growls of the Chairman's assembled soldiers. Rocky's tail became a blur.

Gizmo laughed. "If we can't beat them..."

"Then let's let them beat each other," Max finished.

Rocky and Gizmo both curled up next to Max, taking in deep breaths. Max tried to look as cowed as possible as Dolph neared. The white wolf Wretch was at his side, the rest of his pack at his heels. They looked better fed than the last time Max had seen them. He wondered briefly what they'd been eating on the outskirts of the city—then tried not to think about it.

"I knew you'd come this way sooner or later," Dolph snarled, showing off his sharp, stained teeth. "It was only a matter of time until I'd get to finally kill you."

Max opened his eyes and made them look big and sad, but didn't say a thing.

Dolph took another step. "Is this how you plan to end, mutt?" he roared. "Lying there, giving up? You have no honor. Not like us wolves."

"Hey," Wretch growled, nipping at Dolph's side.

Dolph howled, then snapped at the scarred white wolf. "What?" he demanded. "Can't you see I'm busy?"

Wretch ducked his head, though his pale blue eyes were narrowed in anger. "Just thought you'd like to know we're not alone," he said.

Dolph looked up, and Max craned his head to look behind him. There, walking calmly down the center of the bridge, was the army of Corporation dogs, with the Chairman in the lead. The Chairman matched Dolph's sneer, completely ignoring Max and his friends lying between the two packs.

"I thought I made it clear, wolf!" the Chairman barked. "Your kind are not to infest my city!"

Dolph's fur bristled, and he held his head high. "I'm not in your city," he spat. "I'm on this bridge."

"Close enough."

All the wolves were on edge now, some backing away and nursing recent wounds, no doubt from the Corporation attack days before.

The Chairman and his dogs growled, their limbs tense. They formed a dark, impenetrable line on the bridge, standing from railing to railing side by side. Hackles raised, they narrowed their brows, their ears back flat against their heads. Challenging. Daring the wolves to make a move.

Dolph growled and snapped at those of his pack who had dared to back away, and the thick-furred, wild-eyed beasts, too, formed a line. They drew back their dark lips to show off their sharp, shredding teeth, stained with the blood of all their kills.

For a long moment, neither side made a move. Gray and pale blue wolf eyes met the dark, steely gazes of the trained dogs of the Corporation.

A dog barked a taunt. A wolf howled with rage. Max couldn't tell who had sounded off first.

The Chairman took a step closer to Dolph, and Dolph took a step toward him. Neither would back down, Max knew.

"Uh-oh..." Rocky whispered.

"Get ready," Max said.

The Chairman's ears twitched, and he tilted his head. "Wolves," he muttered. "I could use wolves in my Corporation. I could break you, make you the most vicious guards I have. Then I would fear for nothing."

"Break me?" Dolph bellowed. Then, louder, "You would try to train me as your pet? Never!"

Max's head darted front to back, looking at both packs, judging their postures, their eyes and ears and tails. The rush of the river pulsed in Max's ears, and the air over the bridge felt thick, tense.

"When I bark," he whispered in a growl only his friends could hear, "we jump off the bridge. It's not *that* high up." Max swallowed. "I don't think."

"Not that high up, huh?" Rocky yipped.

"Got it," Gizmo said, fearless as always.

"Rocky?" Max whispered.

"What's with you and jumping into water?" Rocky whined softly. "Fine, fine."

"It's your choice," the Chairman growled at Dolph, lowering his head, bunching his back legs. "You can either submit to the Corporation or you can die."

"Then I gladly choose death," Dolph snapped. *"Yours."* And the wolf raised his fearsome head to the sky and let out a long, commanding howl.

"Now!" Max barked.

Not waiting to see what the dogs and the wolves on the bridge would do, Max rose onto all fours, ran straight to the edge of the bridge, and dove through the guardrail. Behind him, he heard Rocky let out a high-pitched "Hiii-*yah!*"

And Max was flying.

Cool, misty air surrounded him, tugging at his fur,

chilling his insides. He felt like he was hovering forever, watching the glittering ripples of the river come closer and closer ever so slowly. Above him, he heard roars and barks, and over it all, Rocky and Gizmo howling in fear and glee as they fell through the air.

Then he hit the water.

The impact was hard against his body, as though he'd plopped belly-first against a metal floor. The force of it drove the air from his lungs and sent his head reeling, dizzy. He wheezed for breaths, and a wave splashed over him, driving him deep under the freezing water.

The water was so cold that for a moment, he went rigid, eyes wide as he sank beneath the waves. He gasped for air, but water trickled into his nose, his mouth, and his throat instead, burning his insides. Adrenaline pumped through Max's veins, and he was certain he would drown, would almost get away and—

Max's flat paws, made for paddling through water, found purchase in the river's depths. Light glittered, refracted through the waves above, and he pumped his limbs, climbing up and up until he finally burst out into the air once more.

For a moment he bobbed there, hacking up river water and gasping for air, his ears sinking into the shushing silence of the waves before popping back up to catch brief bits of the battle raging on the bridge above: snarls and pained yelps and vengeful cries.

"Rocky!" he gasped as he struggled against the waves. "Gizmo!"

The water surged around him, carrying him downstream faster than he'd expected, the bridge and their enemies growing farther and farther away. His heart thudded in a panic as he paddled toward the far shore, wondering if the river was too much for his friends, if their tiny bodies hadn't been able to handle the impact.

Then, over the roar of rushing water, Max heard their voices calling to him.

Paddling so that he faced the shore, he saw Rocky and Gizmo, soaking wet, racing along the stony ground. They called his name over and over.

"I'm here!" he shouted. Water enveloped his snout, but he spat it out. "I'm coming!"

Max let the current carry him forward even as he swam to the side. The shore drew closer and closer, his two small friends jumping up and down, shouting encouragement.

And then Max's front paws met smooth, wet pebbles. Claws catching, he pulled himself from the water, walked to the dry edge, and plopped heavily onto the shore.

He shivered, gulping in heaving breaths as Rocky and Gizmo laughed and howled with joy.

"We did it, big guy!" Rocky said.

"That was so—wow!" Gizmo yipped. "That was amazing! All those dogs, and then we jumped off, and it was like flying! And then splash! And then you were zooming down the river, but you made it, and now we're all safe! Yay!"

"The current took us right to the shore," Rocky added. "You must have jumped farther out to keep getting swept downriver. I almost thought we lost you, buddy!"

"You can't get rid of me that easily, not after all we just went through," Max said. He got to his feet and shook his entire body, sending water spraying everywhere. Rocky sputtered and darted away, but Gizmo leaped up and down, giggling as she got sprinkled.

For a long moment, the three dogs lay near the water, catching their breaths. The river rushed beside them—heading toward their people, Max guessed.

"So what now?" Gizmo asked, lying on her back and sunning her belly in the afternoon sun. "The Corporation and the wolves will never find us now, not with the water covering our trail and our scent. Should we hike along the river?"

Tail wagging, Rocky jumped to his four stubby legs and said, "I have a better idea." Waddling away, he gestured with his head for Max and Gizmo to follow.

Max couldn't keep his tail from wagging when he saw what Rocky had planned. Up ahead, half on the shore and half in the water, was a small human boat tied to a weathered, moss-covered wooden pole. It wasn't very large, but it would be enough to fit the three of them comfortably—and let them rest while the river did all the work of carrying them to the ocean.

Gizmo and Rocky went to work tearing at the rotting rope with their teeth while Max nudged the boat into the water. Before the rope could break completely, Max had the two smaller dogs jump in. He chewed the rope the rest of the way, shoved the boat entirely into the water with his head, then leaped in just as the waves caught the little ship and pulled it downstream.

The boat bobbed gently on the waves, and the world was quiet save for the sound of the water. No barks or howls, or yips or growls. Just the soft breathing of three friends.

Of course, there were no sounds of the humans, either.

Exhausted, the dogs curled up against one another to sleep. Rocky sniffed at Gizmo's side, and she giggled before letting him nuzzle her.

Max raised his head and looked behind them to the bridge and the city, already growing smaller in the distance, tall shadows in front of the setting sun.

He looked ahead, downriver, where the city gave way to countryside once more—where more towns lay abandoned, more dogs and cats and other animals roamed free, trying to form new lives. But somewhere, far beyond the reach of the darkness that surged in his dreams, were Charlie and Emma, waiting. Madame had promised him. And Max would never forget Madame.

"Our families are out there, at the end of the river," Max said to his friends, even as they began to snore, fallen fast asleep. "As long as we don't give up on them, they won't give up on us. No matter what we have to go through, it'll be worth it once we're together again."

Through a snore, Rocky briefly opened his eyes. Groggily, he said, "You said it, buddy." Then, the little Dachshund curled up closer to Gizmo and sighed comfortably.

Closing his eyes, Max let the boat rock him to sleep, where he would dream of the world he once knew—and the one he meant to find again, no matter what.

ACKNOWLEDGMENTS

The Last Dogs series and *The Vanishing* wouldn't exist without many amazing and hardworking people who helped transform both from a neat idea to awesome reality. Special thank-yous must go out to my fantastic editors, Julie Scheina and Pam Garfinkel, whose insightful notes helped shape *The Vanishing* into the book it is today; to Greg Call for giving life to Max, Rocky, Gizmo, and the rest of the Last Dogs cast through his brilliant illustrations; and to the entire Little, Brown Books for Young Readers team for working so hard to bring this first Last Dogs book to the shelves.

A huge thank-you to Michael Stearns and Ted Malawer of the Inkhouse, who not only gave me the once-in-a-lifetime opportunity to tell such a fun and thrilling story, but who were also there every step of the way to help make this the best book it could be. Thanks also to all my friends in the Elevensies for the weekly chats and the endless support.

And finally, thank you to all the dogs I grew up with: bumbling brothers Salt and Pepper, cuddly Bear, ferocious Prince, friendly Dubby, spunky Spunky, skittish

Cupcake, rowdy Ariel, stoic Shadow, and loyal Brandy—not to mention the dozens of amazing dogs of all shapes and sizes that belonged to friends and neighbors. Each and every one of them inspired the world within these pages, and I can't imagine my life as a kid without knowing and loving them all.

(Yes, even Prince, despite the fact that he and the Chairman would have gotten along just *great*!)

Don't miss

THE LAST DOGS

DARK WATERS

coming June 2013.

Keep reading for a sneak peek!

THREE SUNS

◆———

Max was running through a city.

The street he ran down was long and empty. People had once swarmed the sidewalks on either side of the road. They'd sat beneath the glass bus shelters with the advertisements of smiling men and women on the walls, or laughed as they went in and out of the shops at the base of the tall buildings, arms overloaded with colorful bags.

Now the sidewalks were barren. Stray newspapers and plastic bags were blown by a chilly breeze until they pooled next to concrete steps and in doorways. The windows of the stores were shattered, the rooms beyond them dark.

All the people were gone.

Howls and barks echoed around Max, ricocheting among the glass skyscrapers that rose high to gray clouds overhead. Max looked back over his shoulder as he ran. Dozens upon dozens of shadowy wolves and dogs chased him. Behind them, a dark storm flooded through the mazelike streets, an inky blackness that blotted out the city in its wake.

Leading the pack of shadow beasts were two enormous creatures—a canine the size of a school bus and a wolf as large as a house. They were all sharp angles, with pointed ears and triangle snouts, and both stared at him through bright red glowing eyes. With each step of their giant paws, windows rattled and the ground quaked. Cracks snaked through the asphalt as if the street itself were being torn apart.

Max knew the two towering beasts well. The Chairman, an evil Doberman. Dolph, a vicious wolf pack leader.

Run as far as you like. It was the Chairman's deep voice, but it did not come from the shadowy figure; it spoke directly in Max's thoughts.

You will never *escape,* Dolph's voice snarled.

Max wanted to challenge his pursuers, but there were so many, and he was all alone. Maybe if his friends had been here in this nightmare city, they could have faced the rampaging creatures together. But loyal Rocky and feisty Gizmo were nowhere that Max could see.

So instead, he gasped for air and looked forward, away from the cloud of blackness, away from the howling pack.

He veered around the corner of one building, then another and another. But no matter how many streets he turned down, he never seemed to get anywhere new—each street looked exactly the same. Same darkened storefronts, same two cars parked halfway on the sidewalk, same blank traffic lights swaying as they dangled overhead.

Pain lanced through Max's legs—his muscles were cramping. He couldn't run forever. Already he could feel himself slowing, struggling to catch his breath.

Then he heard it. The sound of rushing water.

A river.

Halfway down the street, Max tried something new: He skidded into an alleyway. It was narrow, grimy, and dim with shadows. Trash was piled along the walls. But this was the way to go—he was sure of it. The gurgles and splashes of the river came from the end of the alley.

Max leaped forward. A break came in the storm clouds, and daylight streamed down from above, sparkling and glinting off the water, which was just coming into view.

As Max reached the end of the alley, a dog stepped into his path. She was a Labrador like Max, only her fur wasn't gold like his—hers was black and specked with white. Her tail wagged when she saw him, though her big brown eyes were sad and weary. She was frail and thin, but she projected a strength that he recognized at once.

It was Max's friend Madame Curie.

Find the people who made this happen. Her mouth did not move, but her voice echoed in his thoughts. Just as the Chairman's and Dolph's had.

"How?" Max asked. "They all left, and we don't know where they went."

Madame tilted her head, and as she did, something on her collar glinted in the sunlight. There was a golden symbol attached—three conjoined circles in a row.

Find the three golden rings, her voice whispered. *They will help you learn what you must know.*

"But what are the rings?" Max barked. "Please, Madame, we don't have much time. I'm being chased. I need—"

But she was gone.

Sadness swelled within Max, just as it had when he'd watched Madame pass away. He was suddenly overwhelmingly tired and alone. All he'd ever wanted was to find the humans who had raised him and loved him—his family. But the farther he'd journeyed, the more horrible things he'd had to face. Losing Madame and fleeing the snarling dogs and wolves was just the start of it.

He didn't know how much longer he could run.

Just then, the sunlight flared, and Max looked up.

In the sky, three suns hovered side by side. They burned like enormous white holes in the blue of the heavens, and Max had to squint to see them.

Three rings. He had to remember. No matter how tired or sad he was, he had to keep trying. If not for himself, then for his friends.

He had to follow the rings to find the people.

Soon, even squinting was no help against the hollow suns—the searing light grew brighter and brighter until Max could see nothing but white. The alleyway around him disappeared in a blaze, and the ground beneath his feet grew too brilliant to look at. All Max could do was close his eyes and surge forward to the river he knew was close by.

The noisy rush of water filled his ears, drowning out the barks and yips of the pursuing dogs and wolves. Running blind, Max felt the pavement fall away beneath his front paws, and he leaped for all he was worth into the light.

Max awoke.